MW01113845

SEASONAL

SEASONAL

A NOVEL BY

BETTY J. BELANUS

Round Barn Press
Rockville, Maryland

SEASONAL
BY BETTY J. BELANUS

First Published in 2002 by
Round Barn Press
Rockville, Maryland

Copyright © 2002 by Betty J. Belanus
All rights reserved.
No part of this book may by used or reproduced in any manner
whatsoever without written permission from the publisher.

Cover photograph by Betty J. Belanus
Author's photograph by M. E. Francis
Cover and book design, typography & composition by
Arrow Graphics, Inc. Watertown, Massachusetts
Printed in the United States of America

Publisher's Cataloging-in-Publication
(Provided by Quality Books, Inc.)

Belanus, Betty J.
    Seasonal / by Betty J. Belanus. — 1st ed.
    p. cm.
    ISBN: 0-9716852-07

    1. Folklorists—Tennessee, East—Fiction.
2. Tennessee, East—Fiction. 3. Murder—Fiction
I. Title

PS3602.E536S43 2002   813'.6
                    QBI33-296

To Steph—
Jenni's "other"
surrogate "mom"—
hope you enjoy
this!
Yours,
Betty
May '03

DEDICATION

For my family and friends, who encouraged me,
but especially for Bobby Fulcher,
our TSPFP mentor supreme.

ACKNOWLEDGMENTS

I would like to thank my friends who read drafts of this book and made useful suggestions, including Hanna Griff, Jan Rosenberg, Judy McCulloh, Debora Kodish, Diana Parker, Erica Brady, Cindy Houston, Barbara Bennett Howell, Erin Roth, Carla Borden and Jean Freedman, and researcher Hayden Roberts. Many of the examples of folklore used in the book were inspired by the collections of the Tennessee State Parks Folklife Project (TSPFP) fieldworkers, Ray Allen, Jay Orr, Elaine Lawless, Denis Kiely, Bob Jeffries, Betsy Peterson, Tom Rankin, Brent Cantrell, Ingrid Gensler and myself. The TSPFP collection is housed in the Tennessee State Archives in Nashville. Several other examples of folklore were inspired by the collections of the Western Kentucky University Folklore Archives in Bowling Green. All events in this book are fictional, and any resemblance of characters and events to real life is purely coincidental.

Chapter I

INTRODUCTIONS

May, 1979

I piled the last load of equipment on the narrow bed: camera bag, tape recorder cases, mike stands, boxes of tape and film, backpack full of notebooks and ballpoints. Propped my old Samsonite suitcase next to the bed. Everything was dripping, including me. My sneakers were spongy—the VW bug's floorboards still leaked, despite my liberal application of Bondo the week before.

It was four o'clock in the afternoon, but the rain following me east from Nashville made it dark, both inside and outside. My roommate was propped up in his bed, studying what looked like a textbook by the light of a small lamp. I thought he resembled a grasshopper—long thin legs and arms folded at odd angles. His rhythmic chewing added to the resemblance; the smell of Juicy Fruit mingled with the damp woolen odor emanating from my blanket. I introduced myself. "I'm Rob Anderson, the folklorist."

"Folklore," he drawled. Obviously a local. "What's folklore?"

A third year graduate student, working toward a Ph.D. in folklore, I was used to this question. I gave him my favorite definition, brief and to the point: folklore is the study of traditions. Things learned by observation, imitation, not from a book. Folklore passed over space and through time: blues singing, basket making, fairy tales, flat foot dancing, herbal remedies, knock-knock jokes.

He was quiet for a while. I figured he was satisfied. I found a towel in my suitcase and began wiping off the equipment.

Then he stopped chewing and said, "You know what the folklore of the '70s is?" I didn't answer. "I'll tell you what the folklore of the '70s is. The folklore of the '70s is apathy." Pause. "And, the folklore of the '80s is going to be decadence."

I squeezed the water out of my socks. Great, I thought, I don't know anyone in a 150-mile radius of this remote state park, and I'm stuck with this joker for the summer. The soggy bed made a wet spot on the seat of my jeans.

I tried to recall the enthusiasm I had had for the summer ahead—the rush of adrenaline when the project director called in March offering me the job. My first real chance to get out into a community and collect the material I loved so much. Music and stories and hand-crafted objects that came straight from the heart. People carrying on traditions that stretched back in time for centuries, yet adapted to fit changing circumstances. Last night in Nashville I had barely slept, staying up and drinking way too much beer with the other folklorists working on the project in Middle and West Tennessee. We talked for hours about our graduate programs, what led us into the field of folklore, and our grand ambitions for our careers.

But, here was the reality. It reminded me suddenly of Summer Camp from Hell. Surly roommate, damp and gloomy quarters, hundreds of miles from family and friends. Maybe I should have stayed at school this summer and gotten my second language requirement out of the way as my advisor had suggested.

I saw a flash of movement on the floor. A big spider skittered across the gray linoleum and disappeared in the shadows. I unpacked the rest of my suitcase, moved the equipment off the bed, and fell asleep in my clothes to the sound of the unrelenting rain.

The next morning, it was still raining. I couldn't even make out the mountains in the near distance. During the first cup of coffee—black—I was sitting across the desk from Ed Daniels, the editor of the local weekly, The Jakesville Gazette. I had set up this interview following the suggestion of our project director before leaving Nashville the day before. The caffeine jolt helped—I hadn't slept well on the hard, narrow bed. And, besides, graduate school hadn't prepared me to be coherent at 8 a.m. "Tell me again what you're looking for, Mr. Anderson."

"Well, sort of the history of the area and its traditions—things that have been carried down over the generations. Stories and music and crafts."

"And you're going to have programs at the park on these things. For the tourists."

"For the local people, too."

"Give me some specifics, son, and maybe I can give you some names. I've lived in this town all my fifty years, know lots of people."

I swallowed the "son" bit, since I knew that I looked even younger than 24—especially with my new, conservative haircut. And I had to learn to project the polite, respectful demeanor that a successful folklore fieldworker needs to gain people's confidence. "How about musicians? Fiddlers, banjo players, that sort of thing. People who used to play for dances?"

He stared out the window and took a long sip of his coffee. He twirled a pencil, then fidgeted with some paper clips. "Yeah, too bad about old Boyd—he sure could've given you some good old tunes. He sure could play a fiddle like the devil himself."

"Who was that?"

"A fellow named Boyd Jenkins. But, that's another story entirely. I'll tell you who to go see—Carl Wallace. He used to play in a bluegrass band and now he has get-togethers on Friday evenings at his place. All the musicians go and just play."

I grilled him for another twenty minutes, gathering names of quilters, rug weavers, old-time preachers, gospel singers and an ex-coal miner or two. The remains of the coffee were cold by then, and I left the Styrofoam cup perched on the edge of his desk. It would still be there in a week or month judging by the clutter.

Cup of coffee number two occurred at the office of the county farm agent, Dave Rodifer. It came in a mug advertising Radio Station WHIL, "Music for the Hill Country." I wondered if they had any knowledgeable disk jockeys I should contact. "Traditions, you say. Kind of like—uh—what, for instance?"

"I was hoping you could give me some names of older farmers in the area that might know about farming with mules and that sort of thing. And, maybe some information about the logging camps that used to be in this area." I swirled the coffee around trying to melt down the globs of non-dairy creamer floating on top. Half an hour later I had five more pages of Notebook #1 filled with names and bits of pertinent information. I was writing so fast that my hand hurt, and I hoped I could read my own writing later.

"By the way—do you know anything about someone named Boyd Jenkins?"

He tapped his fingers on the desk and ran his right hand through his sparse dark hair. "Why?"

"The newspaper editor, Mr. Daniels, mentioned him. Said he played the fiddle."

"What else did Daniels say about Boyd Jenkins?" Rodifer narrowed his eyes.

"Just something about his story." His attitude was making me more curious about this Jenkins fellow.

"Boyd Jenkins was a no-good drifter who kept turning up around here because he had kin. Little good they did him in the end. Don't let anyone tell you Boyd Jenkins was any kind of hero, son. He was no good. You go visit some of those folks I've told you about—they're good people. They'll help you out with your project."

I thought it best not to ask about Boyd Jenkins over the third cup (the best one to date, with real milk and brewed in a clean pot) with the public librarian, Mrs. Dougherty.

"Well, first you just must meet Harriet Peacham, she's our county historian and she knows all there is to know about everything here. Then, Miss Georgia Daniels—yes, Mr. Daniels's maiden sister, she's a wealth of information, too. And the ladies in the Homemakers' Club, well, they have meetings every Wednesday where they learn crafts and such as that." I promised to come back and look through the file on local history. I wondered if I'd find any clippings on Boyd Jenkins. I beat a retreat to the men's room. I didn't find any good graffiti, but I really hadn't expected any. It was an occupational duty to at least look for some, however.

My next stop was the park office. I was scheduled to meet the park superintendent, David Bird, and brief him on my work. He'd already received some information over the phone from the project director in Nashville, but face-to-face interaction, I figured, counted for something.

He was a small man with a ruddy complexion, and he shook my hand very firmly. "So, you are Anderson. I was expecting someone a little older—I heard you had graduate training. Tell me, Anderson— I don't quite get the gist of this whole thing. This project is called, I understand, the State Parks Folklore Project. You're going to collect the folklore of the area around the park, present programs on that folklore, and put all the information you collect into the State Archive. And, you're a folklorist." He nodded to himself. Then, he looked at me. "What is folklore, anyway? What sorts of things are you after?" The receptionist came in with coffee. I felt a dull caffeine headache coming on as I launched into another explanation of my work. He seemed satisfied and began reeling off a list of possible leads, all of which I dutifully copied into my notebook.

"Sir, is there anyone on the staff itself who knows the area well?"

"There's old George Whitelaw, the groundsman. His family—and, believe me, it's extensive—all live around here and have for years. You might catch him having an early lunch up at the restaurant if you hurry."

Eleven fifteen. George must start working before I'm awake. After four cups of coffee and no breakfast, an early lunch sounded good. Maybe it would help soak up the caffeine.

George was sitting at a table near the kitchen, drinking coffee and smoking a filterless Camel. A younger man sat next to him, also smoking. Great, I thought, now I'll have a cigarette smoke headache to add to the caffeine one. The hazards of folklore fieldwork were mounting.

"George? Hi, I'm Rob Anderson."

"You're one of them seasonal kids, huh? Come here from college, have you, to give us a hand this summer?" About half of his teeth were missing, but his grin made me feel more comfortable than any greeting I'd received so far. We chatted about the area and its occupations, religious traditions and musical talent over ham sandwiches and potato chips. The younger man, whom George had introduced as Fred "everyone calls him 'Spike' " Dooling, the other park mainte-nance man, listened in silence the entire time.

Finally, I hazarded the inquiry, since I felt that my rapport with George merited it. "George, tell me about Boyd Jenkins." I thought I saw Spike throw a sideways, slightly interested glance toward us.

George lit up another Camel and took a long drag. He smiled. "Folks been telling you stories about Boyd already?"

"A couple of people I met this morning mentioned him."

"Boyd was a great feller. Played a mean fiddle."

"And?"

"You don't want to get into all that now, do you?"

"I am sort of curious."

"Well"—another drag—"There's them that'll tell you Boyd was no good. But he helped a lot of folks. The government did him in, buddy, uh-huh. The FBI shot him down in cold blood."

"What?"

"That's right. Listen. I ain't got time to tell you the whole story of Boyd Jenkins, me and Spike gotta get back to work. Tell you what— there's a feller will tell you all about Boyd, and he's got all the time in the world. That's my uncle, Earl Whitelaw. Go out here, turn left on the first gravel road. At a fork in the road, go to the right. You'll see a blue trailer. About a mile past there is a mailbox, says, 'E. Whitelaw.' Turn in there. If he ain't there sitting on his front porch chewing tobacco, he ain't far away."

My first instinct was to go directly to Earl's and get the full story. A combination of love of delayed gratification and the thought that the story of Boyd Jenkins was not the sort of thing I was supposed to be collecting kept me on track. I returned to the Nature Center, the squat one-story building that served as program space, work station and seasonal living quarters to make some sense out of my scrambled notes for an hour.

I decided to jump right into my work by visiting some beekeepers, the Otis family, who lived close to the park. They came highly recommended by the superintendent, and he had given me directions to their home, saying he was sure they wouldn't mind if I just dropped by. Still, standing at their front door with my hand poised to knock, I wondered what I was doing. Would they really welcome a complete stranger, arriving unbidden? I was almost ready to turn and retreat to my car when the door opened and a solemn woman with lots of red, unruly hair swung the door wide.

"Can I help you?" she asked.

I could feel the sweat collecting at the back of my shirt. "Uh, my name is Rob Anderson and I'm working at the State Park." I could see a puzzled look creeping over the woman's face. I rushed through the rest of the explanation. "We're working on a folklore project. The superintendent, Mr. Bird, suggested I visit you and ask about your beekeeping."

The woman's face crinkled into a laugh. "Oh, that Dave Bird! Always getting us in some sort of trouble! Well, come on in and we'll see what we can help you with."

I spent the balance of the afternoon talking to Mr. and Mrs. Otis, who knew a lot about the wild plants of the area and told stories about hunting wild bees and the folk law of whom a "bee tree" belonged to. They took me to the backyard, crammed with white-painted, boxy beehives, whirligigs made out of scrap metal and plastic Pepsi bottles spinning in the breeze. The expansive vegetable garden was already producing lettuce, early green beans and peas. I shot a roll of film.

With their permission, I hauled out the tape recorder—a heavy, expensive reel-to-reel Nagra lent to the project by the Library of Congress's American Folklife Center. It was the first time I had set up the recorder on my own, and I fumbled for several minutes with the cords and mikes before getting it right. The beekeepers watched patiently with more than a little amusement.

I had just turned the first tape over when the interview took an abrupt shift toward religion. One minute Mrs. Otis was telling me about the healing properties of ginseng, the next she was quizzing me on my faith.

"Are you saved?"

"Am I—uh—yes. Uh-huh, sure."

"Praise the Lord. Then you know Jesus. Won't you come to church this Sunday? Our church is just down the hollow here, the Mount Airey Primitive Baptist. A nicer bunch of folks you won't find anywhere. I know you're far from home but we are all at home in the house of the Lord, isn't that right? And in fact we're having our

Homecoming this very Sunday and we'd be most honored for you to be our guest. There'll be a dinner on the grounds and special singing and just a mess of folks all praising Jesus."

I didn't have the heart to tell her that I was raised Catholic (at my maternal grandmother's insistence), even though neither my mother nor my father ever set foot in churches except for the odd wedding or funeral they couldn't avoid. Or that I myself hadn't been to church in at least three years. I didn't want my own checkered religious history recorded for posterity on the tape. I agreed to go to the Homecoming because I figured the music would be of interest and the food would be great. The couple, especially the Mrs. was delighted.

I declined an invitation to dinner, even though the idea of a home-cooked meal was tempting. I had an urgent desire to be alone for a few hours, not to talk to anyone, not to explain myself to anyone. Just relax and observe.

I drove back into Jakesville, the small county seat seven miles from the park which everyone referred to as "town." I found a small, storefront diner and ordered a burger. Sitting under a large poster of Elvis in his sequin period, I watched the cook sizzle my meal behind the Formica counter. Later, I walked up and down the quiet main street, reading posters in the store windows. I noticed a number of events that I had to attend in the next few weeks: a pie supper, a revival, a political rally, a gospel sing, and a fiddler's contest at the local music barn.

On the way back to the park, I had the VW windows rolled down, and the cool air streamed in, bringing with it an almost sickly sweet smell. I remembered that smell from the hedge along my grandmother's garage: honeysuckle. My brother and sister and I used to pick the white, trumpet-shaped flowers and suck the sweet tips. But it had bloomed later than this in Northern New Jersey. Still, it made me feel a little bit more at home in this strange place.

I hit a bump in the road nearing the park entrance, and the VW radio, which I always left turned on in the usually vain hope that it would work, burst into life, blasting out Michael Jackson's "Don't Stop 'Til You Get Enough." Maybe it was a portent of the amount of folklore collecting I should be doing this summer? With all of the names I had gathered in only one day on the job, I doubted whether I'd ever feel that I'd gotten enough documentation.

It was just beginning to get dark when I returned to the Nature Center. Long pink and purple streaks still hung over the mountains. My roommate, the oracle, was reading Hemingway when I walked into the bedroom. He didn't even look up.

I forced myself to sit down on my bed and write an entry in the field journal I was supposed to be keeping. I wrote about my coffee-drinking escapades, my meeting with George, the religious bee hunters. And the interesting, conflicting reports of Boyd Jenkins. I'd begun to get a mental picture of Boyd: a big man, with a long scraggly beard and a wild look in his eyes. I could imagine him sitting outside on his grassless front yard, playing mean fiddle tunes.

I grabbed last week's issue of *Time* magazine out of my backpack. I had brought it with me from the land of graduate school, which seemed further and further away. It assured me that there was an outside world. A world where President Carter was refreshed after his Georgia vacation, and the Roche Sisters were billed as "folk singers." Good thing the VW usually ran for weeks without a fill-up—the gas shortage was raising prices.

When I finally turned off the light attached to my clock radio, it was nearly midnight and the naturalist was already snoring. I dreamt crazy, scary dreams about wild-eyed fiddle players chasing me through the woods, and woke up twice in the middle of the night wondering where in hell I was. And more importantly, why.

Chapter 2

ADJUSTMENTS

I climbed out of bed the next morning, ready to face new folklore adventures. I gave myself a little pep talk while I shaved. I had made it through my first interview. I was putting to practice all the great stuff I had learned in my fieldwork seminar and getting paid for it to boot. Living in a beautiful state park rimmed with green mountains. It was a wonderful opportunity, I would gain so much. I ate some Cheerios I had bought in town, and hurried down to the office.

My excitement flagged a bit when I picked up the receiver to dial the first number. Fifteen minutes later, after getting three no-answers, and one person who hung up on me after telling me in no uncertain terms that he was "not interested in whatever the hell I was selling," I connected with Bessie McMann, someone the librarian had suggested was a great quilter. She invited me to come right over. She was expecting an "insurance feller" to come sometime that morning, but didn't think that would interfere much with our visit.

I got to her house without taking too many wrong turns, and she welcomed me in like a long-lost relative. She started talking as soon as she opened the door of the small, tidy house and didn't stop for an hour.

"Now, here is my latest one I just finished. It's called a sunbonnet, see, here are the little girls with their bonnets. It took me two months of steady work and I'm giving it to my granddaughter for her room. She'll be so tickled to get it. She's been wanting one for so long but you know she is the youngest and I've made a different one for each of the nineteen grandkids and she was last so she had to wait longest, bless her heart. But my Mom always said 'Good things come to them that waits,' so I guess it's okay."

She opened her bedroom closet and lifted down quilt after beautiful quilt, unfolding them lovingly on her bed. Fans, Dresden plates, flower gardens, log cabins, nine-patches, and a special heirloom crazy quilt made from old silk ties and scraps of black velvet. My mother, an afficionado of "country stuff," as she insisted on calling it, would have been drooling at this bounty. I complimented Mrs. McMann on the wonderful craftsmanship and excellent choice of colors, and she beamed. "Just something I learned from Maw and Grandmaw and kept up with all these years," she remarked.

I was in the middle of taking photos of the quilts when the doorbell rang.

"Oh, there's that insurance feller. You see, I had me a little grease fire in the kitchen last week and they sent this feller out to check on the damage for a settlement," she explained as she padded off to answer the door.

I was expecting to see a middle-aged three-piece-suit type, sent up from the nearest city, Knoxville. When he passed by the open bedroom door and gave me a nod, I laughed to myself. He was just a few years older than me, tall and rangy, dressed in crisply ironed tan slacks and a striped button-down shirt. It made me feel like a schlep in my graduate school uniform—jeans and a t-shirt.

"So, Mrs. McMann, I hear you've had a little trouble here," I could hear him saying. He was a Yankee like myself.

"Oh, you don't know the half of it. See, here, how it charred up my good woodwork and window frame and all?" I went about my business, photographing the quilts and jotting down notes on a photo log form while they discussed the problem. In a short while, I heard Mrs. McMann calling me from the kitchen. "Son, won't you come in and have some tea with us?"

I packed up the camera equipment and joined the cozy scene in the kitchen. Bessie had gotten out some homemade molasses cookies, and the insurance feller was putting some finishing touches on his own forms.

"This here is Mr. Anderson, he is doing a folk-lore project out here at the state park. See, he's been taking pictures and getting some information on my quilts."

"Is that so?" The insurance feller looked amused. "And what, pray tell, are you going to do with the information, Mr. Anderson?"

"Well, I was hoping to get Mrs. McMann to bring out some of her quilts and give us a demonstration of quilt making, actually. And all of the documentation will go to the State Archive for future use by students and scholars."

"Hmm. I'm pretty sure your home owner's insurance would cover any possible damage to any of your quilts if you brought them to the park, Mrs. McMann."

"Oh—we'll be very careful, and we wouldn't let anything happen to them!" I exclaimed, and I could feel myself reddening. I looked over at the insurance feller and saw he had laughter in his blue eyes.

He closed his notebook and took a casual sip of his tea. "I have some interest in the folklore of the area myself. You can't help but pick things up when you're traveling around like this. People tell me stories—I enjoy it."

"Have you heard any stories of a guy named Boyd Jenkins?" I ventured, throwing it out casually. I wasn't sure I liked this guy but he might be a good source of information.

Mrs. McMann chimed in. "Oh, Lord, has folks been telling you stories of that feller? Well, don't believe all you hear because there's a pack of lies about old Boyd. I don't see what all the fuss is. I knew Boyd when he was just a bit of a kid. He was a wild one, but always polite and respectful of his elders. Just got on the wrong side of the law, is all."

"Yeah, I've heard a few Boyd stories," The insurance feller said, speading his long hands on the edge of the table. He didn't elaborate.

"Well, best to leave all that to history, I say," Mrs. McMann said, and the conversation turned to the fine late spring weather we were having, and how good the strawberries were this year. I made a mental note to collect some fresh strawberry recipes. After another half hour, the insurance feller excused himself. I left at the same time, walking out with him. He drove a small Honda just one step up from my beat-up Volkswagen bug.

"By the way, my name is Chris Demond. I live just outside the park grounds, in that little blue house near the east entrance. I'm usually home after seven. Stop by sometime, if you get a chance, and we'll talk folklore." He chuckled to himself as he got in his car and drove off.

In the next few days I buried myself in work, visiting an old-time fiddler and a wood-carver, attending the rehearsal of a family gospel group, following up leads on a crafts cooperative and a water-powered grist mill. I started taking lots of pictures of local architecture set against a backdrop of rolling hills, wide valleys, narrow hollows and distant mountains. The landscape at first reminded me of Vermont, where my family had spent our vacation a few summers. But, as I drove around the three-county area, I began to see the landscape as an organic part of the culture, touched by tradition. My head swiveled constantly as I noticed a log barn here, a small family graveyard there, what might be a root cellar in the corner of a house lot. I almost ran off the road several times, and once stopped so short to take a picture of a dogtrot house that the guy behind missed rear-ending me by inches. When I tallied up my mileage for the first week on the job, I was surprised to find I had driven almost 250 miles.

I gave up on the radio, which had started working off and on again. Somehow, the sappy top forty disco tunes or popular country and western music available on the local airwaves didn't seem proper background music for the scenery. Instead, I started playing copies of my music field tapes on the portable cassette tape player as I drove. "Sherman's Retreat" and "I'll Fly Away" seemed much more appropriate.

As I got more interviews under my belt, I picked up a few more details about the life and death of Boyd Jenkins. I couldn't resist asking everyone I interviewed to tell me what they knew about the story. I learned that Jenkins had indeed been an outlaw, had killed someone, and had hid out for weeks (maybe even months or years, depending on who was telling the story) in the woods before the final showdown with twelve state troopers (or, twenty-five FBI men). Opinions seemed divided as to whether Boyd deserved his fate. I longed to go to the library and read some written accounts of the story, but every time I found myself in town with a few minutes to spare, the library was closed.

At the end of the week, I decided to reward myself by visiting Earl Whitelaw and getting at least one whole oral version of the story. I found him, just as George had said I would, sitting on his front porch chewing tobacco. Perhaps "gumming" tobacco would be a better term for it. If Earl had any teeth left in his mouth, I couldn't distinguish them from the wad of tobacco.

"Howdy," he said, and aimed a spit into the overgrown hydrangeas.

"Mr. Whitelaw, I'm Rob Anderson. Your nephew George suggested I talk to you about a project I'm working on up at the park."

Earl chewed on that information for a minute or so, took another spit. "George, did what, now?"

I raised my voice. "He said I should visit you."

"Why for?"

"To ask you some questions."

Another minute, another spit. "Hold on." He disappeared inside the run-down house, and returned affixing a hearing aid. "Okay, young feller. Start over."

I did my best to explain the project, and asked him about his former occupation. He told me he had been a logger, and we discussed that awhile. When the conversation lagged, I jumped in with a question about Boyd Jenkins.

"George says you might be able to tell me a little about a fellow named Jenkins that I've been hearing some about."

"Jenkins? You mean ole Boyd, huh?" Spit.

"Yes, that's the one."

"You ain't heard the real, whole, honest truth about ole Boyd, I'll bet, 'cause there is few that knows the real, whole, honest truth. You hear all sort of half-true stories and downright lies, is what you hear." Spit. "I learned Boyd's whole story by listening to this and that feller I worked with or either met up with; kind of studied on it, you could say, 'til I guess I know most of the facts." He paused and I thought he'd spit again. Instead, he squinted at me as if gauging my level of interest. "Now, if I tell you the whole story of Boyd, what are you going to do with it? Are you going to take it down?"

"Well, I have a tape recorder in the car. If you don't mind, I would like to tape the information."

"Well, go get the thing. This here is the real true story and I want you to get it straight." He motioned me off toward the car, and I scrambled up out of the comfortable old rocker I'd settled into and dashed for the cumbersome Nagra tape recorder. It took two trips to get the two heavy metal cases, mike stand, and reel-to-reel tapes.

"Hell, that's some rig. I thought you probably had one of them little bitty old things. Hell, this here is something." He looked a bit apprehensive as I fumbled with the connections, remembering our project director's words: "People are always intimidated by tape recorders. You might as well intimidate them with the best."

I rolled on a tape and adjusted dials. "Oh, it looks bad, but it's not too awful." I placed the mike on its stand and brought it near Earl.

"I have to talk into here?"

"Yes. Let me just say a little identification piece here, and we'll be ready." I swung the mike toward me. "This is Rob Anderson for the State Parks Folklore Project, I'm here with Earl Whitelaw in Sharp's Church Community, and we are going to talk about Boyd Jenkins." I swung the mike back toward Earl. He took another spit, shifted the wad of tobacco a little, cleared his throat, and started.

"Now, this here is the real, honest, true story of Boyd Jenkins, of this section. I am telling this story so that the future generations will have it right, and nobody will call Boyd a coward and a no good for nothing son of a bitch like some do now, even here in this county.

"It all started many years back. Now, if Boyd had lived, he'd be in his fifties now, but he was shot down in cold blood by the FBI when he was—oh, twenty-five or so I guess. But let me start at the beginning."

And so began the real, honest, true story of Boyd Jenkins, according to Earl Whitelaw, master storyteller, recorded for posterity by the Nagra. I was to learn that it was just one version of the real, true story, but it was one of the most detailed and downright exciting versions I collected in the course of the summer. During the telling, Earl paused only to allow me to turn over the tape—and, of course, for the regularly timed spit, which added an agreeable rhythm to the story. His narrative was so detailed, and his hearing was so bad, even with the hearing aid, that I decided to forego asking questions while he spoke, just adding a nod of encouragement here and there.

Chapter 3

BOYD, TAKE ONE

"Boyd, he was always sort of what you'd call a renegade, a troublemaker maybe. He had spirit, I call it. Came from a family of coal miners on one side and loggers on the other—hardworking people, not schooled, you know. But not ones to make trouble. I don't know where Boyd got that mean, feisty streak—some say from his mama's grandpa. He got hung for killing some feller he caught with his wife, but that's a whole other story. Well, Boyd wanted out of this part of the country when he was young, so he joined the military. Went to fight in that Korean War—told everyone he was going to go kill him some gooks. Well, I don't know about that, but I do know he got sent back with an honorable discharge. Caught some disease over there, I heard. Came back, right back to his hometown. Lived with his folks and lived off some money the military sent him home with. His family is musical—always have been as far back as anyone can recall—and Boyd played the fiddle. He'd set on the front porch and play all night—slept during the day. Once in awhile someone'd ask him to come play a dance, and he would for a little money and as much whiskey as he could hold. I believe it was that whiskey that was his downfall as much as anything. He'd get to drinking, and someone would say some little thing to make him mad, and he'd get to fighting. Put one guy in the hospital—I know him.

He's still got a scar over his eye where Boyd broke a bottle on his head!

"So, this one night Boyd was playing a dance over in Sunrise. He kinda took a fancy to this one lady. Of course, she was with some other guy. So, this guy says to Boyd, 'Keep your eyes on your fiddle, soldier boy, and off my woman,' or something like that. Boyd doesn't say anything right then, but he asks around to find out who this guy is. Turns out he works at the grocery store—the manager I think he was of the little grocery in Sunrise. I say 'manager'—that sounds kind of grand. I think actually his daddy owned the store and this feller helped run it. He traveled a good deal checking on new items and such. Boyd found this all out and set up a plan. Next time this feller left town, Boyd went calling on the lady. She'd heard about Boyd being a bad boy and all—I guess she thought she'd live dangerous and go out with him. They thought no one would recognize them—went over to Knoxville to some gin mill. So happen that some buddy of the grocery feller saw Boyd and the lady, and told him about it next chance he got. Maybe a few weeks later. Boyd was laying low—guess he decided he really liked this lady and didn't want to mess up by courting her too strong while this other feller was in the picture. He'd call her on the phone and try to persuade her to tell this other guy it was quits so he could have her free and clear, but I reckon she was playing both sides of the fence.

"So, this feller told the grocery man about seeing Boyd and his woman all cozy in Knoxville, and that grocery guy got really mad. Everyone talks about Boyd's temper, but the grocery guy had one to match. So, the next day Boyd's mother comes to town to buy a few things and this grocery man comes up to her when she's about to pay. He says to her, 'You Boyd Jenkins's mama, ain't you?' She says yes, and says, 'You a friend of my son's?' He says, 'No, I ain't no friend to such a no good son of a bitch like him. You tell him he'd better get his ass out of town but soon or I'll fry it for him but good.' Then he tells the cashier, 'Sorry but we don't serve trash here—void this order.' And he walks away, leaving Boyd's mama with her mouth wide open wondering what in hell Boyd had done to this guy. Well, she's madder than a snake herself, but not sure who to be madder at—this guy or Boyd for doing whatever made the guy treat her like that. She had to drive clear over to Jakesville just for a few groceries.

"Meanwhile, it seems this grocery guy was so mad at the girl, too, that he went over to her house that same night and roughed her up some, calling her a tramp and a whore and every other name in the book. She tried to tell him that all she and Boyd did was go out for a few drinks, but he told her he knew she slept with him and she could go to hell with him for all he cared now. Well, Boyd got such a dressing down from his mama all day that he decided to escape to town for some recreation that evening. He was hanging around talking to some fellers and drinking whiskey when one of them said he lived next to that girl's house and he'd heard that grocery guy screaming at her and her screaming back and then, he thought, crying after the guy left. Boyd jumped up at that and said something like, 'That no good bastard, I'm going to go give him something to scream over.' He took another big swig of whiskey and marched on over to the grocery store.

"The feller lived above the store, Boyd knew, and there was a light on in the upstairs window. Boyd stood under that window and yelled up, 'Come down, you little bastard, you woman beater, you coward,' and other such things to get a rise out of the feller. In a bit, the guy hung his head out of the window and told Boyd where he could go. Boyd just kept on hollering, though, so the guy went and got his gun. He aimed it at a spot near Boyd's foot and fired away. Them that saw this whole scene say Boyd never even flinched. Instead, he laughed. 'Is that all the better you can aim?' he said.

"Meanwhile, somebody from inside the house there grabbed the grocery guy and hauled him away from the window, saying something like, 'Don't do anything stupid, Tom, that piece of trash Jenkins is not worth going to jail over.' I guess that was his daddy or somebody. So, Boyd stood there for a while more, hollering that this guy was a big coward and that he'd be back to settle the score later so the guy'd better be ready for a fight then. When he got nowhere with that, he went over to the lady's house but she wouldn't let him in, telling him he was drunk and she was done with both him and the other guy—they was nothing but trouble and she didn't need trouble. There was a little two-bit gin mill on the edge of town, and that's where Boyd went next, sitting in a corner and not talking to no one. After a couple of hours, he got up and left. From what I gather, he went home to his mama and daddy's house and got a gun—they say it was his daddy's hunting rifle, I don't know for sure. Well, I guess you can see where this is leading. Somehow Boyd got that grocery guy to come out behind the store, and the grocery guy had a gun with him—would have been crazy not to with Boyd in that mood. They shouted some at each other, and then shots were fired—at least two. When the grocery feller's daddy came out to see what had happened, he found that son of his lying dead. And, of course, Boyd nowhere to be found. Well, he woke the whole town of Sunrise up, believe me, screaming and carrying on, and the sheriff took off after Boyd directly. First place he went, of course, was to Boyd's folks, but they was sound asleep and didn't know anything about the situation until the sheriff came to their door, or so it seems. Anyway, the sheriff searched their house and came up dry. The only thing they found out was the gun was missing, and several rounds of ammunition. Oh, and Boyd's fiddle, too.

"Next the sheriff visited Boyd's lady friend, but she said she had told him she was done with him, and after searching her house and finding nothing they figured she was telling the truth. By then it was way past midnight, and the sheriff told the grocery feller's daddy that there was no sense chasing after Boyd until they could find some tracks or other evidence in the morning, and told everybody to go to bed. By morning, the grocer's daddy had called every county and state lawman he could think of, complaining about the sheriff not doing his job and how this case had to be dealt with right away. By noon, Sunrise and thereabouts was crawling with all sorts of lawmen.

"Meanwhile, the sheriff hadn't come up with much. Boyd, y'know, was familiar with all the woods in this country, since he and his daddy had hunted them since Boyd was young. Also, Lord only knows what sort of skills being in the military had taught old Boyd about survival and covering your tracks. So, it was about like he'd just disappeared. The lawmen searched for weeks, and then most of them gave up. Their bosses probably told them it was no use spending so much time and effort trying to find Boyd when he was probably long gone somewheres they'd never find him. Don't guess none of them cared much, that grocery family wasn't liked much by people around there anyhow.

"There was a couple of fellers, I believe they were FBI men, who kept on the case. They hunted through the woods, sometimes with a dog, and they tracked down all of Boyd's kinfolk who lived both this side of the border and over into Kentucky. None of them had seen him, or so they said. They poked around every abandoned logging camp, every cave, even every hollow tree I guess that they could locate. Once in a while, they'd run into somebody who'd claimed to see him, or they would find some empty whiskey bottles, but they never did find Boyd or even a warm trail—and they were at it for over a whole year.

"Meanwhile, the stories started. You know, someone claimed to have seen Boyd somewheres in the woods when they was out hunting, or else someone claimed to have given him a meal when he wandered up to their door. Some fashioned him a regular Robin Hood, say he stole stuff from rich folks and gave poor ones money or jewelry in exchange for food or whiskey. In some stories, he was supposed to have grown really long hair, all greasy and scary looking, and to have lots of wild hound dogs following after him. Or else people would say that he was all barbered up and looking like a dandy, passing himself off as some rich tourist.

"I say all of it's bunk. Boyd had such a mess of kinfolk who lived way out in the woods, I say that one or the other of them hid him from time to time, giving him food and clothes, and the rest of the time he hid out in one or the other cave. The cave part is true, at least, because that's where these lawmen finally tracked him down to. This was a good two years after he shot the grocery man. Somehow, these guys got wind that Boyd had himself a hideaway way up in the Kentucky woods, far from anywhere a road would take you. I heard it's part of a state forest preserve now, come to think of it.

"So, they kinda spied around to make sure he was really there, and I guess Boyd got a little too confident that he'd never be found up there and had sort of settled in. These guys weren't about to take any chances. They radioed in twenty or so of their buddies to help them bring old Boyd 'to justice' as they say on the TV. So, here's just one lonely criminal holed up in a cave probably with just one rusty old hunting rifle, and more than twenty FBI men with high-powered guns surrounding him. Guess they figured he'd be a fool to try to outshoot them and escape. But, they didn't know the Jenkinses—they're a stubborn lot.

"When they called out one of those things lawmen say, like 'Come out with your hands up, we've got you surrounded,' Boyd just laughed and opened fire. Shot three or four of them, I'm told—I think one died later. Boyd was having such a good old time shooting these guys—or else, he decided to make a run for it—but anyway, Boyd directly come out a little into the opening of the cave, and that is when they let him have it. Eighteen, or whatever was left, lawmen let loose just about all at once, and you don't need a college education to guess what the results of that was. And that was the end of Boyd.

"Some say he died with his gun in one hand and his fiddle in the other. Guess he had carried that old fiddle with him throughout his running. He sure was a hell of a fiddler. I remember some of them dances he played—my wife loved to dance, and we would go and dance and dance on those Saturday nights. Sure do miss her, too, every day. But, I guess you heard all you want to because that's all I know about Boyd. After he died—and it was all in the papers, you can read that part at the library, I guess—people quit talking about the whole thing and it only comes up once in awhile when us old timers are sitting around remembering stuff. So, did I tell you what you wanted to hear?"

I assured Earl that he had, and I turned off the tape recorder. We sat in companionable silence for a few minutes, then I asked Earl if I could come back some time and interview him about his logging experiences. After the intensity of the "real, true story" I didn't have the energy to continue the interview, and Earl was looking a bit tuckered out himself. He said he didn't mind if I came back—I knew where to find him. I packed up all of my gear and roared off in the VW.

It was two o'clock. I had a four o'clock interview with a farmer who owned draft horses. I longed to blow it off and spend the rest of the afternoon relaxing and catching up on my field notes, and listening again to Earl's taped story of Boyd. I settled for making myself a quick peanut butter and jelly sandwich back at the Nature Center and playing back enough of the tape to assure myself that the Nagra had indeed recorded Earl's story. I knew I had a great folk narrative on my hands, and I tingled with the anticipation of collecting more versions. I could see a dissertation topic on the horizon.

Chapter 4

LOCAL COLOR

A few days later, I was driving along on my way to an early morning appointment with a chair maker, when I turned a bend and started following the broad river which sliced through two of the counties I was working in. The sun was brilliant, but the air streaming in through my half-open window was cool and dewy. An ethereal fog rose off the river, hovering just above its calm surface in opaque swirls. Few cars passed. Just me and the river. I pulled the car over and reached for my camera. But, as I stood there with the viewfinder between me and the river, I reconsidered. What did this scenic slice of river have to do with folklore? The other pictures I had taken of the scenery in the area were part of a cultural context: farmscapes, mountainside log houses, entrances to old coal mines. The film in my camera belonged to the state park system and the pictures would end up in the State Archive. Did mist on the river serve any documentary purpose?

I just stood there for a few minutes, enjoying my own mental documentation of the morning, and thinking that I really should get another decent 35mm camera to take my own personal pictures. It was then that I realized how attached I was growing to this place, how I was already sadly anticipating leaving it and going back to "normal life" in my college town. I raised the camera and snapped.

My first program took place on my two-week anniversary at the park, a Sunday. It was, I thought, a sure thing. I had booked a local family gospel group to play at two in the afternoon in the campground's rustic amphitheater. The weather was good, the group showed up on time, the rickety portable sound system worked as well as could be expected. We even had a pretty good audience of campers and a few staff members—well, about a dozen people altogether. But, hey, it was a new concept for the park and it needed some time.

Afterwards, however, I decided that I needed some advice on attracting locals into the park for programs, which was one of the goals of this project. Bright and early Monday morning I was back in the cramped and disheveled office of Ed Daniels, newspaper mogul. I declined a cup of coffee this time.

I had convinced Ed to put a small notice about the program, with some basic information about the project, in the paper. Somehow, it hadn't captured the attention of the populace.

"I was thinking, actually, that it'd be a good idea to write a feature about your work," he announced, scratching the two-day stubble on his chin. "Things are sort of slow, newswise, here just now and it might be a human interest thing—local color, family stories, crafts. Yeah." He rifled through the mess on his desk for a steno pad and a pencil that had a point.

I squirmed as he studied me and scribbled some notes. "So, what sort of stuff have you uncovered so far?" I rattled off a list of folks I'd visited—quilters, musicians, beekeepers, the church homecoming, the chair maker. "Oh, and I collected a couple of versions of the legend of Boyd Jenkins."

Daniels stopped scribbling and looked up, amused. "The 'legend' of Boyd Jenkins?" he snorted. "I'll refrain from mentioning that one." He shook his head a little. "Boyd doesn't need any more posthumous publicity."

"Why not? It must still be a popular story around here, judging from the number of people who seem to know about it."

"Well, there are so many lies that people like to tell about Boyd, embroideries on the truth, that the 'truth' is totally obscured. And it has been since the moment Boyd Jenkins pulled the trigger and killed that man. Even the newspaper stories probably didn't get the whole truth." He tapped the pencil for a few seconds. "Besides, don't you know that the fellow who does the insurance work—Demond I think his name is—collected a whole bunch of information about Jenkins already?"

"Chris Demond?" I blurted, incredulous. "But why?"

"I think he said he was writing some sort of article or book or something. But, he gave it up and went into the insurance business, and settled down here. Darnedest thing. I guess he just liked the area. I don't think he ever published anything—least I don't know about it if he has." He poised the pencil to write again. "Okay, tell me about some of the upcoming programs you're planning."

I thought about this new, disturbing development as I left Daniels's office for my first interview of the day. I remembered Demond's comment about having "heard a few Boyd stories." I wondered if Earl had given him his rendition of the "real, true story." I hadn't thought to ask Earl if anyone else had collected the story. I had assumed I was treading on virgin territory. I felt violated. I wanted the Boyd story to be mine, for the research to be fresh, for my insights to be brilliant. I didn't want to follow the footsteps of some dilettante who had abandoned this fascinating episode of local history to become an insurance adjuster. Professional courtesy would be to at least ask him about his research, but I wasn't feeling very courteous at that moment.

Later that afternoon, I was following Mrs. Ruth Taggart down her hall to the sunny room where her quilting frame and rag rug weaving loom were set up. "Have you met my granddaughter up there at the park? She's a lifeguard and her name is Ruthie—that's right, she's named after me and I'm proud of it. She's a lovely girl, very smart— in her third year of college, you know—and she wants to be a veterinarian last I heard." She paused in the doorway, looking expectant.

"No, I haven't had the pleasure of meeting her yet," I said in my politest fieldworker voice. "I'm afraid I've been so busy I haven't gotten to the swimming pool yet."

"Lord, son, don't work yourself so hard. Here it is summer and you young folks should be having some fun. I tell Ruthie the same thing. You know, she doesn't have a boyfriend—least wise she hasn't brought one around lately—and I say, now, Ruthie, I know you are young, but you should have yourself a beau to take you places. Why, by the time I was her age I was already married with two little ones. But, now, I'm not saying she should rush into that, mind you, a smart girl like her with a chance for a career and all, but she should have someone to take her out to the pictures and all, that's what I'm saying, you understand."

With some difficulty, I finally got Mrs. Taggart off the subject of Ruthie and onto the subject of quilt making and rag rug weaving. Even so, she worked Ruthie's name into the conversation as often as humanly possible. "This is Ruthie's favorite quilt," and "I made Ruthie a rug out of her old blue jeans for her dorm room," etc., etc. I was getting pretty sick of hearing about Ruthie and dreading the logging of this interview tape when I would have to hear all about Ruthie all over again. But, Mrs. Taggart's work was intricate and she knew Bessie McMann well. ("She and I met when Ruthie's father and her son Henry were in school together, years and years ago. . . .") They would work well together for the quilting program I had in mind.

As I was leaving, I got one more, "You really should go introduce yourself to Ruthie down at the swimming pool." Then came the clincher. "Tell her to bring you to dinner here some night—I'll cook her favorite chicken and biscuits. I taught her how to cook it, and she is a right fine cook, too." She gave me a suggestive wink as she was closing the screen door.

Just what I needed, I thought, driving to my next interview. An aggressive grandmother trying to fix me up. I suppose I should have subtly—or not so subtly, since Mrs. Taggart didn't seem like someone who needed subtlety—hinted that I was involved with someone. I couldn't very well tell Mrs. Taggart I was actually living with someone, "in sin," as it were. I decided to tell Mrs. Taggart, and any other grandmother with similar inclinations, that I was engaged next time the problem arose although it wasn't true. But, then I began to worry that the information could somehow get back to my significant other, who was due to visit in two weeks.

In the next few days, a heat wave hit the area. The temperature was over 100 with a nasty, humid haze that obscured the mountains. Driving around—despite the natural air conditioning provided by the rusted-through holes in the VW's floorboards—was hell. Sitting around logging tapes and writing notes in my field journal in the unairconditioned Nature Center was hell. After a couple of days of this, I decided it was time to visit the swimming pool.

I swam a few lazy laps and then sat, dripping, on a poolside chair. I had spent so many hours that spring studying for finals in the library and typing term papers that I had gotten little exercise and no sun. I contemplated my white body with the little roll of flab bulging above my swimming trunks before turning my attention to the rest of the pool clientele. There were plenty of campers and day-use visitors splashing around, kids screaming, mothers yelling. I closed my eyes and savored the barely perceptible breeze cooling my half-dry body. A long, shrill blow on an athletic whistle broke my reverie. "You— Bobby! How many times do I have to tell you not to dive off there?" An authoritative voice rose over the happy pool noises.

Squinting in the hazy sunlight, I looked up toward the voice which came from about fifteen feet away. I first noticed the mass of long, curly black hair framed in the light. Then, the tanned face, nose white with sunscreen, and a lithe body with long, athletic-looking legs dangling off the lifeguard chair. The curve of those legs made me catch my breath. If this was Ruthie, being "engaged" had suddenly lost its appeal.

I considered my options. Should I go right up to her, in my faded trunks with my pasty, pudgy body, and introduce myself? Would grandma have told her about the "nice young feller working over at the park"? Or, should I try to meet her sometime later, fully clothed and feeling less self-conscious? Why was I feeling self-conscious, anyway? I wondered to myself exactly what I was planning to do with young Ruthie besides sample her granny's chicken and biscuits. I realized that, as I pondered all of this, I had been staring at her profile— strong and classic, framed by that incredible hair. She turned her head and stared back.

"Is there something wrong?" She called over to me, shading her eyes.

I threw my towel over my shoulders and straightened up. "Uh, no. No. I was just wondering, um, if your name could be Ruthie by any chance."

She scrutinized my face. "How'd you know that?" she said, quickly surveying the pool, then hopping down off the chair.

I pulled the towel closer around me. "I met your grandmother. Maybe she told you about me?" No sign of recognition in her dark brown eyes, just a slight confusion.

"Granny Taggart or Granny Bigelow?" she asked, coming closer. (My first thought was, oh, there's another one? I'll have to find out what kind of folk talent she has.) Ruthie stood over me with her hands on her hips. I squirmed a little under my towel.

"Taggart. I interviewed her about her quilting and weaving."

"Oh, you're that folklore guy. No, granny didn't tell me she met you, but I read about you in the park bulletin." She turned her attention back to the pool, making sure Bobby and his cohorts weren't misbehaving.

"I'd like to talk to you sometime, 'cause I'm thinking about taking a course in oral history next fall, so I can get some of our family history down. I need some humanities credit and it looked like fun."

I ignored the suggestion that my chosen field of study was merely "fun." "I'm staying at the Nature Center. If you come over, I can show you the notes I took on your grandmother's interview." How about the etchings while we're at it, I thought. I laughed, a self-conscious little chuckle. "Your grandmother said I should tell you to bring me back to her house for chicken and biscuits."

She turned back to me and looked closer, up and down. I couldn't read her face. "That's Granny Taggart—always trying to fix me up with somebody." She didn't laugh, but she didn't look disgusted, either. She turned back toward the pool. "I'll stop by sometime after work," she said, and strode back to her chair.

I slunk off to take a shower and to make some notes in my long-neglected field journal. I didn't write anything about Ruthie.

Chapter 5

HEADS UP

The next day—not quite so hot—I was driving to an appointment with a banjo maker who lived way out in the countryside. The road twisted and curved, revealing something scenic at every turn: a half torn-down barn, cows chewing their cud in the afternoon heat under the shelter of some scrub pines, a sweeping view of the distant mountains. It was a long drive and I was beginning to get sleepy. I turned a sharp bend and stomped on the brakes. There, by the side of the road, was a small shed with hundreds of baby doll heads nailed to its side. I considered the fact that I might be hallucinating. But no—as I got out of the car and approached the building, it was real enough.

I stared up at the disembodied heads. Blond, brunette, bald. Painted on or molded features—some with those awful glass eyes that look too real. Dirty, stained faces, some with cracks or holes in them. Most of them weren't staring back at me, but had their eyes (if they were open) fixed on some remote point, seeming to yearn toward whatever lay there. I found myself turning in that direction to see if I could figure out what it was they yearned after. It was so eerily quiet that I could hear the wood bees buzzing in and out of the building's roof line. Suddenly, I heard a crunch of gravel, and a big man dressed in a short-sleeved blue work shirt and dark blue pants came around the corner of the building and laughed. I jumped—which made him laugh harder. "I see you're interested in our baby dolls," he said in a scratchy but friendly voice, which reminded me of that guy on the old Howdy Doody show. "Uh, yes," I managed.

"Oh, she—the missus you know—likes to 'rescue' them from the dump. You know, kids get sick of them or they get broke, and they toss them out. Now, too, people'll bring them to her 'cause they know she has this collection, you know. Call her the Doll Lady. Lots of people stop and it's good for business."

"Business?" I asked. He pointed to the front of the building. In my fascination with the doll heads I hadn't even noticed that it was a small country store. "Billings One Stop" was printed on a sign which also advertised Sunshine bread. "Well, I am pretty thirsty!" I admitted. He led me inside to an old-fashioned chest-type cooler filled with soft drinks that I had never heard of. I chose a small glass bottle of something yellowish called "Doctor Enuf." When I paid for it, Mr. Billings handed me a bottle opener on a long string.

"Been in business here long?"

Billings sat his heavy frame down on a worn stool behind the counter. "Fifteen years this September," he grinned. "I used to work at a grocery store in Sunrise, then I got to hankering to start my own. Wife's family had this bit of land out here in the country, and so we saved up for stock and me and two of my brothers built this here shed and it serves the folks around here that don't like to go way into town just for a loaf of bread or such as that." He watched as I guzzled down the drink, which tasted vaguely lemony like weak 7-Up. "You a traveling salesman or something?"

"No, I'm working over at the state park on a folklore project." As soon as the words were out of my mouth I anticipated his response.

"A what project?"

"We're collecting stories and information about traditions in the area—things that have been in people's families for a long time. Quilting, hunting, coal mining, string music, all of those kind of things."

"Then what you going to do with all that information?"

"Well, I've been presenting programs up at the park, and also the information will go into the State Archive."

"I see." He scratched his head again and fell silent. I asked if he wanted the bottle back, and he took it behind the counter. I was just about to turn around and head out the door when I realized what he had said.

"You say you worked in Sunrise at a grocery? Which one?"

"Ain't more than one, or was then."

"Then you probably heard about that business with Boyd Jenkins."

"Heard about it, hell, son. I lived it." He paused for a moment and then, seeing the interest in my eyes, opened his mouth to begin what I knew would be a long story. I quickly intervened.

"Wait! I want to hear all about this, but I have another appointment in a few minutes, with T.L. Wilson, the banjo maker. Maybe you know him?"

Billings looked disappointed. " 'Course, he's my daughter-in-law's uncle. Nice feller."

I promised that I would come back as soon as possible to record his story and to take some pictures of the baby dolls (if that was okay with Mrs. Billings). I got the phone number and address for my files and hurried on to the Wilson home.

When I mentioned that I had met a sort-of relative, Mr. Wilson chuckled. "Oh, him. Now, don't go believing much of what he tells you. He likes to hear himself jawing." I thought that was as good a recommendation for a storyteller as I was likely to get.

Two days later, I was sitting on a ratty, overstuffed easy chair at the back of the Billings One Stop. Mr. Billings sat across from me, with a good view of the front door, in case a customer should wander in. The tape recorder and mike were arranged on a couple of orange crates between us. Before the interview began, I happened to glance up toward the rafters and noticed several stray baby dolls, who hadn't made it to the wall yet, staring down at us.

First, I asked Billings a few questions about himself and his family's history in the area. His father and grandfather had been farmers and, interestingly enough, split oak basket makers. I wanted to pursue this awhile, but Billings was so anxious to tell his version of the Boyd story that he steered the conversation away from the subject of basket making so skillfully that I hardly noticed the transition.

"Yes, Pap and Grandpap made baskets and in the off season of farming, they'd bring them to these little towns around here in a wagon. And they'd bring them to people's houses, but also try to get some of the grocery stores to carry them, you see, kind of on a commission, you see. Well, I usually went around with them, and I guess you could say that's how I got interested in the grocery business. It just kind of fascinated me, you see. We'd go into one of them little old groceries, and I would just wonder and wonder—where did all this stuff come from, and how did you know what people wanted and how much to order and all that, you see, and I was always asking questions like that of the owners.

"Finally, one of them—this feller over in Sunrise, like I was telling you when you stopped the other day, he says, joking like—'Hey, Garrett (that was my Pap's name), I could give this son of yours a job when he gets old enough.' Says, 'He has asked me so many questions since you been bringing him around, I figure he knows all about the grocery business as much as if he took a college degree in it!' " Billings laughed heartily. "So, that's how I got that job in Sunrise, and how I happened to be there through the whole business with Boyd Jenkins. 'Cause, you see, I didn't just work there, I boarded there as well, since my folks lived so far out in the country and all."

Billings paused and took a deep breath. I knew I didn't need to ask any more questions for a while.

"I came to work at Ralph Atkinson's grocery in Sunrise when I was just fifteen. Times were poor on the farm, you see, and the family needed a little something extra to see them by. I was never much of a scholar, and so high school wasn't going over too good with me anyhow. I'd miss a lot of school to help on the farm, anyway, so what was the use. I always liked to read, though, and do to this day—read everything I can get my hands on." He waved his beefy hand in the air, and I noticed a bookcase on the wall behind him weighed down with books of all sorts.

"Anyway, like I said, this Mr. Atkinson was willing to train me and also board me. He was a right nice feller, that Mr. Atkinson, I learned a lot from him. But, that son of his—Tom—could be a mean bastard, and he didn't like me for some reason from the very start. He was maybe ten years older than me, and always trying to pick a fight.

Calling me a hick, or making fun of the way I talked, or something. If I so much as made a face at him, though, he would complain to his Papa about how I was bothering him. So, you see, there was no love lost between us. Not that Boyd Jenkins was one of my favorite people in the world, either. He was, you see, one of my cousins on my mother's side, and whenever I used to see him at some family gathering, he always picked on me, too.

"So, you see, I guess you could call me 'impartial' in these goings-on, since I really did not like either of these fellers even if one was kin and the other's daddy was my boss." Billings laughed again. At that moment, the bell sounded at the store's front door. An elderly lady with a basket full of eggs under one arm walked in. " 'Scuse me," mumbled Billings, and hauled himself out of his chair. I put the recorder on "pause."

As soon as Mrs. Ross had exchanged her eggs for a loaf of Sunshine bread and a jar of Skippy, Billings was back into the story as though he'd never left off. I quickly un-paused the recorder. (Earlier that week I had lost twenty minutes of incredible banjo playing, forgetting to do that, and I didn't want to miss one word of a complete version of the Boyd legend.) "About a year and a half after I came to work there, this trouble with old Boyd began. I usually went home of a weekend, you see, after the Saturday morning rush, so I didn't get to go to these dances. Too bad, but anyway, I didn't get to witness Boyd moving on old Tom's girlfriend. I knew her all right, though, because she came into the store a lot when his daddy wasn't around, and he was always taking her back into the stockroom and—hey, you are a grown feller, I guess I don't have to tell you what they were doing back there." He winked.

"His daddy didn't like this girl—guess she wasn't good enough for his only precious son, you see—and, they were always having an argument over him seeing this girl. 'She will bring you down, Tom, I'm telling you,' I remember him saying. Well, the old man started sending young Tom out on buying trips more often to get him away from this girl. This is when the trouble really began, I guess. 'Cause this gave old Boyd a chance to move in on her, you see. Can't see what she saw in Boyd, no how. He wasn't a looker like that Tom, and he could be mean as a snake sometimes. But that was her business I reckon.

"Anyways, one night, I was sound asleep when all of a sudden I hear these voices, angry, shouting. I didn't need to eavesdrop, you see. The window of the little room I slept in was right next to where one guy was yelling and one floor directly under where the other guy was yelling back. Didn't take long to figure out that the guy outside was ole cousin Boyd and the one upstairs was Tom.

"'Come down here, you son of a bitch,' Boyd was yelling, only he was already so drunk that it sounded like 'sumofabish.'

"'You're crazy if you think I'm coming down there, you drunk bastard,' Tom yelled back. 'Speak your piece and get the hell out of here.'

" 'You such a sorry piece of shit that you have to beat up women to feel big,' " Boyd yelled. Later, you see, it was told around that Tom had knocked around that girlfriend for going out with Boyd when he was away. I had no proof of that but wouldn't 've put it past him to do something like that.

"'Go back home to them trash you call folks and get sober, Jenkins,' Tom yelled back.

"Old Boyd yelled some other stuff that you can guess was not too complimentary about this feller Tom, and presently I heard some shuffling going on upstairs. I wasn't sure what was going on but the next thing I knew there was a very loud bang. Judging from the sound, Tom fired a shot into the air, sort of a warning, you see. After that, things were quiet. I guessed that the shot had brought Boyd back to his senses and that he had slunk off to drink some more. Anyhow, I went back to sleep.

"Next thing I know—well, it must have been a few hours later—I heard more yelling, Boyd and Tom again. Directly, I heard feet on the stairs and someone running out the back door. Now, I never will know if that stupid old Tom meant to run off and avoid Boyd altogether, or wanted to face him, but Boyd met him in the back alley and they had more words. I couldn't hear exactly what they were saying, but the tone of it was even more angry than before. Then, bang! bang! bang! Three shots. Two from Tom's gun, that was a revolver his daddy kept around to scare burglars away, so he used to say, and the other one from a shotgun—that was Boyd's.

"Well, I guess Boyd would've had to have been a better shot, having been in the army and all—that Tom had got exempted from the military somehow and he was too much the city slicker to be much of a hand with a gun anyhow. Killed that Tom dead with the one shot. Well, I guess blew a pretty big hole in him with his daddy's ole hunting rifle, they say.

"Pretty soon the whole place was full of folks—the sheriff of course but also the whole town, it seemed. Nothing too exciting ever happened in Sunrise, you see, so this was big news. A murder! Tom's daddy, of course, was pretty hysterical, you can bet, and calling for the hanging of Boyd, who of course was long gone by then. I got questioned by the sheriff, and later other lawmen that came to investigate. But, it was a pretty cut and dried case. All they had to do was find Boyd. But, that was the hard part, you see.

"Ole Boyd knew the wild woods in these parts and just where to hide. Then again, both sides of his family live all up and down this section both on the Kentucky side and here, and some kinfolks will help their own no matter what he's done. I guess that's why they got the FBI on this, chasing him across state lines and all. Tom's daddy started going a little crazy, especially since the whole town seemed to be telling stories about where ole Boyd had been seen, here and there, and all that foolishness. When something like that happens, folks just naturally like to gossip about it, and make up all manner of lies about it just for the sake of flapping their lips. Like I said, nothing as interesting as this had happened in Sunrise since—well, I guess as long as I could remember. Anyway, I didn't believe any of the fancy tales being told about Boyd and his whereabouts. Seems like he was being turned into a hero of sorts, but in my mind he was just a feller who'd gotten drunk and shot another feller. I felt pretty neutral about the whole thing, you see, from the start. The only way it affected me was, I got sort of promoted at the grocery, since the son was dead and the old man was going around half crazy. I got most of the responsibility, me and another guy they hired, and I learned more than I ever would have if ole Tom had stayed alive. Guess Boyd done me a service there."

Billings chuckled at his grisly joke, and leaned back in his chair. I thought the story was over, but waited a little while in silence just in case there was a postscript.

"Of course, they caught ole Boyd finally, as I knew they would sooner or later. And, to give him credit, he went out with a show—the stories started all over again when that happened. How brave he was to stand up to those FBI men, and all that. Heck. Just stupid, is all I say. And, must have been pretty crazy himself by then.

"I say I wasn't that interested in the whole story, but I did have a hankering to see the cave that Boyd holed up in all those months. Just a natural curiosity I guess. So, the fall after they brought him down, one of my hunting buddies and I asked around and found out where the cave was located. We found it after a good search—it's a wonder that the FBI found it at all, not even knowing those woods. We knew it was the right cave because we'd heard tell about the paintings."

My ears, which along with the rest of me was beginning to get a little numb, perked up. "Paintings?" I asked.

"Don't tell me nobody told you about the paintings! Well, I guess it's not really all that common knowledge. You see, Boyd must've had a lot of time on his hands, holed up in that cave. He wasn't really traipsing all over Tennessee and Kentucky doing all the things folks tell stories about, he was just plain holed up most of the time. So, I guess he had to find something to keep him busy or he'd go crazy. Well, I don't know if it worked, 'cause he probably was crazy already."

I was getting a bit impatient with Billings's digressions. "So, he painted?" I urged.

"Painted the walls of the cave, with scenes. I guess he got hold of some paint and brushes somewheres—stole them, probably, out of someone's tool shed or something. Kinda crude, you see, but still you could recognize who and what things were. There was his daddy's home, and a kind of 'self-portrait' of Boyd and his fiddle, and his hound dog—I remember that dog, too, he used to follow old Boyd wherever he went. I think he called him Bob, 'cause his tail was bobbed off—a black and tan and bluetick mix if I remember correctly." Billings fell silent, musing over Bob's proper pedigree.

"Were there other paintings? And what happened to them? Are the wall paintings still in the cave?" I was violating one of the first things a folklore fieldworker learned: ask only one question at a time.

Billings scratched his big nose. "Well, just about the whole cave was covered with them. Like I said, he didn't have nothing but time to work on it. It's kinda like those prisoners who start doing art while they're in the pen, you know, I saw an article about it once in the Sunday magazine. But, it's funny you should ask about other paintings, because there was a story going around that Boyd also painted on other stuff, like I guess slabs of wood or whatever he would get his hands on, and that he sometimes traded these paintings for food or other stuff from the local folks. But, I don't hold no stock in that story, no how. Hobos used to do that during the Great Depression, with things they'd make out of old cigar boxes and such, so maybe folks just started telling tales about ole Boyd doing the same. Ain't nobody ever brought out one of these so-called works of art to serve as evidence, you see, that I know. And, there weren't any left in the cave as far as I heard. Or, any sign of his painting stuff, brushes and such, you see. So, I guess he really only kept his art work to the walls. And, I guess you can figure what has happened to them over the years, painted on rock that gets damp and dry according to the seasons. From what I hear tell, there is still a little of the paintings if you look real hard, but not much. Why, you fixing on making a trip up there?" Billings chuckled.

"Is it far?" I asked, knowing full well that I would want to go even if it were several hours away.

"Maybe a couple hours' drive, almost up to the Kentucky border, and there's a road that goes partly into it now. Some big out-of-state outfit is fixing to do something up there. That bothers the locals—they can't see a bunch of city slickers wrecking their woods, you see! But money talks, and they bought that piece of land for a right smart bit of it—more than it was worth, I hear. First there was rumor that the state had bought it for a game reserve, but I hear now it's a private outfit."

I cut off this new line of gossip. "Could you give me directions to get up there?" I asked, putting pen to notebook. Billings stirred, and reached for something behind the counter—a map of a county just south of the Kentucky border. "Well, if you really want to know, I guess there's no harm to it." He spread the map out and gave me explicit directions. I figured I was bound to get lost anyhow.

Chapter 6

RESEARCH FELLOW

The day after interviewing Billings, I was checking my messages at the park office. I found one from Chris Demond. I had almost forgotten Mr. Insurance Feller in the weeks since meeting him. I had become preoccupied with my documentation chores and the impending visit of my graduate school girlfriend. "Come for dinner Wednesday night at 7:30—call if you can't," Demond's message read. The note had a tone of command that irked me, but I really did want to find out how far he'd gotten with his Boyd research before he gave up on it, and what the nature of the research was in the first place. Maybe he had merely been collecting some information for a freelance article and it hadn't sold. Maybe he was a failed novelist who attempted to use the legend as the basis for a plot. Maybe he was just curious about murders. Maybe over a casual dinner I could get some of these questions answered? Besides, unlike myself, he might be a good cook. And I could use a little intellectual stimulation.

When I walked into the small house, I smelled something spicy and delicious, altogether different from the tasty but mostly bland Southern fare I had been served at diners and homes in the past month. It was 7:40. "You're late," he said as showed me into the living room. He noticed me appreciating the aroma. "I used to live with a Pakistani woman," he explained. "It's vegetarian. It'll be ready in about five minutes." He sauntered back to the kitchen to stir something.

I looked around what I could see of the tidy cottage. Some nice folk crafts—maybe I should ask him about their makers. Worn furniture, not much different from my own back at grad school (known affectionately as "Early Salvation Army"). A small TV set, a low bookshelf with popular fiction and some well-kept plants. There were a couple of doors to other rooms, both closed. One led upstairs, I speculated, and the other—maybe a home office?

"Something to drink?" he called from the kitchen. "I don't drink alcohol, but I have a couple of beers here somewhere."

A beer sounded great, although I wasn't sure it was good etiquette to drink in the presence of a non-drinker. I accepted a Bud that he produced from the recesses of his well-stocked fridge. The kitchen was also small but tidy. Demond stirred a pot of what turned out to be a very hot, very delicious vegetable curry. Brown rice and a salad waited nearby.

"So, how's your research going?" he asked as we started eating.

"It's been great. Today I interviewed a guy who makes these intricate canes out of tree branches, with snakes and sayings carved into them. He had some great snake stories, too—"

Demond broke in, "—Hoop snakes; snakes that divide themselves into pieces and then reattach; snakes that drink milk out of children's bowls. Thompson Motif number ex-one three two one, Aarne-Thompson Tale Type two eighty five."

I think my mouth was hanging open, like a cartoon character's pantomime of surprise, because I choked a little on the curry. It was the reference to Stith Thompson and Anti Aarne, two scholarly figures rarely heard of outside academic folklore circles, that threw me. He smiled, and chuckled a little.

"Masters in folklore from Penn, 1976; all but dissertation towards the Ph.D."

I swallowed some beer to encourage the curry down the right hole. I had figured on just about any explanation of why he was so interested in legends, crafts and other folk stuff except this one. To make matters worse, his academic folklore training was further advanced than my own. And, from the biggest rival of my own graduate school,

Indiana University. I had passed my masters exam the year before, and I was only one year into the rest of my coursework toward the Ph.D. I waited for him to continue. Surely he wanted to relate the story of why he quit—maybe philosophical problems with the department chair whom I heard could be difficult; a sudden reversal of fortune that made gainful employment necessary; or just a desire to be more involved with the "real world"? Or, I thought, horrified, maybe he was still working on his research here, just doing the insurance thing to make some bucks towards expenses. Or to have a better "in" with the locals. That was it. He was going to write his dissertation on the Boyd legend. Damn!

While I was speculating, I realized that Demond was watching my face with obvious pleasure as he sipped his Sprite. And my face was probably as easy to read as a large-print copy of Reader's Digest.

He said, finally, "I've decided not to finish the degree." He paused again, draining the soda can and crushing it in his hand in a bit of male bravado. "Of course, I'm still very interested in field collecting. It's so easy to do in this job—incredible stuff just falls into my lap." I glanced again around the visible portions of his home and took more notice of the folk crafts that served as decor. A fine Dresden Plate quilt hung on the wall; rag rugs were scattered on the wood floor; some split oak baskets and old woodworking tools took up shelf space among the stereo equipment. Obviously, he was making good use of the stuff that fell into his lap. "So, all the advantages of studying this stuff without the hassles."

"By the way," he began again. "I thought you'd like to know that, before I decided not to finish my degree, I was working on some research for the dissertation, which included collecting a number of versions of the Boyd Jenkins legend. I understand the story interests you. Instead of wasting your time collecting versions of the legend, I'd be happy to show you what I've collected. I don't have any plans to do anything with it myself at the moment, but you never know. I might decide to finish the research someday and write something. So, I would appreciate it if you wouldn't plan to use it in any way yourself. I just thought you might like to see what I've collected to satisfy your own curiosity about the legend and its variants." He turned the crushed soda can over thoughtfully in his hand. "After all, I'm sure you have plenty of other work to do in your short time here, setting up programs and all of that. Working on the sort of public sector project you're engaged in this summer—well, you get such a short amount of time to do any research in an area, don't you? That's why I like living here and working at a job that allows me to travel around and collect at my leisure." He looked up, smiled an annoying smile, and offered to make some coffee.

I pondered my options while he brewed the coffee in the kitchen. Was his offer sincere? I itched to see his versions of the Boyd legend, to see how they compared with the ones I had collected, and to find out whom he had interviewed. I was sure he must know about the paintings, and might even have some. But something made me hold back. He was, after all, tying my hands by asking me "not to plan to use" the material he had collected in any way. While his own research had preceded mine, and he had been thinking about using it for his dissertation, he had also just told me that he wasn't going to finish the degree. This all seemed to fall into some crack of professional ethics that was beyond my limited experience. I decided to postpone any decision and subtly changed the subject when he brought in the coffee.

I told him about the impending visit of my girlfriend, and how it would interrupt my research. He smiled and put down his coffee. "I'll give you a friendly warning," he said. "You can get caught up in the culture here. There are kind people, willing to share little portions of their lives with you. But you'll be leaving at the end of the summer, going back to another life. Keep that other life in your thoughts and your heart. Don't be seduced by this temporary experience. Learn all you can from it, and bring that back to grad school. But always remember you'll be leaving. This is only one of many folklore experiences you'll have in your career." He held my eyes for several long moments and I felt almost mesmerized with his words.

His laugh broke the spell. "And, hey, I envy you. It's hard to get a piece of action around here. Although there are some noteworthy young lasses around—case in point, the lifeguard down at the park. I think her name is Ruth. I met her grandmother this past spring at a community function and she was singing her praises, and for once it wasn't just a grandmother's prejudice." He wiggled his eyebrows rakishly.

I tried to return a man-to-man joke grin, hoping the disappointment didn't register on my face. I finished my coffee and headed back to the Nature Center to log some tapes. I still wasn't sure what to make of this guy. But, I had decided that I would be damned if I would ask to see any of his research on the Boyd legend. I felt that doing my own research on the legend was going to be a test not only of my scholarship but of my manhood. I'd show him that a folklorist working on "a public sector project" is capable of some serious research.

Of course, my attitude was acerbated by that bit about Ruthie. He might be envying the visit of my girlfriend, and just doing some male swaggering—after all, how would he have known that Mrs. Taggart had done her song and dance about Ruthie for me as well? And why should I care so much?

I tried to put myself in his position. I guess I would be pretty pissed off if some out-of-towner came nosing around my territory. But, I couldn't help feeling that there was something more malevolent behind his "friendly warning," and something more than posturing about his interest in Ruthie.

I realized that my mind was straying from the tape I was logging, Mrs. Annie Rankin describing her mother's loom house, and dwelling too much on this Demond business. I tried to put it out of my mind and concentrate on logging the tape. Actually, it was quite interesting. I hadn't known that people had separate loom houses; I always figured the loom was right there in the house with everything else. But those looms were really huge sometimes, so it would make sense. And, I remembered from watching a demonstration at a living history farm, really noisy, too.

But my mind kept returning to Demond's words. I realized that I was looking upon the impending four-day visit of my girlfriend not as a welcome break, but as an annoyance. Maybe he was right in his own strange way. I was getting too involved in this job, in this place, in the rhythm of the summer, the seduction of the landscape and culture. I gave up trying to log the tape and fell asleep over an article in the current Journal of American Folklore, which had been forwarded to me from my other life.

Chapter 7

VISITOR FROM THE OTHER WORLD

When she walked in, the quilting program disaster was already in full swing. The quilt frame that Spike had rigged up collapsed, spraying needles, pins, thimbles, spools of thread, cardboard patterns and chalk across the floor. Mrs. McMann and Mrs. Taggart both sat with needles in mid-air and the frame dangling off their generous knees. Startled, a young woman who had been absorbed in watching Mrs. McMann's gnarled but deft fingers executing twelve stitches per inch jumped back, right into my clever clothesline quilt display. The Boy Scout knot I was sure would hold gave way, and six quilts tumbled into a heap at the feet of three other bystanders. Attempting a speedy getaway, the boy who had started it all (via a well-placed kick to the corner sawhorse holding up the frame) slipped on a spool of thread and sprawled on the floor, wailing. His nose hit something hard, and blood spurted out—perilously close to the spotless, priceless quilts. As far as I was concerned, the kid deserved to bleed to death, as long as he didn't get any on the Double Wedding Ring or Grandma's Flower Garden inches from his face. I couldn't decide what to dive for first—the frame, the quilts, or a cloth to mop up the blood.

The Nature Center door opened, and she walked in carrying the lumpy tapestry bag she always took on trips. The scramble to undo the disaster was largely out of my hands. Mrs. McMann and Mrs. Taggart both calmly stood up, set their sides of the frame down on their chairs, and moved together to replace the sawhorses. Helpful bystanders quickly scooped up the quilts and set them with reverence on a nearby table. The boy's mother produced a huge wad of Kleenex, affixing half to his nose and mopping up the mess on the floor with the other. By the time I regained some sense of usefulness, all that was left to do was pick up the scattered sewing supplies. This is how Melissa, my graduate school girlfriend found me—on my hands and knees, spearing pins into a tomato-shaped pincushion. "So, this is the important cultural work you've been doing all summer?" she said, looking down at me, laughing.

We had met in an introductory anthropology class our first semester in grad school. She already knew that she wanted to learn an African language, get a Fulbright and go study somewhere "exciting and worthwhile" that would further the world's understanding of the intricate workings of humanity, and then get a tenure-track position at a university. She was already an academic anthropologist. I, on the other hand, although I didn't know it at the time, was already a public sector folklorist. I had a vague but enthusiastic desire to study something just as exciting and worthwhile but considerably closer to home, to preserve whatever treasures I found in an archive, museum or other public institution, and to present programs, exhibits or whatever to the public. For me, the Southern U.S. seemed an exotic enough locale to study. Teaching, quite frankly, frightened me.

We argued from our first cup of coffee at the local coffee house (where a cup of coffee could last at least 100 pages of a required text) about the relative worth of studying your own versus someone else's culture. I guess it was this argument, which we never resolved, that set off the sparks of the first intellectual/sexual relationship I had experienced. Not that I hadn't had my share of sexual experiences for a healthy male college graduate. But I had never tumbled into bed discussing comparative paradigms of the psychological symbolists before. The intellectual stimulation fed the sexual.

We had great times in our narrow, creaky first-year grad dorm beds, and by the end of that year we were searching for an affordable apartment where we could coexist with the cockroaches. We found one, minutes from campus and just around the corner from her favorite vegetarian restaurant, where you could get a big bowl of fried brown rice and veggies for a buck.

The apartment was small, with the living room, kitchen and dining area all jammed together and a drafty bedroom with just enough space for a double bed and two small dressers. The price was right, though. The next year, we moved to a slightly larger place and, despite constant arguments—not all of them intellectual—we lived there still.

Or, rather, she lived there this summer while I lived here in the back of the Nature Center with the naturalist. She was furthering her essential anthropological education, honing her African language skills and spending long hours in the library amassing what would be the bibliography of her dissertation. She had agreed to come visit between summer sessions.

At the time we had planned this, I saw it as a respite from my monk-like existence as a folklore collecting machine. After a month and a half here in the field and meeting Ruthie, I must admit, the visit seemed less and less like a good idea. In fact, I had begun to dread it like a sore throat that wouldn't go away no matter how many Sucrets you popped. I had begun not to miss anything about her, neither her good features nor her annoying ones. Not her long silky, reddish-brown hair or her smirky lips. Not her blueberry pancakes with real maple syrup (she was from western Massachusetts; her father was an Economics professor at Williams) or the habit she had of burning the toast. Not her books on Africa in their orderly rows on the bookshelves or her subscription to the Sunday New York Times. Who could love a Sunday paper without comics, anyhow? Not even making love to her. Somehow, none of it seemed to matter. In fact, none of it seemed quite real.

But it was real enough, I realized as I carried her bag into my room after the quilting program ended. She had sat patiently, observing the people coming in and out of the Nature Center oohing and aahing over the quilts and asking Mrs. Taggart and Mrs. McCann the same questions over and over again: "How long does it take to make one of these?" "Is this one for sale?"

My roommate had gone away for a few days to attend his grand-parents' fiftieth wedding anniversary party several counties away. As far as I could tell, he hadn't taken a day off from his naturalist duties the whole month we had been here, so he deserved it. And, it conveniently coincided with Melissa's visit, so we could have a little privacy. Despite his absence, the room still had a gloom about it, like his ghost was lurking in the shadows reading The Sun Also Rises. I raised the dusty venetian blinds in a futile effort to make the place look cheery.

"God, you never told me what a dump this place is!" she said, plopping down on my bed. "Well, now that your little show is over, why don't you come here and show me how much you've missed me." I stood there for several seconds holding the carpet bag, which felt like it had bricks in it. Then I dumped the bag onto the floor, narrowly avoiding serious damage to my foot, sat down next to her, and kissed her. As she slid her hand down my t-shirt, I guessed I had missed her just a bit after all.

Over dinner, at the one halfway decent restaurant in the largest nearby town, she chattered enthusiastically about what great progress she was making on her bibliography, and how she was just beginning to really "feel" the language, which was called Hausa. She had met a native speaker, an engineering student, and she had gone to lunch with him a couple of times to practice. "So, tell me more about what you've been finding out here. Did you collect any more stories about that guy who killed somebody?"

I told her about the latest Boyd stories I had collected, plus about the Child ballad singer, the incredible wood carver, and the herbal medicine specialist. I had to explain to her, again, that a Child ballad was not a ballad about a child, but one of the corpus of the most famous ballad collector in the English language, Francis J. Child. Finally, I told her about the baby dolls. Her eyes widened.

"That's so similar to fetish worship in tribal societies!"

"No, it is not!" I countered. "It's just a woman who likes to collect old doll heads from the trash. She just has a collecting thing, not a religion thing."

"Well, of course you cannot expect these people to express the meaning of what they're doing in so many words. But, it's a fetish worship, believe me. How does she refer to the dolls?"

"What?"

"You know, Mr. Big Researcher—how does she refer to them? As inanimate objects, or as real?"

"Of course she doesn't think they're real!"

"Of course she doesn't express the fact that they have a real, religious significance to her, you mean. How does she refer to them?"

I looked down at my iceberg lettuce and tomato salad. "She calls them, 'her little babies,' " I mumbled.

"See! I told you!" She ripped into her spongy white roll and smeared it with a pat of margarine. "Fetish worship!" She grilled me on other details of the interview I had done with Mrs. Billings a few days after talking to her husband, all the while analyzing each facet of the woman's doll-collecting habit. I began to wonder—was I just being non-intellectual about the analysis of the information I was collecting, or was she being overly intellectual? This wasn't a graduate course, it was a folklore collecting job. Collect, present, preserve. I knew that I would feel silly suggesting that Mrs. Billings was a fetish worshipper in my daily journal, which would be made public record. But had I suppressed my analytical skills (such as they were) in favor of mere collecting of information? Should I be spending more time on interpretation, keeping a journal of my own? Did I have the time and energy? Was it possible, after all, for a folklorist to do serious research in one of these short-term summer gigs?

Dinner was one big argument. Afterwards, we took a walk down the main street together. She took my hand. "I miss you. I don't have anyone to cook blueberry pancakes for." Or, anyone to argue with and feel superior to, I thought.

In the next few days, I took Melissa on a couple of interviews, which she sat through looking bored, and on some architectural photo ventures ("Why are you folklorists so preoccupied with architecture? I can't get too excited over a perfect two-thirds I-house, whatever that is"). She had to admit that the scenery was beautiful, and she expressed the opinion that the people seemed "nearly unspoiled examples of a simpler time," which almost made me gag. This was the first time we had been in the field together, and I was beginning to see a side of her that I hadn't really noticed before. She was a died-in-the-wool Yankee snob. Southerners, and perhaps all rural people, represented backwardness.

To her credit, she did try hard to lend the Nature Center some hominess. This was always something that I had admired about her, I had to admit. Along with her intellectual skills, she was Susie Homemaker at heart. She picked chicory and Queen Anne's lace from the side of the road and stuck it in an old peanut butter jar on the kitchen table. She even cooked a couple of meals on the beat-up stove.

Still, we were both keenly aware that she didn't belong in this part of my world. As her visit progressed, no longings to be back in the rarified atmosphere of graduate school and the convenience of a large university town overcame me, no matter how many times she asked me things like "Don't you miss the library?" or "Isn't there anywhere you can get a decent cup of coffee around here?"

Coming back from an interview one afternoon, we were both hot and sweaty. "Didn't I see a pool here somewhere?" She asked, fanning herself with my field journal.

"Uh, yes," I said. "But, it's so crowded. Jammed with little kids and fat old ladies with smelly suntan lotion," I elaborated. "And dirty, very dirty." I wasn't even sure that Ruthie was on duty that day, but I didn't want to take any chances.

She looked at me strangely, and shrugged. "Okay, I get the idea. Let's just take a shower together instead."

Her visit lasted four days, after which she was ready to get back to her studies, and I was ready to resume my monastic existence. I managed a tight hug and lustful kiss before she climbed into her car, a slightly-used Volvo, given to her by her rich grandmother who bought herself a new one. "Can't wait for you to get home," she breathed in my ear, nibbling it a bit. I just smiled and nodded. I couldn't wait to get back into the field.

Chapter 8

PERSONAL HISTORY

A day later, I was on my way to an interview with a retired coal miner who might or might not sing ballads and/or tell great tall tales (depending on whom you asked) when I noticed a little side road with the enigmatic name "Hangman's Chapel Road." How could I resist taking a detour? There were a few homes—new ranch style, neatly landscaped—near the turnoff from the main road. Soon it turned into gravel, and meandered deeper into woods on either side. The road wound around, crossing a small creek by a rickety wooden bridge. Suddenly there was a clearing and a dilapidated wooden church with a small graveyard, fenced in by rusty wrought iron, appeared. I braked, scattering gravel, and pulled off in front of the church. The dust caught up with me as I got out, coating my face and arms.

I felt compelled by something stronger than ethnographic curiosity to inspect the graves. The silence was deep, broken only by the hum of insects. The tall hardwoods fringing the cemetery threw long shadows across the graves. The first headstone I stopped at was mundane: Mrs. Trudy Sharpe who had died in 1957 and had a modern-looking grey granite headstone inscribed "loving wife and mother." I wandered around, recognizing a few surnames from my research. The older stones dated back to the mid 1800s, and were mostly carved with willows and urns, sprays of lilies, or open Bibles. Then, I caught sight of some graves in a corner. Jenkins, Arny and Mabel. Died 1899 and 1910. Some relation to Boyd? I ran over. Who knows, maybe even ole Boyd himself was buried here.

There were lots of Jenkins graves, although no Boyd. Maybe the FBI had confiscated his body and donated it to the Smithsonian, like certain portions of John Dillinger. Except for a few infants, the Jenkinses came in pairs. Mary, born 1880, died 1910. How sad to die at 30. Joshua, her husband, born 1885 and died 1970, lived to a ripe old age. If he ever took another wife, there was no evidence here. Sadie, born 1903, died 1975, was paired with Melvin, born 1900 and died 1955. Although I hadn't learned Boyd's mother's and father's names (I bet Demond knew), I remembered a stray comment by one of the many people who had mentioned the legend. "Sent his daddy to an early grave, the whole mess." Fifty-five didn't seem like an extremely early age, but the wife had lived twenty more years, so maybe it was a comparative sort of thing. Could this, then, be Boyd's parents?

I ruminated over the plain graves. My eyes followed the path of a lazy bee sampling the dandelions in between the graves. I noticed something about the set of graves I had just passed. Stanley, born 1920, died 1965 and wife Lucy, born 1920 and no death date. Lucy Jenkins, still living. Around here? I felt like rushing back to the county seat to find some records, then I remembered my interview— I was going to be at least a half hour late. I also realized that I had no idea which county I was in at this point, anyhow. I dashed back to my car, wrote some hurried notes in my field notebook, and retraced my route to the main road in a cloud of dust. Once again, Boyd was on hold.

Later that evening, I was sitting with Ruthie at a small card table in a side room of the Nature Center that the naturalist and I used as an office/dining room. She had dropped by after the pool closed— I was in the middle of logging some tapes when she knocked, and I hadn't heard it through my headphones. The Nature Center was a public building, and she just walked in. Absorbed in my work, I literally jumped out of my chair when I looked up to see her peering at me across the room. I forgot I was attached to the headphones, and nearly choked myself in the process. I had just finished transcribing a ghost story, a version of "The Graveyard Wager." It was such a perfect example of the genre that I had decided to transcribe it verbatim. I had just gotten to the part where the girl pins herself to the grave with the knife.

"Hi," she said, looking over my shoulder at my writing. "Oh, I know this story. Grandpa Taggart used to tell it to us all the time to give us a good scare. Want me to tell you what happens? The girl gets so scared that she dies from fright. Like that would really happen." She chuckled at the memory. "Who told it to you?" Without waiting for an answer, she found the name on the white cardboard lining the plastic cassette tape box. "Mr. and Mrs. Samuel Reynolds. Great Aunt Florence and her husband—her second husband, I might add—Sam. We call him Sam the Sham, not to his face. He's an old blowhard, I hope you realize."

Before I could get a word in edgewise, she continued in her musical accent, not quite as sharp as her grandmother's but still distinctive. "I came by to see if I could get a copy of the interview you did with Granny Taggart and maybe see how you do this type of oral history stuff. How much would a copy cost and how long would it take to get one?"

I assured her that I could make a copy right that very moment. Attempting to impress her with my mechanical prowess, I whipped out my handy patch cord and plugged it between the Nagra and the cassette recorder I used for logging. "This will take an hour to finish," I said, trying to sound important. "If you can wait, you can take it with you tonight, no charge." (What a clever ploy to keep her around for an hour while I got to know her a little better! No matter that I had no authority to give away free tape copies of archival material without any prior approval from the state.)

I offered her some iced tea—I even had a lemon that hadn't gotten moldy yet in the recesses of the ancient refrigerator the naturalist and I shared. I remembered to offer sugar—I had learned that folks here in the South liked their iced tea with plenty of it. So far, so good. We sat out on the porch of the Nature Center, until the mosquitoes drove us inside. From the front room, we could hear the June bugs buzzing on the screen door.

Ruthie settled herself in the old armchair, the one semicomfortable chair in the whole Nature Center. I sat at my desk chair, and tried not to stare at her. She was beautiful, with her healthy tan, dark eyes and all that hair tumbling around her shoulders. It was the hair that got me, deep black and shiny in the glow of my desk lamp. But, there was something about her eyes, too. A spark—maybe a hint of mischief.

"Your work sounds pretty interesting. I heard a guest lecturer at school talk about the 'folklore' of this area. It made me think about all the old tales that my own relatives tell, and the stuff that they do like quilting and whittling—"

"Who whittles?" I broke in. I'd been searching for a good whittler for a couple of weeks now.

"Oh, well, Grandpa Bigelow used to, but he's got arthritis so bad now he can't do much." She laughed. "Don't look so disappointed, I know some other whittlers I can tell you about sometime."

I considered getting up and fetching my field journal, but decided it would spoil the moment. "So, what was it like to grow up around here?" I asked, then regretted that it sounded too much like an interview question.

"Well, I always thought it was like growing up anywhere, really. It probably seems pretty isolated to you, but the city—we always call Knoxville "The City"—isn't that far away. And, my family lives in town, not out in the country. Grandparents on both sides are plain old country folks, though, and in the summers us kids used to spend two weeks each with both sets of them. So, I am sort of a country girl myself." She took a sip of tea. "Yup, just a plain old country girl." She had turned the southern twang up several notches and her eyes were laughing at me. "And yourself?"

"I'm a plain old suburban boy, I guess," trying to emphasize my New Jersey accent to match her tease. "Raised up in a totally boring suburb of New York City."

She smiled. "Ah, New York. There's some place I'd love to go. Almost did once on a 4-H trip, but I got the flu and they went without me." She made a face. "Did you go there often?"

"Not too often. My father works there, but once he gets home he never feels much like venturing back out again. He's totally suburban—coaches a Little League team, leads Boy Scout troops, mows the lawn. He's an accountant, what can I say."

"And your mother? Is she 'totally suburban' too?" she asked, half-mocking.

"Oh, she got a degree in history, and worked in a museum for awhile, but then did the housewife thing when my sister and brother and I came along. I guess she got me interested in folklore. She was forever dragging us kids to some out-of-the way museum or other, or to farms or antique stores or estate sales. She likes the country and loves rummaging."

I was used to interviewing people about their lives, but not used to having the tables turned. It made me feel uncomfortable.

Ruthie looked surprised. "I never thought of the suburbs around New York as - um - country."

"Aha!" I said. "Beyond the suburbs, there's still a lot of country in New Jersey and New York, and I guess I've seen most of it. My sister and brother hated it—you know, another Saturday afternoon in the back seat of the station wagon, blah blah. I thought it was fun. My mother would always lose track of me and then find me talking to some old farmer. . . ." I trailed off, smiling to myself at the memory of the time I had fallen into a wet cow flop at a living history farm, and my sister and brother had held their noses all the way home. "That's why I became a folklorist, I guess."

Ruthie laughed, as if she had shared the unspoken memory with me. Her laughter was contagious, and I chuckled. "I think you're geting the hang of interviewing. You're probably ready for that oral history class."

"Oh, I may need a little more coaching . . ." She smiled and leaned forward, smoothing her hair away from her forehead and catching it in back as if she were making a ponytail, then letting it bounce back around her shoulders. I caught my breath, and took a swig of my tea.

Suddenly, we heard a car door slam, and my taciturn roommate came ambling by. Leave it to him to ruin the moment.

"Hey, Ruthie," he said, giving her a little salute on his way by.

"Hey, yourself, Dwayne," she said, waving at his retreating back.

"You know him?" I asked, as if knowing the naturalist were some-how unnatural.

"Sure. We took an ornithology class together last fall. A bit weird, but not a bad guy." That was being generous, I thought. "I'm mad at him, though."

"Why?"

"If it wasn't for him, I would have gotten the naturalist job this summer. But he's already done with his degree and working on his pharmacy license, and I was only a junior. Still, I know a lot about nature and the environment around here, and it would have been more interesting than lifeguarding again. Not to mention better pay. There's always next year. By then, he'll be filling prescriptions somewhere."

"Hey," I said, with sudden inspiration. "Want to go on a field trip with me sometime?"

"Maybe." She looked a little suspicious. "Where?"

"You've heard of Boyd Jenkins?"

She laughed. "Well, we can't go interview him, I guess!"

I glared a little despite myself. "I'd really like to go see his cave. You know, the one he supposedly 'holed up' in?"

"Of course I know. But here's something you probably don't. Up to the time that that big company bought up the land and posted it, Boyd's cave was a hangout for teenaged boys, my big brother included in his wilder days. They'd go up there and smoke dope, far from 'parental supervision,' so to speak. It was even sort of a 'rite of passage' I think you anthropology types call it to stay overnight in the cave." She raised an eyebrow and winked. "If you smoked enough, you might even see the ghost of Boyd Jenkins!"

"You've been there?" I asked.

"No, sir! Girls were strictly forbidden." She grinned again. "But I always wanted to go. After I got old enough to not be scared anymore."

"What do you mean?"

"When we were little, my daddy would use Boyd like the boogie man if we were bad. You know, 'You'd better behave or ole Boyd will come out of the woods and carry you back to his cave.' " She did a plausible Wolfman imitation, clawing the air and growling.

"So, if we took a trip up there—in broad daylight of course—you'd be game?"

"You bet, bud. I'd almost forgotten all about it, but I'd still love to see it. I even sort of know the way, since I made my brother tell me one time. He said there were some, like, paintings or something there. Very spooky." She smiled. "Sounds like an adventure, and I'm overdue for one. Yelling at bratty kids all summer isn't my idea of fun. Just say the word and I'll tag along. But I won't tell my parents, and especially not Granny Bigelow, where we're going."

"How come?"

"They think the whole Boyd thing is kind of a low point in this area's history, if you follow me. Granny Bigelow, you see, is a second or third cousin to the guy that Boyd shot, and she really had enough of that whole business when it was happening."

"Does she ever talk about it?"

"Not really. Once she told me that no one liked the guy, but that's no reason why Boyd should have shot him. I guess everybody thought he was raising the price of groceries just to make some extra money or something. Anyway, he was a jerk, but I guess I agree with Granny. It's an interesting story, though."

The tape in the reel-to-reel recorder made a loud snapping sound. The first side of the dubbing was finished. I turned the tapes over to dub the other side.

"Got any more tea?" She asked. We sat, talking more about families. I learned that she was the youngest of three, that her brother and sister were already married and living nearby, and she had two nieces and a nephew. And that she was the first in her family to go to college, and the only one with any ambition to leave the area and do something other than work in the family construction business.

She ferreted out of me that I was the middle child of three, and that my sister and brother were both headed for high-paying careers in computer science and medicine, respectively. And that folklore was a career almost guaranteed not to earn me a nice house in the suburbs.

The conversation came back to the Boyd legend. I told her about the stories I had collected so far. She sat listening, with genuine interest, asking intelligent questions. Something reminded me of Demond's comment about meeting her grandmother.

"Do you know a guy named Chris Demond?" I asked.

She looked puzzled for a moment, then grimaced. "Oh, that other guy Granny tried to fix me up with. I haven't met him yet." She looked at me. "Friend of yours?"

"No, I just met him, but apparently he's been collecting information about Boyd Jenkins for awhile. He has some folklore training and was thinking about using the story for his dissertation."

"And you don't like him."

I looked at her in surprise. She laughed. "It's written all over your face, bud."

"I'm just not sure I trust him," I said. "There's something, um, I can't explain it. Just a feeling."

"Sure you're just not jealous he got the Boyd story first?"

I was beginning to think Ruthie could read minds. I looked her in the eye, then tried to wipe out the impure thought I was having about her at that moment, just in case.

"Well, if I meet him, I'll give you my own opinion," she promised.

The second side of the tape started snapping. I retrieved the cassette, labeled it with my best penmanship, and handed it to Ruthie. Our fingers touched as I handed it to her, the brief contact sending shivers up my whole arm. She thanked me and disappeared into the warm, mosquito-filled night.

Chapter 9

COMMUNION

The time had come for my first trip back to Nashville, the capital, the hub of the project, for a staff meeting. The idea of driving three-and-a-half hours and losing two days in the field wasn't pleasant, but the chance to hang out with my colleagues in the "big city" made the trip tolerable. The drive gave me some time to take a mental stock of the first portion of my summer.

So far it had been interesting, I had to admit. Lonely sometimes, even boring at others, but generally eventful. In my five weeks on the job, I had interviewed 34 people, recorded 65 hours of tape, taken over 250 photographs. I had carried out four programs—the gospel sing, the quilt debacle, a campfire storytelling session featuring one of the rangers who was a real character and a medicinal wild herb walk (Dwayne knew the herbal expert, a local feedstore owner).

I still had a long list of possibilities to interview, with a big square dance program lined up for the following weekend. Should I have phoned the caller again before I left? What if the band didn't show up? I'd heard the fiddle player had a "little drinking problem"—what if he arrived for the program totally plowed?

I decided to worry about all these things later. For a while, I zoned out and enjoyed the scenery. The highway paralleled a mountainside with a steep drop leveling out to green countryside and more distant mountains. Picturesque farms dotted the greenery. After awhile, even the view wasn't holding my interest. I hadn't brought the cassette recorder with me, and when I tried the radio I found that it was on the blink again. So I sang old Beatles songs out loud to keep myself awake. Ob-La-Di, Ob-La-Da.

I finally arrived at the Department of Conservation building around 1 p.m. The other project members were all waiting on me to go to lunch. Our director's tastes ran to down-home plate lunch joints. By the time I'd eaten my meatloaf and gravy with three sides and cornbread, I was ready for a nap. I ordered a cup of black coffee.

We began our meeting informally over lunch. The director wanted to know how the local folks were reacting to the park programs. We all agreed that the majority of our audiences were, so far, tourists. We brainstormed methods to get more locals to come out for the programs. The director explained that some people still had a bad feeling about the parks because, in some cases, the state had taken over private lands to build them and hadn't paid what was considered a fair compensation for the land.

I glanced around at my fellow fieldworkers. The group was basically amiable, but there were underlying tensions—unspoken competition among us folklorists hung in the air like smoke. All three of us were from different graduate programs. Mine was the only Ph.D.-granting program of the three, so the others assumed I was more academically inclined than they were, and set out to prove as often as possible that they knew folklore theory as well as I did. For my part, I envied the practical approaches the master's programs took, encouraging their students to get more fieldwork experience and working on job skills like photography and recording. I was afraid the quality of my documentation was not going to measure up to theirs. So, we over-compensated by exaggerating our accomplishments.

I actually liked both of my summer folklore colleagues very much. The mid-state folklorist, Ann Shaw, originally from Ohio, had served as a Peace Corps volunteer for two years in Central America, then worked for several more years as a translator before starting graduate school. She wore flowery, flowing skirts and had a long dark blond braid down her back. She reported that her "rustic" log cabin in the park grounds reminded her of her housing situation in the

Guatemalan jungle. I joked that the weather this summer probably reminded her of it, too. She seemed much more mature than the rest of us—even than our director, who was younger than she was. She was particularly interested in material culture and local history. But she was also a damned good old-time banjo player, as I had learned during the training session we had prior to going out in the field. She described herself as "an old folkie from way back," but she was probably only about thirty-two or so.

The other guy, C. Jackson Bancroft III (just Jack to us) was a laid-back Southern gentleman, a couple of years older than me. He was always dressed impeccably in starched white shirts and chinos that looked as if he'd just pressed them, and he seemed at first meeting terribly stuffy. But we soon learned he had a dry sense of humor and an uncanny way of putting people at ease. He had a special interest in African-American music and narrative, and his position in the western part of the state allowed him ample opportunity to indulge it. He was collecting great toasts, blues music, and had even found some black shape-note singers and a fife and drum band. I was jealous. My three counties were almost totally homogenous—Anglo-Saxon and Scots-Irish with a smattering of German and a suggestion of Native American ("My great-grandmother, so they say, was a full-blood Cherokee . . .").

The project also included a work-study student who served as a coordinator. Blake was a friendly, open-faced bear of a guy, older than most college students. His family was native to the middle part of the state, and he described them all as "a big, rowdy bunch of 'billies" who laughed at him when he said he wanted to go to college. Instead, he went to vocational school and became a draftsman, following the trade for several years until he had saved up enough money to do what he really wanted—to go to the state university in Middlesboro and study anthropology and history. One of his professors was on the advisory board of the project, and had recommended him for the position of coordinator.

Our director was, by training, a naturalist. His current position was State Naturalist, which allowed him a lot of freedom and travel time. He had begun his work, like Dwayne, as a seasonal naturalist in his undergraduate days, working his way up to full-time jobs at a succession of the larger state parks that hired naturalists all year long. Early on, he had started interviewing local people who knew a lot about the natural environments around the parks where he worked, and this interest had grown to include musicians, craftspeople, storytellers, and others. The parks had let him slip a few folklore programs into the schedules. Eventually, when he reached the state level, he had convinced them to let him apply for National Endowment for the Arts funds for this project.

He loved his job as a naturalist and had no desire to go back to school and study folklore, but he had done more interviews and carried out more successful programs than most professional folklorists—certainly more than all three of us combined. He had a childlike enthusiasm about folklore that made our outlooks seem jaded. He had developed an impressive network of traditional musicians, storytellers, and craftspeople around the state. Several of these folks lived in the counties I was working in, and whenever I encountered one of them, they spoke of our project director as if he were a son. He visited as many of them as possible on a regular basis, collecting more stories and songs each time. To me, he was the epitome of a great fieldworker.

All afternoon and into the early evening, the fieldworkers took turns reporting interesting interviews and adventures. Everyone had made incredible finds, and the project director looked pleased. At about seven, we broke for dinner at a pit barbeque, then adjourned to our coordinator's favorite country and western watering hole on Lower Main Street near the old Ryman Auditorium to drink and listen to some music. I was telling Ann more about the Boyd legend, yelling over the twanging of the steel guitar. She perked up at the idea that some of Boyd's paintings might still exist. If I found enough of them, she suggested, I could do a small exhibition at the park.

"I haven't even seen one of them, much less enough for an exhibition."

"Have you tried any art galleries or big antique stores in the area?"

"No—I haven't had time. There's a big antique complex near Hancock, maybe I could try there."

Our director, who was listening, chuckled. "Don't expect to get much information about anything from Gary Joe Pierce, the guy that runs that place. He keeps any information he has close to the vest. He's spent years talking the folks around there out of their heirlooms and he's not about to give anything away to anybody. Tell you what, though. You might ask Cyrus Daniels to sing you his musical version of the 'Boyd Legend,' as you call it."

"Who's Cyrus Daniels—any relation to the newspaper owner, Ed Daniels, and his sister, the local historian? They didn't mention him." Our director never ceased to amaze us by revealing information about tradition bearers he knew in our areas. He seemed to be holding out on us, as a sort of test—the "real folklorists" versus the self-trained— to see what we'd come up with on our own.

"Probably, although if he is, he's not the sort of relative most people'd want to claim. He's quite eccentric. Lives way up on the top of a mountain with no electricity and lots of hound dogs. Not exactly the type of person who'd want to do a program at the park, but you might find it interesting to visit him some afternoon. I passed a fine afternoon up there one time myself, a couple of years ago."

After way too much beer, we all retired to our motel rooms. The next morning was devoted to equipment checks and exchanges, turning in our film and tapes, and other business. I entered the Department office building with a throbbing hangover headache. Over coffee and huge, sugar-crusted donuts, the director announced, "Blake needs to get out of the office and see some experienced fieldworkers in action." He dragged out the word "experienced" elaborately, in a subtly sarcastic manner. He turned to me. "I think a week in the East would be a good place for him to start. Want some company? You take him back with you today, and I'll pick him up next week."

I looked at Blake. He grinned—I could tell he was anxious to get out of the office. "Why not?" I asked. Secretly, of course, I was thinking of how this would delay my further contact with Ruthie for another week, but on the other hand, it might be nice to have some help with the Saturday square-dance program.

Before taking off for the trip back East, we stopped by Blake's cramped studio apartment and he packed for "folklore camp." The Nature Center floor would have to serve as his pallet. "I hope you like spiders," I joked.

"Welcome to Bugs-R-Us," he countered, pointing to an ant trap and a roach motel.

Chapter 10

COORDINATED EFFORTS

B lake had an agenda. As I had already found out, he loved local
c&w music, the twangier the better. Moreover, he was attempting to convince our project director that we should not only be
looking for the purest examples of old-time music in the field, but
discovering what types of contemporary music local folks were listening to (such as, of course, country and western). "This is the old-
time music of the future," he argued. "Why not collect it now in its
heyday instead of waiting till it's almost gone?"

The first night he was with me, after a long day of fieldwork, we
had to go scope out a series of smoky c&w bars. Each subsequent
night of the week, except for Saturday, because of the square dance,
we somehow managed to find at least one live band playing in various larger towns within an hour of the park. Blake was in heaven, and
he was even beginning to convince me that the music was worth
studying. I listened carefully to his aesthetic opinions on the merit of
this singer or that bass player over another. And, when I got a bit
bored, I practiced my low-light photographic skills, experimenting
with the tripod on loan from the Department of Conservation.

Needless to say, after the second night I stopped planning any
morning interviews. Blake, who had about five inches and fifty
pounds on me, could down prodigious amounts of beer and still wake

up cheerful and ready to roll. This was the one thing about him that I hated. Otherwise, I found his company congenial on both personal and professional levels. He had an inexhaustible repertoire of dirty jokes, but he also had interesting opinions on the future of the fields of applied anthropology and folklore. We were having a great week.

On Wednesday evening before we departed for our journey into c&w land, I invited Ruthie to join us at the park restaurant for dinner. Blake and Ruthie hit it off immediately, swapping stories about their more bizarre relatives. Since my relatives were fairly dull in comparison, I sat back in amazement, more than a little jealous. Later, Blake declared Ruthie "a fine gal, though a bit skinny for my taste," and gave any future relationship that she and I should develop his hearty blessing.

On Thursday night, we happened into a bar early in the evening, before the musicians were set up, and sat down to chat up the bartender/owner. I looked up and noticed an unusual painting on the side wall. It was done in what art historians love to call a primitive or naive style, painted on something other than canvas and framed in rough barnwood. The subject was a deer being chased by what looked like large dogs or wolves, the wild-eyed buck in mid-jump and the voracious-looking hounds nipping at his heels. Dark forest was suggested in the background. The light was eerie. It reminded me a little of the paintings of Albert Pinkham Ryder which we had studied in my undergraduate Art 100 class. I stared at it a long time. The bartender followed my gaze.

"Kinda gives you the chills, don't it," he said, grinning.

"Where'd you get it and who painted it?" I asked, holding my breath.

"My aunt died and left me some stuff 'cause she didn't have any living children of her own to give stuff to. This was among it. I'd never seen it before in her home—guess she had it stuck away somewheres. Hardly seems like a good choice for your living room or dining room." He chuckled.

I exhaled. "No idea of who painted it?"

"Well," he said, "there's the interesting thing. As you see, it doesn't have a—what you call it, signature? But, if you turn it over—" He walked over and reached for the painting, bringing it to us, turning it as he came.

We squinted in the dim light of the bar. He brought it closer. There was some scratchy writing in black pencil on the light background of what I saw was some sort of heavy paper. The bartender interpreted. "Near as I can make out, it says, 'To Sarah'—that was my aunt—'Thanks for the meal and kindness. Remember me, Boyd'— something that begins with a J."

"Jenkins," I suggested, swallowing hard.

"Maybe," he said, shrugging.

Blake and I looked at each other, blinking in disbelief. Then we both looked back at the bartender. His smile was fading. "What is it?"

"Do you know who Boyd Jenkins was?" I asked.

He mulled that over a while. "Now you say that name, I'm beginning to recall. Yeah, he was some sort of bandit or something from up around Sunrise?" He looked at us for confirmation.

"Did your aunt ever speak of him?"

"Well, tell the truth, I wasn't ever very close to her. She was my Mama's eldest sister, we only visited of a Christmas or some other family gathering."

"Where did she live?"

"Here and there. That is, she married a logger and they lived up toward the state line. Sometimes in logging camps, sometimes in town. She cooked for the logging camp off and on. Retired to a little town up there."

That made sense, I thought, or so it would seem from the stories of Boyd trading paintings for a meal. The location was right, too. I looked back at the painting. Narratives were one thing, but this material manifestation made the man and the legend so much more immediate. I shivered.

"If I were you, I'd hold on to that. Don't let any art or antique dealers talk you out of it. I've been learning a lot about Boyd Jenkins this summer, and a piece of his art work is something pretty unique."

The bartender laughed. "Not many art dealers come through here, buddy, believe me." He asked me why I'd been collecting stories about Boyd, and I gave him a short explanation. He wanted to know more about the legend. I gave him a thumbnail sketch, piecing together bits of the story learned from one informant or another. I realized as I spoke that I was beginning to create my own pastiched version. Was I becoming a folk conduit?

A flurry of new patrons drew the bartender's attention away, and soon the music began. But my eye kept returning to the dark vision of Boyd. I asked the bartender's permission to photograph the picture. "Is it worth any money?" he asked, looking hopeful.

"I doubt it," I said. It really didn't occur to me that anyone would pay the bartender large sums for a painting by Boyd, legend or no legend. "But it is worth a great deal from a historical point of view."

He grunted, and turned back to mopping up the bar.

On the way home, the holes in the VW airing out our smoky hair and clothes, Blake and I discussed the painting and the Boyd legend. "The dogs obviously symbolize the authorities chasing him," Blake mused, imitating one of his professors. "The deer is Jenkins, of course."

"How do you think he'd be categorized as a painter? Folk, visionary, idiosyncratic, naive?" I asked.

"I don't know enough about the distinctions," Blake said, "but I'd categorize him as damned good. I liked it, wouldn't mind one on my wall." Considering the gloom of his apartment, I thought it might make an improvement.

"Would someone, you think, pay a lot for a painting like that?"

Blake snorted. "Some people will pay a lot of money for the damnedest things. My Uncle Tilson paid a hundred bucks at an auction once for an old ringer washer—he's got it setting out in front of his house with petunias growing in it." He chuckled.

"Let's go visit the infamous Cyrus Daniels tomorrow," I suggested.

"Why not." Blake said, taking a draw on the beer he had brought with him for the road.

Chapter II

HUNTING STORIES

"Cyrus? Why in hell do you want to visit him?" I had called Ed Daniels to see if he knew how to get to Cyrus's home. He did, and gave me directions after railing on awhile about what an unsuitable choice Uncle Cyrus would be to represent this part of the country. Not that he'd come down to the park, ever, for a program—but even documenting him seemed somehow inappropriate. "Be prepared for some raw language and dirty stories," he warned, but I could hear a hint of amusement in his voice. I was tempted to tell him that one of my professors always told us that ninety-nine percent of folklore is obscene, but I wasn't sure how he'd take it.

Blake and I chowed down on a big breakfast at the local Cracker Barrel, just off the interstate near the park. One of the occupational hazards of folklore fieldwork is never knowing when or where your next meal is coming from. We doubted that Cyrus would be long on hospitality.

It took us about an hour and a half to reach the foot of Cyrus's mountain, which was actually a very steep hill. It was fairly easy to find, since Ed Daniels had given us a fail-safe landmark. It seemed that, when he was working, Cyrus was a stone mason. At the foot of the hill, he had constructed a most curious wall, embedded with local stone, bottles of all descriptions, parts of old cars, sea shells (where he got the latter is anyone's guess) and other various found objects. The whole thing was about six feet high and ten feet long, flanking one side of the turn up the hill. On the opposite side of the dirt road stood two equally curious figures, a crude representation of a man and woman, both also six feet tall, built from similar materials.

"Wow," said Blake.

"Should we take pictures now or later?" I asked. We opted for later. Our director had said nothing about Cyrus's art work. No doubt he thought the surprise would be worth it.

The VW barely made it up the rutted dirt road. At the top was a beat-up house trailer, with stacks of junk scattered in all directions. Broken bricks, scrap metal, bottles and aluminum cans lay in half-sorted piles near the house. Several old cars, two without wheels and all missing some external parts, were perched at one side of the trailer. A very dilapidated pickup truck, the one vehicle with most parts intact, was parked at the front of the trailer with the hood up.

As soon as we reached the top of the hill, while I was looking for enough square footage to park without running over some trash, the yard came alive with dogs. The barking and baying was deafening. They descended upon the VW like hornets disturbed from their nest, from under the trailer, behind the junk piles, and Lord knows where else.

Blake started opening his door. "What are you doing?" I cried. He looked back in surprise which quickly turned to amusement.

"I'm getting out of the car. Don't tell me you're afraid of a few hound dogs."

"There must be fifty of them, and they don't look too friendly," I said, almost yelling over the noise. I liked dogs, but not in large packs.

"You just gotta know how to talk to them," Blake said, opening his door and shooing the dogs nearest him back. "Get outa here, dogs," he bellowed. Most of them slunk away a safe distance. A few stood closer to him, wagging their tails tentatively.

A grizzled head poked out from under the truck hood. "Hey, dogs. Back, dogs," the man yelled, and all the dogs retreated toward the trailer, turning to inspect the visitors from a safe distance. All of Cyrus—for who else could this be—emerged from behind the truck hood. He was filthy, from his stained John Deere cap down to his mud-encrusted work boots. His hands and face had car grease smeared on them, and his dark green work clothes were covered with dried mud, grease and unidentified dirt. I could smell his unwashed body from ten feet away as he approached.

"What can I do for you two young fellers?" he asked. The question was somewhat obscured by his lack of teeth, but the tone implied suspicion.

"We're from the state park," I began, but decided a long explanation would lose him. I cut to the quick. "We heard you tell a good story and also can sing some old songs. Do you remember a fellow coming up here a couple of years ago to get some of those stories and songs from you? We work with him."

He grinned, showing the four or five teeth he did have.

"Yeah, another young feller. He wanted to know about some of those stories. I learned them from my Granny and uncles when I was just a shaver. I still remember all that stuff, think about those days all the time."

"Do you have a few minutes to tell us a few tales?" I ventured.

He laughed, a raspy sound that ended in a flurry of coughing. "Do I look like somebody in a hurry, son? If you're interested in setting around here for a couple of hours, I am happy to oblige." He slammed down the trunk hood. The noise started up a small flurry of barks from the hounds.

"Too stifling hot in that trailer house, damned old tin can. Lemme get some chairs and we'll set right out here if that's all right with you." He turned back from the door. "Sorry I don't have a thing to offer you but a drink of water."

He re-emerged with a couple of creaky-looking wooden kitchen chairs, with faded and cracked orange plastic seat covers. Blake jumped to help him. Cyrus went back into the trailer and brought out one more chair and a jug of bottled water. The third trip inside yielded three jelly jar glasses.

"Okay," he said, settling himself in one of the chairs. "Ask away." We hadn't even introduced ourselves. When we did, it didn't seem to make much of an impression. When I asked if he minded if we recorded, he shrugged. He started talking before Blake got the Nagra set up and hardly stopped for two solid hours. This was a man who, it seemed, didn't get much chance to talk. He was like a bottle of seltzer that had been shaken before opening, bubbling over with information, animating his tales and songs with his hands and even leaping up to do an impromptu buck and wing.

He moved from story to song to story with dizzying speed. It took a lot of concentration for me to understand what he was saying. I sensed by Blake's chuckles that I was losing some of the subtler humor. I decided that it would be a good exercise for our coordinator to log this tape himself. I guessed that Cyrus reminded him of some of his more colorful relatives.

His repertoire moved seamlessly between Jack tales, riddles, bawdy songs, ghost tales, a few mournful ballads and even an old-time hymn or two. He paused every few minutes to take a sip of the lukewarm water. During one of these pauses, I interjected. "I've heard that you've written some songs. Isn't there one about Boyd Jenkins?"

Cyrus took a longer draw of water and poured some more, then looked into the half-full glass as though gazing into a crystal ball. Then he looked me hard in the eyes, holding the gaze for a full minute.

"I can tell you're actually interested in Boyd. Some folks just want sensation. You came to the right place to learn about Boyd here, son, because I probably knew him better'n any living soul. Y'see, Boyd was my huntin' buddy. And there ain't no better way to get to know a man than to hunt with him."

Blake looked at me with his eyebrows raised. He got up without a word and went to the car for more blank tapes. We were in for the long haul.

"Folk'll tell you a piece of the Boyd story, what they've heard, but most of it's half truth at best. I can tell you the whole story as I heard it from the horse's mouth, like they say, from talking to ole Boyd his-self." He looked at us and paused.

"You mean, you talked with Boyd after the shooting?" I asked.

Cyrus laughed, slapping one thigh, which caused a puff of dust to rise. "Talked to him—son, didn't I just finish saying I hunted with him?"

"How did you know where to find him?"

"Hell, son, most people in these parts had a pretty good idea of where ole Boyd was holed up. Half the country's related to him, after all. And most people didn't blame him one bit for shooting that good-for-nothing grocery man's son. It was self-defense anyhow. Jest that other feller's tough luck that Boyd was a better shot. He should've been. He'd been hunting those parts with his daddy since he was knee high. One of the best shots I've ever run acrosst.

"His daddy and mine knew each other well. They used to trade hounds. If he'd come to look at our hounds, Boyd'd come along, and same if my daddy went over there. Boyd and me played marbles while they were wrangling over a dog or two. I was a little older than him, maybe five years, but that didn't matter much. Yeah, he was a damned good rolly hole player, too. He was always winning all my best marbles, the scoundrel." Cyrus swirled the water around in his glass.

"Well, anyway, we stayed friends. Didn't see each other too often. Once in awhile he'd come by to see if I wanted to go hunt, or to talk dogs. He had a great coon dog, Bob he called him, and I was always trying to get him to trade me Bob for some one of mine, but he never would do it.

"Kinda lost track of him—he joined the army and went off to Korea to fight. When he came back he was a changed man by all accounts. Drank too much, didn't have much interest in anything 'cept playing the fiddle. He was always a great fiddle player, I reckon, from what I'm told. I knowed him as a hunter—I wasn't ever much for that sort of Saturday night dancing.

"So I heard he had taken up with a girl in town, from somewheres up north, and that it led him to this trouble. Heard he shot that feller, and I said to myself, well, that feller probably deserved what he got for one reason or t'other. Then, they said Boyd ran off, and no lawmen could find him. Even sent in the Feds 'cause they figured he'd crossed over into Kentucky.

"I had a pretty good idea of where he went, myself. It was a favorite spot for us to go hunting, up in the woods about an hour from here. We'd drive up there as far as we could with my truck—not this here truck," he chuckled, following our gaze. "I had another one, way back then."

"Anyways, then we'd walk in and there was some fine game up there. Depending on the season, deer, rabbits, coons, wild turkeys. We had good hunting up there, never came home empty handed. Onest, we got caught up in a big rainstorm up there and we holed up in a cave. There's plenty of caves up that way, amongst the cliffs.

"So, when I heard about Boyd I jest figured to myself, I'll jest bet that's where he is. Up there holed up in some cave or other. And, sure enough, it turned out I was right.

"No lawmen ever came to ask me any questions, and I wouldn't 've told them anything if they had. But, next time I felt like going hunting, I figured I'd see if I could find ole Boyd and see if he needed anything. Plenty of folks, I heard, had seen him and helped him stay hidden. He'd a lot of relations all up and down this country, like I said, after all, and they were true to their kin. Anyway, I went up there and I'll be damned if I didn't find him, too."

" 'Cyrus,' old Boyd said, 'You and me go way back. Can I count on you to help me out?' Course I told him I would. 'What do you need?' And he rattled off a few things he wanted to get. He already had some stuff for cooking, and blankets for sleeping and all. Fact is, that cave was fixed up pretty cozy.

"One thing he wanted, and I thought it curious at the time, was some stuff for painting. I don't mean painting houses, neither— painting pictures, I mean. I asked him, 'Boyd, since when do you paint pictures?' And he said it was jest something to pass the time. Said he'd always thought about doing something like that but didn't never try because he figured everyone'd laugh at him. But now he wanted to put down his life in pictures, kinda like. Something every- one could remember him by. 'Cause, you see, he already figured his goose was cooked, and of course he was right. It would jest be a mat- ter of time before they caught him.

"So, anyways, I did oblige him and brought him some stuff—paint, brushes, some heavy paper. I went up there a few more times—spaced out my visits and always tried to make sure nobody was following me. The last time I went up there, he gave me one of his paintings. I still have it and I'll show you before you leave. Story has it, he traded those paintings for food and such all over this section, though I haven't seen any 'cept my own. He painted up the cave, too, you may have heard tell of that."

"Can you still see any of that in the cave?" I asked.

"Oh, some traces, kind of chipped off and faded. I was up there about a year and a half ago, but they've closed it off for hunting now, some fancy Northern outfit bought the land and posted it."

Cyrus took another swig of water, but seemed anxious to continue.

"There's something that has been bothering me these many years. Like I said, there were FBI men hunting old Boyd for a couple of years."

We nodded. "Well, first there were two, but they pulled one of them off the case and that left the one. He stuck around a good long time. More'n a year before they took Boyd down. Boyd told me that he was sure this feller had a good idea of where he was hiding, and he was really jest waiting to blow the whistle. What he was waiting for was never clear to Boyd, or to me neither. Some say this FBI feller had a girl in a nearby town—local girl I mean—and wanted to stay around the area because of that. But I'd wager there was something else keeping him around and I've never been able to figure what that was. Some sort of scam, I'm sure, but what?"

Cyrus looked at us, questioning. Blake shrugged and I raised my eyebrows in a "beats me" gesture.

"Well, anyways, there are plenty of Boyd stories around. In fact, there was another young feller who was gathering some of the stories up. He came up here but I didn't like the looks of him. I told him I didn't know nothing about Boyd, jest we was friends when we was boys was all. I didn't show him the picture, though he asked if I knew anything about Boyd's 'art work' he called it."

I had a pretty good idea of who that must have been, and I was greatly relieved that Cyrus had held out on him.

Blake nudged me. "The song," he whispered.

Leave it to Blake to remember what started this whole line of inquiry.

"Cyrus, what about your song about Boyd?" I asked. "When did you write it?"

"Right after they shot him down, I wrote this. Sort of a tribute to old Boyd." He cleared his throat and began singing.

Boyd Jenkins is my name
That name I'll never deny
I shot the grocery man's son
And left him for to die.

But here's the honest truth
He fired the first that night
My aim was truer was the fact
That led to the awful sight

As he lay bleeding in the dust
I saw my race was run
I lit out for the woods right quick
I'll never see the sun.

Goodbye, farewell dear Mother
Goodbye to Daddy too
I shot the grocery man's son
And now must pay my due.

The last note quavered and Cyrus looked at us, in turn. "That's it, boys. That's the God's honest truth about Boyd. He wasn't a bad feller, really, and he was as good a friend as I've ever had."

No one spoke for a minute or so, a moment of silence in honor of Boyd. The only sound was the hound dogs snoring in the late afternoon heat. Then Cyrus rose. "Let me show you that picture I have."

I had almost forgotten the promise of seeing the picture, and Blake and I both shook ourselves out of our reverie, grinning at each other.

Cyrus came out of the trailer with the painting, which was about the same size and with the same sort of frame as the bar owner's aunt's picture. This one depicted a hound dog with a mottled black and white body and brown muzzle and legs. The dog was barking up a tree at a large raccoon, perched in one of the upper branches. The hound had a curiously short tail.

"Bob!" I exclaimed, a little too loudly. A couple of Cyrus's hounds lifted their heads and gave short growls.

"Sure enough," Cyrus said, grinning. "When Boyd gave it to me, he said, 'Cyrus, I knowed you always wanted to get your hands on my coon dog, so here he is!' Folks say Boyd had gone crazy out there in the woods all by himself, but I know different. He was jest as sane as you or me to the end."

I contemplated that for a few seconds, suppressing a smile.

"What happened to the real Bob?" asked Blake.

"Why, Boyd had him with him when he run off—that dog always went everywhere with him. Nearly killed the old hound when Boyd left for the army, you know. Yep, Bob stood his ground when the FBI men come to shoot Boyd down, and went out with him."

"They shot Bob?" I said, surprising myself with the emotion in my voice. My mind flashed briefly to Disney's Old Yeller—the scene where they shoot the dog had stuck with me for years after I had seen the movie at about age seven. Somehow, hearing that the FBI had shot Bob made Boyd's story that much more real.

"They sure did. And you know, some says they buried Bob next to Boyd, too." He looked into the distance. "Boyd would've wanted it that way."

"Where is Boyd buried anyhow?" I asked.

"Can't rightly tell you, son. I heard they took him off for identification by his family and for police evidence and all that, but what happened afterward I don't know. There sure wasn't any proper funeral I know of, anyways. More's the pity—Boyd was actually a God-fearing man, down deep. He used to do a little preaching here and there before he went off to the army."

"In a church?" I asked.

"Naw—just around, to anyone who'd listen. His ma was a regular churchgoer, that's a fact, though his daddy wasn't much for it. Boyd got born again as a teenager and commenced preaching to anyone who'd listen, me included. He saw I wasn't much interested, though, and gave up." Cyrus grinned. "I think he got some of that spirit back out there in the woods, 'cause part of the painting inside the cave was religious type stuff."

This certainly shed a whole new light on Boyd. Cyrus fell silent and looked tired. Blake gave me a little nod, and we rose. We thanked Cyrus and shook his hand in turn, getting oily smears on our own hands as a token.

We packed up the equipment and shoved it in my back seat. As we turned to leave, Cyrus called after us. "If you ever find out what that FBI man was up to, you come back and let me know, won't you?"

We agreed and I headed the VW down the steep drive, hoping my brakes held out. We paused to take some shots of the stone entranceway. I noticed something I hadn't at first—the male statue had something that crudely represented a fiddle tucked under his left arm. "Boyd?" I asked Blake, touching the statue's arm.

"Hmm," said Blake, considering the possibility. "Who's the gal, then?"

"Girlfriend?" I offered. From up the hill, we could hear the faint barking of the hound dogs. Cyrus was probably feeding them their dinners. We headed back to our home away from home, the Nature Center.

The square dance went much better than I had anticipated. There were about seventy-five people there—many, I learned, from a local square dance club. Blake was in fine form, dancing nearly all night with a succession of women, all of whom seemed charmed by his attentions. For his size, he was very light on his feet, and I envied his skill. The fiddler was just drunk enough to be having a good time, which didn't adversely affect his playing. I looked for Ruthie, but she wasn't there.

Blake left two days later, and I missed him as soon as he and the project director pulled away from the Nature Center. It was a lonely business, this folklore work, and it had been comforting to have someone to shoot the breeze with, bounce ideas off of, drink with. Now he was barreling back to Nashville in a state car with our project director, telling him Lord knew what about our fieldwork experiences. And, I was back to work, solo, as usual.

Chapter 12

READING ROOM

The last week had been exciting and exhausting, but through it all I hadn't forgotten my field trip date with Ruthie. At the park office Monday morning, I checked the schedule to see when her next day off was. Friday, just a few days from now. So I made some interview appointments to keep me busy until then and left a note for Ruthie with the receptionist.

Back at the Nature Center, I packed up my equipment and started to head out. Spike was fixing a broken part of the Nature Center porch railing when I came out. Just five minutes before, when I entered the building, he'd been nowhere in sight. He had a habit of popping up like a phantom, I had noticed.

"Howdy," he mumbled as I passed.

"Hi, Spike."

"Off to talk to more folks?"

"Yeah. I'm visiting a chair-seat weaver this morning and a mandolin player this afternoon."

He straightened up from his work. "Get any more stories about old Boyd?" He grinned, his rotten-looking teeth showing.

"Oh, a few people have told me some more about him."

"That right." He pulled a pack of Camels and a book of matches out of his work shirt pocket and lit up a cigarette, drawing deeply.

"Hard to sort the lies from the truth of that story. Hardly worth it," he said.

"Could be," I replied, getting into the spirit of his minimal conversation style, which reminded me of dialogue in a grade B western movie. "Interesting, though."

He took another long drag, exhaling a cloud of smoke in my direction. "If I were you, I'd lay off that story."

I was on the verge of asking him why he felt that way, but he bent low to his work. As I continued down the stairs, he flicked the smoldering cigarette butt into my path.

The next day, my interview with a tatter who lived in town fell through. When I reached her house, I found a note thumbtacked on the front door: she had forgotten that she had to take her husband to the doctor's that day. It was hot and sticky again, and instead of going back to the park and trying to line up another appointment, I felt like finding a cool place to hide out. It occurred to me that I could spend the day at the public library, something I had been meaning to do for quite a while. Hopefully, it was open.

It was. There were a few sluggish-looking customers, old men reading newspapers and middle-aged women flipping through needlework magazines. I headed for the microfilm area and tried to calculate what the dates of the Boyd misadventures would have been. If Boyd had served during the Korean War, his discharge would have come somewhere between the beginning of the war in 1950 and the ending in 1953. He had been hanging around the area for at least a year afterwards. I began with the 1951 papers, local and city, and after about an hour and a half finally came up with my first reference, in the local paper, dated August 7, 1954.

"Jenkins Shoots Grocer.

Criminal at Large.

"Local and state police are searching for Boyd T. Jenkins, of Truman's Gap community, who according to witnesses is alleged to have shot and killed Thomas D. Atkinson, son of Ralph Atkinson, grocer, late Sunday night.

"The two men were said to have been quarreling, and gun shots were fired. There is some confusion over whether Atkinson was armed, but apparently Jenkins was not wounded. He administered at least two shots, one of which struck Atkinson in the chest and killed him instantly, according to county coroner, Dr. Clifford Peebles.

"Jenkins then fled on foot before anyone could apprehend him, and later drove his truck to his parents' home in rural Truman's Gap. His parents claim not to know his whereabouts, since they say they were sleeping when he arrived at the house, and they did not hear him enter and exit. His truck was later found abandoned near the entrance to the Piney Branch State Forest.

"It is believed that the fugitive may have entered Kentucky through the dense forest. The Federal Bureau of Investigation has been called in on the case and will join local law keepers in Tennessee and Kentucky in the manhunt.

"Anyone with knowledge of the whereabouts of Boyd Jenkins should call the sheriff's office immediately. It is to be remembered that Jenkins is armed and dangerous. It is also to be remembered that aiding a criminal in the evasion of justice is a serious offense."

The story had no byline, but I guessed by the style that it was the work of a younger Ed Daniels. The Knoxville paper ran the same story, which had apparently been picked up by the news services. I decided to concentrate on the local paper. The next week, this follow-up appeared:

"Jenkins Still at Large.
Suspected Hiding in Woods.
"Boyd Jenkins, accused of the fatal shooting of Tom Atkinson of Sunrise, is still at large. He is presumed to be hiding out in the dense forest that borders the state line. The FBI has several agents investigating the crime.

"Local and federal lawmen are currently interrogating Jenkins' relatives and will organize a massive manhunt to begin late next week. Anyone who knows any details of the whereabouts of Jenkins are reminded to contact the sheriff's office immediately."

The article went on to describe Boyd as a white male of medium build, about five foot eight or nine, dark hair close cropped, green eyes, and twenty-five years old. I stared at the page for a minute, all of my mental images of Boyd suddenly shattered. None of the versions of the legend I had collected so far had described Boyd physically, so I had concocted my own vision, far different from reality. This could have been a description of me.

Several of the versions of the legend I had collected had given me Boyd's age, but the fact that I was almost the same age Boyd had been when he shot Tom Atkinson hadn't registered until I read it on the screen. Boyd had seemed older, more experienced, tempered as he was by tragedy and bad luck. Boyd and me: same age, same height, same hair and eye color, same build. It gave me the creeps. It took a couple of minutes to recover and resume reading.

The article from the following week gave a more detailed account of the manhunt. It had turned up a few promising leads, but no Boyd. Several people had alleged to have seen him, but their information conflicted. Agents combed the woods with dogs, but the trail led nowhere. The article concluded, "It is as if Jenkins has disappeared without a trace."

The next week reported that the FBI was leaving three experienced agents in the area to follow leads. Stories continued to surface of Boyd being seen here or there, although the article quoted one local lawman as saying, "He could be in Mexico by now for all we know."

The final paragraph in this article described the death of Jenkins's father:

"Jenkins' father was stricken with a heart attack and died early last week. His death was attributed to the actions and disappearance of his youngest son. He is survived by his wife, two daughters and two older sons."

I spent an hour tracing the story as it continued to be covered over the next two years. Follow-ups did not appear every week; Boyd's disappearance became unnewsworthy after awhile. There were brief reports of the FBI agents—two, then down to one—who remained on the case, following leads that indicated Jenkins was still in the area. Finally, according to the last story I could find, dated May 1955, the FBI guy caught Boyd's trail in a remote part of the forest near the state line. A logging foreman who was reputedly helping Jenkins stay in hiding was watched carefully for a couple of weeks. It was this man's trail that led the agent to Jenkins's cave hideout, and the FBI man forced the logger to confess that he had been supplying Jenkins with food and other necessities. At this point, four other agents were called in. They enlisted local lawmen to help them "bring Jenkins to justice," as George Whitelaw had quoted. The rest of the story was delivered in a breathless prose:

"Early on Tuesday morning, thirty members of state and local police forces from both sides of the state border joined four Federal agents, surrounding the cave with their firearms trained on its entrance. Jenkins was called out repeatedly, but made no reply. The lawmen remained on the alert all day, making entreaties every few minutes to Jenkins to give up and turn himself in. Toward nightfall, Jenkins rushed out of the doorway of the cave with a large hunting rifle and began blasting in all directions. He was felled almost instantly by the lawmen, but not before he managed to wound three of them, one seriously. Jenkins was pronounced dead at the scene."

That was it. No, "thus ends the saga of Boyd Jenkins" or other flourish. No mention of what had become of Boyd's remains. No epitaph whatsoever.

There was a photo of the principal FBI agent, the one who had kept on the trail all that time. His name was Peter Livingstone, which meant nothing to me. The picture wasn't very clear, but there was something vaguely familiar about his features. Especially around the eyes.

The machine that makes copies of microfilm was broken, so I went through the stories again, and copied down the newspaper accounts longhand, for what they were worth. I wondered if they were any more accurate than some of the oral history accounts I had collected. Who could say what the real truth of the Boyd story was. With that deep thought on my mind, I headed back to the Nature Center to take a nap under the coolish breeze of the electric fan I had purchased at a flea market the day before.

I was jarred awake from a dream about rabid hound dogs chasing me through the woods, by a loud knock on the front door of the Nature Center. I pulled on my jeans and trudged to the door. It was twilight, and streaks of dark orange and fuchsia stood out against the cedar trees on the horizon. Ruthie stood framed in the light of the porch like an apparition.

"Tomorrow's good," she said, stepping into the room.

"Tomorrow?" I repeated, still groggy from the nap, and suddenly very self-conscious without my shirt on.

"You know, for the trip up to Boyd's cave. Listen, everyone says that the people who bought that land haven't started doing anything up there yet—some environmentalists have a legal case to make them preserve the area instead of developing it." She stopped, continuing almost to herself, "Hmm, that would make a good topic for a report in my Environmental Law class this fall."

I nodded, beginning to come out of my fog.

"Anyhow, I wanted to check on that—we don't want to run into a construction crew, or find out someone's bulldozed the cave away."

"Good thinking," I said.

"You're sure you have good directions? Mine are sort of hazy."

"I have the directions right here in my field journal," I assured her. I didn't tell her that I was notorious for getting lost. I figured she'd find that out soon enough.

"Okay, I'll meet you here tomorrow." She started to leave, then stopped. "Oh, you remember that Chris Demond guy? You told me you met him."

I was fully awake now. "Yeah."

"He was over at the pool yesterday and we got to talking. Then he asked me out to the movies next week." She looked down at her flip-flops, then up at me. "I said yes."

Chapter 13

FARTHER ADVENTURES

The next morning, Ruthie was at the door again, holding a large picnic basket. "Lunch," she said. I could see that having her along on a field trip would have its advantages.

"Where did you tell your parents you were going?"

"I told them that you were taking me with you on an interview, so I could get a head start on my oral history class."

"And they weren't afraid that I would take you into the woods somewhere and have my way with you?" I joked—well, half-joked, because seeing her this morning in her well-fitting jeans and lavender tank top gave me a few thoughts along those lines.

"Granny Taggart told them that you were a nice young man, and very smart. Aren't you?"

"Well, my graduate school GPA is 3.5." She stuck her tongue out at me, and handed over the heavy basket. I put it in the back of the VW with my camera equipment and we headed off.

It took us almost two hours to reach the general vicinity of the cave. Ruthie asked me a few questions about what kind of things folklorists studied and whom I had interviewed so far. But the roar of the VW's engine laboring up and down hills made conversation difficult. For the last half hour, we climbed up a mountain that was extremely steep, with deep drop-offs into the woods to the right, and more woods sloping upwards on the left. There was no sign of life, just forest punctuated by bright orange "Posted, No Hunting" signs every hundred feet or so.

When we reached the top of the mountain and began heading down the other side, we started looking for the turnoff. The road was more even on this side, with gentler slopes. According to the directions Mr. Billings had given me, it was the second road on the right. He had said that it looked like a dirt logging road.

We passed an indentation in the woods that resembled a road and looked at each other. Should that be counted as one or not? We came to the second, which was more obviously a road. I slowed the car, and Ruthie shrugged. "I guess we should try it," she said.

We followed the road a short distance until it dwindled to two paths with high weeds growing between the ruts. It did look as though someone had driven on it fairly recently, but it didn't match Billings's directions at all. "Guess that other one wasn't a road after all," she mused when I stopped the car. There was a clearing where the road ended, with some smooth stumps. One of them had something on the top of it. I got out to investigate, and Ruthie followed. The remains of a baloney sandwich, the meat slicked with grease and the white bread beginning to curl at the edges, stood frying in the bright noon sun shining on the stump. An empty Pepsi can and some cigarette butts littered the ground near the stump. "Logger's lunch," Ruthie quipped.

"Looks like the logger wasn't here so long ago," I said, noticing that the Pepsi can still had sweat on it, and one of the cigarette butts was still smoldering a little. I crushed it out with my sneaker. "He had the right idea, though—nice place for a picnic. What's in that basket, anyway?"

Ruthie took out a couple of deviled ham sandwiches with pickle relish and two Granny Smith apples, and we settled on the stumps. I was glad the sandwiches weren't baloney. I took out my camera, feeling compelled for some reason to document the logger's lunch, and then on impulse took a picture of Ruthie sitting on her stump eating the apple. A bit of juice dribbled down her chin, and I had a sudden wild desire to lick it off. She wiped it with the back of her hand. "So, what should my strategy with Demond be?"

Last night, after the revelation about her date, she had told me that she'd only said yes because she wanted to get more information about Demond. "He seems kind of slimy," she confessed. "Although he does have a nice bod." I'd only known her for a couple of weeks and already she knew how to push my buttons.

"Well," I thought, chewing my own apple. "Try to get him on the subject of Boyd. See what he knows. Why he's so interested in the story." I thought another moment. "And try to find out if the name Livingstone means anything to him."

"Livingstone?" she asked. "As in, 'Dr. Livingstone, I presume?' "

I explained what I had discovered in the old newspaper clippings. It was a long shot, of course, and I really didn't think Demond was the type to reveal anything pertinent, but it was still worth a try.

We got back in the car, turned around, and soon found the right road. It went fairly deep into the woods, and ended at a gate of sorts, with a heavy padlocked chain. A sign hung on the gate warned, "Private Property, Do Not Enter." I retrieved my camera equipment, Ruthie reached in the basket and brought out some cookies and two bottles of IBC root beer, which she jammed into the pockets of her jeans, and we started out down the path beyond the gate.

I felt as if I were on a pilgrimage. The tall hardwoods towered above us, and our shoes crunching the underbrush was the only sound, except for an occasional bird call. Last year's leaves gave off a spicy smell under our feet. The light came dappled through the canopy of leaves above, mottling Ruthie's face and bare arms. Suddenly, a squirrel ran across the path and we were both startled. Ruthie grabbed my shoulder in alarm, then started to laugh.

"Spooky," I whispered. Then we were silent again. The path was not exactly well worn, but discernable through the thick underbrush—the legacy of years worth of teenagers and others seeking a thrill, I guessed. I tried to imagine the place as Boyd had seen it. A profound quiet, with only the whisper of the trees overhead. The intense greens and subtle browns, dotted with wild flowers. The evidence of unseen animals—a half-chewed nut, a pile of scat.

After we had walked what I judged to be the "couple of miles down the path," I consulted the directions again. Take the left fork in the path, follow about a mile and a half to a cliff. Follow the cliff around about 180 degrees and you should see the opening of the cave behind some ash trees.

"I hope you know what an ash tree looks like," I said as we started down the left fork.

"Of course I do, silly, I took Forestry when I was a second-semester freshman." We were talking in normal voices now, the long walk building confidence.

I told her more about the visit to Cyrus's and how he puzzled over the motivations of the FBI man. "What do you think this guy Livingstone was waiting for?" I asked her.

"Maybe he was just sick of his job and wanted to hang out in this part of the country. You have to admit, it is gorgeous," she said, sweeping a hand around the lush woods. She stopped and squatted down, lifting a flower with reverence. "Look, a jack-in-the-pulpit." She pointed to a nearby fern. "A fiddlehead. They're good to eat, you know. There's so many species of plants in this square mile, we could spend days counting them." I bent close to look at the flower. She turned her head and her hair brushed my cheek. I had to restrain myself from burying my face in her hair and kissing her neck. She straightened up.

"Lots of people 'seng in these woods."

"Sing?" I asked, rubbing my cheek. I imagined some sect of tree worshippers holding a singing service.

She laughed. " 'Seng, you goof! Go hunting for ginseng. Hasn't anyone told you about that yet? There's a good profit in it. Maybe that's what the FBI guy was doing, who knows. Let's get this show on the road." She started marching down the path, unscrewing an IBC as she went. "Want one?" I hurried after her and reached for the soda.

Finally, we reached a jutting of rock which must have been the cliff. We followed the base until we judged ourselves to have gone 180 degrees and started looking for a cave entrance. Ruthie identified the ash trees, and we climbed up and started parting branches until we found an opening about six feet square. We peered in. I had borrowed a flashlight from Dwayne, remembering to check the batteries before sticking it in my camera bag. I shone the light around the interior, half expecting a bunch of bats to fly out.

The entrance opened into a circular, living-room-sized space with smooth walls and a rather level floor. It didn't seem too damp, and the ceiling was high enough for a fairly tall man to stand up in. At least as tall as Boyd, and me. We stepped inside. I took a deep breath and shone the flashlight around the walls. They were hard to see at first, but when our eyes adjusted to the meager light entering through the opening, we picked out bits of color. I stepped back and illuminated a larger surface. The colors began to take shape.

They were badly peeled, and some whole parts of the pictures were missing. But they were still impressive. Near the entrance was a life-sized portrait of a man, with a dog beside him. Ruthie pointed out a shotgun in one hand and a fiddle in the other. He wore what appeared to be bib overalls and a checked shirt. The peeling paint obscured his face, giving him an eerie appearance. A short distance down the left side of the cave was a painting of a house, which must have been white when it was painted but now looked grey. It had a dark green roof and a chimney with some smoke curling out. The front door was open and someone—it looked like a woman, possibly with an apron on—stood in the doorway. What was left of her arm extended as if in greeting. A tree, probably apple judging from the red blobs among the green top, stood near the house.

Next came the facade of a church, its simple lines reminiscent of many I had seen in my drives around the countryside. A truncated steeple, a wide blue doorway, some colored glass in the front windows. There were some gravestones to the right of the church. Next was a scene that at first neither one of us could make out. Not that the peeling of the paint was any worse, but the scene itself was more abstract than the others. Finally I interpreted, using my knowledge of Boyd's personal history as a guide. There were army boots, a rifle, and a greenish helmet. There was barbed wire, and a big pile of bodies, some with yellowish skin and slanted eyes. The bodies were all sizes, including some that were obviously supposed to be children, and there was a swath of red paint at the base of the pile. Three black jagged lines that looked like lightning bolts reached from the ceiling to the floor. I shuddered, explaining to Ruthie that this must have been Boyd's view of his experience in Korea.

Next was what must have been a pretty woman when it was painted. There were vestiges of a blue dress and high heels of the same color. A little bit of bright yellow around her head indicated blond hair, and the shadow of a red lipsticked smile still played around her lips. She held a flower, barely visible now, in her right hand. Then, there was the facade of another building. It had a sign on the front, which was unreadable, and what looked like a big picture window, with a smaller window in the gable. "The store," Ruthie whispered. "The grocery store in Sunrise."

I nodded. I moved the flashlight and saw the inevitable: a prone body with a big red blotch still visible in the area of the chest. A tall stand of trees came next, and we could barely make out the cave, or what we imagined must have been the cave, at the center.

We had almost completed the circle of the room. The last painting was, again, a life-sized portrait in the same clothing as the first picture. But this time the figure held what looked like a stick in one hand, with a bright blue dab at the end. In the other hand, he held a sign, with lettering in the same color. There were four words. G, something, maybe a t. Maybe an r, something, something, possibly an h, maybe another t. V or else a w, something, another t maybe, a straight line that could have been part of another t, or any other letter that had a straight line. A large C or G, part of what looked like an o, and—I gave up. I could see Ruthie's mouth moving and a look of great concentration on her face. Finally she spoke. "Get right with God." The words resounded against the smooth stone walls.

"I beg your pardon?" I said.

"'Get right with God,' that's what it's gotta say. Haven't you seen any of those signs along the highway? They're usually in the form of a cross, with the words 'Get right with God' on them?"

I had, in fact, seen one of those when Blake and I were driving home from one of our late-night escapades just the week before, and had vowed to return and photograph it in the daylight. "Yes," I said.

"It seems to me that Boyd would have been in the state of mind near the end to 'get right,'" reasoned Ruthie. "You know that he was sort of a preacher when he was young? Granny Bigelow told me that. I guess she figured we'd be less likely to think of him as the boogie man if we knew he'd been a preacher. Although, Lord knows, I've seen some pretty scary preachers in my day." We both laughed quietly, and the sound echoed around the room.

I shone the light around the floor to see if any traces of Boyd had been left behind. There were a few beer cans, Moon Pie wrappers and other trash of a more recent era, but nothing seemed to be left of the outlaw whose home this had been. I shone the light once more around the circle of the room, dwelling awhile on each scene.

"Sad, isn't it?" Ruthie said in a hushed tone. "Laying his life out so—I don't know, out in the open."

"Well, I wouldn't exactly call this out in the open."

"No, I mean out in the open for himself. He lived here, or so they say. He had to look at these paintings all the time. He had to be constantly reminded of what he left behind, what he did, the things he suffered. Do you know what I mean? It's like, well, having your personal photo album blown up and put all over your wall to stare at—and to stare at you—all the time. Except the bad memories are there as well as the good."

I did understand what she meant. And I felt as if I were beginning to understand the kind of man Boyd must have been. "I think he needed this connection to his history, good and bad. He kind of exorcized his demons by painting this stuff."

"Hmm." Ruthie took the flashlight from my hands and did yet another sweep. "So, what do you say, shall we get out of here?"

"Sure you don't want to smoke a joint and look at the paintings some more?" I quipped.

"You got one?"

I took the flashlight back and led the way out of the cave. The relatively bright light outside the cave made us blink. We started back the way we had come. Ruthie handed me a couple of cookies.

About a mile down the path, Ruthie turned to me. "Do you think he was a good artist?"

"I'm not exactly an art critic. I think he was a good folk artist."

"What's the difference between a good regular artist and a good folk artist?"

"Well," I tried to remember some pithy phrases from my material culture class two semesters ago. "A good 'regular artist' as you put it, would be a good, fine artist I guess? Picasso or Leonardo da Vinci.

They come out of a fine art aesthetic. Folk artists, well, they are work-ing from a folk aesthetic."

"Huh?"

"In other words, fine artists are producing work that is considered masterful in their time period by connoisseurs, collectors, gallery owners, rich people. Folk artists are producing work that is appreci-ated by their own community."

Ruthie wrinkled her nose. "That's about as clear as mud. I always thought that 'folk artists,' or people like Boyd that just painted what they knew whether it was good or not, were not trained, and regular artists—or fine artists, as you call them—went to school or studied with other famous painters or whatever. That's not the distinction, I guess."

I realized that my training had prepared me to answer questions about quilts, baskets, rag rugs and the like, but paintings were barely touched upon by our material culture professor. The whole idea of this type of artist was still touchy. Were these people actually working from a folk aesthetic or from their own vision? Boyd's paintings were not folk art in the same sense as his fiddle tunes, which he had undoubtedly learned from his relatives and other older fiddlers. Chances are Boyd had never seen another folk painter, and certainly didn't learn from one.

"What are you thinking about?" Ruthie asked.

"Oh, Boyd and why he decided to paint in the first place. I mean, how did he know he would be any good at it? It isn't that easy, not everyone can do it."

"Yeah, I remember that from my high school art class!" Ruthie laughed. "My people always looked like—well, they didn't look like people, let's put it that way. I guess that's what I was talking about when I asked if Boyd was a good artist. I think he was. At least you can tell what he was painting. His people look like people and his houses look like houses."

I thought about that for awhile, eating the homemade oatmeal raisin cookie.

Ruthie broke the silence again. "I think you're right about what you said before. Boyd just had that art in him. He wanted to paint—had to paint. All this time on his hands, and he wanted to leave something behind. Maybe he felt that his life had been wasted, to a big extent. Or at least had gone terribly wrong. Maybe painting was a way to make it right again. To 'get right.' "

"He did smaller paintings and gave them away, in exchange for food and other stuff, they say. I've seen a couple of them."

"Oh, yeah. I know that. I know someone who has five of them. Boyd's sister-in-law, as a matter of fact. She was my fifth grade teacher, Mrs. Jenkins. She brought the paintings into school once to show the class."

I looked at her, wide-eyed. "Why didn't you tell me that?"

She looked back, in amusement. "Well, you didn't ask! I can call her and maybe she'll let us come over and see them sometime. She still lives outside of Sunrise."

I could tell that Ruthie would continue to amaze me. All I needed to learn was how to ask the right questions.

Chapter 14

ALMOST HEAVEN

We reached the VW and climbed in. Ruthie threw the empty IBC bottles, which she had been carrying all this time in her hip pocket, into the back seat. A true environmentalist. I had to back up until I found a space wide enough to turn around. We started back up the mountain, reached the crest, and began down the steep side. I downshifted to slow us down, trying not to use the brakes too much for fear of burning them out. But it was necessary to step on them now and then on the turns.

I started noticing that the brakes were not responding very well. That was strange, because they had never given me any trouble before. Then, on a particularly sharp turn, I pumped them and nothing happened. Stomped on them and nothing happened. We careened around the turn, swerving briefly into the other lane. Ruthie, not expecting this, jerked over and bumped into my shoulder.

"Hey, watch those turns!" She yelled over the engine. Then she looked at my face. I must have turned a couple of shades whiter. "What's wrong?"

"I think the brakes just went out." Another turn was coming up. "Hang on!"

The car kept accelerating at an alarming rate, and I barely made the turn. The next straight away, so steep it looked pitched down in a forty-five degree angle, loomed ahead. "Hang on," I repeated, "I'm going to try the emergency brake." I looked over to make sure she had her seat belt on, then pulled on the emergency brake. Nothing. Then I remembered that the stupid thing hadn't worked for at least three months.

I concentrated on trying to keep the car on the road. We kept picking up speed and it was getting harder and harder to control the car. In moments like these, they say, your life flashes before you. But all I could think of was that I was going to get Ruthie killed and her family would never forgive me. But, then, I'd probably be dead, too, so what did it matter?

Suddenly, a runaway truck ramp sign loomed up and passed in a flash. "Hold on!" I managed to scream, just as I saw the steep ramp and turned the car sharply into it. I could sense Ruthie bracing herself as the car plowed into deep sand and came to an abrupt, bone-shaking halt about fifty feet up the ramp.

My heart was beating so fast and so hard that I looked down to see if I could see its outline through my t-shirt, like in cartoons. Then I looked at Ruthie. She was looking straight ahead, up the ramp, in disbelief. Suddenly, she screamed out loud—one of those horror movie screams that made my heart beat even faster, if that were possible.

"Oh my God, are you hurt?" I yelled.

"No," she said in a calm voice, taking deep breaths. "It just happened so fast that I didn't have time to scream. And, it seemed like a good opportunity."

Without thinking, I reached over, still in my seat belt, and hugged her. She returned the hug. We both started laughing, bordering on hysterics.

"You know," she said when we had recovered ourselves a bit. "I always wanted to know if these things really worked." She indicated the ramp with a toss of her head.

"Now you know. But I'd have preferred to have seen a driver's ed movie instead of going for firsthand experience." We laughed again.

"Now what?" she asked.

"Well, the first thing is to get out of here." I tried my door. The car was so entrenched in the sand that I could only open it a few inches. When I did, sand tumbled onto the floor so fast that I had a vision of us trapped in sand as if in a giant hourglass. But, it reached a sort of equilibrium when it was ankle deep, and I managed to open the door wide enough to squeeze out. I waded over to Ruthie's door, scooped enough sand out of the way to get her door open, and she climbed out.

"We'll never get it out of here," she observed, looking at the back tires under almost a foot of sand.

"Guess we'll have to hitchhike back," I said. Easier said than done, since we hadn't met a car or other vehicle for the past several miles, coming up or down this mountain. We sat by the side of the road, at the base of the truck ramp, until we got bored. I got out my camera to document the sorry state of the VW. Maybe the pictures would be useful for insurance purposes if the damage went beyond my deductible. Ruthie leaned back into the car and fished around the picnic basket, looking for something else to drink. She pulled out a banana and held it up. It was bruised—in fact, almost mashed. I winced.

"I could have gotten you killed," I said.

"Us. These mountains are tough on brakes, especially in older cars. You're not used to it, driving in New Jersey, I guess, where there aren't any mountains."

"There are too mountains in New Jersey," I corrected her, even though the Ramapos couldn't hold a candle to these mountains.

She gave me a look that said I had totally missed the point. "Look, we're okay, and that's what's important right now. When's the last time you had those brakes checked, anyhow?"

I shrugged. I wasn't exactly scrupulous when it came to car maintenance, since I had never had to rely on my car for a job before this summer.

"And here I thought Boy Scouts were always prepared," she said.

"How did you know I was a Boy Scout?" I asked.

She laughed. "You act like one, bud. Polite to old ladies. Camping out in that nasty Nature Center. And too much of a gentleman to kiss a girl on the first date."

"Some date," I mumbled, stepping closer to her. "I never made it to Eagle Scout." I put my hand in her hair and pulled her face to mine. Just when our lips were about to touch, the shuddering grind of a heavy truck downshifting made us jump apart. A coal truck was barreling down the hill. We waved our arms in desperation. The truck driver applied his brakes with a sickening squeal. I ran down to the truck and opened the passenger side, looking up at him hopefully.

He rolled down the glass and called out over the roaring engine, "Looks like y'all have had some trouble here, son. Get that pretty girl and climb in, I'll give you a lift into town." I waved to Ruthie and we were on our way. The driver took us to the closest town and let us off at a small diner. He wasn't going our way. We discussed hitching another ride the rest of the way, but Ruthie decided she'd better call her father to come get us. I sat and watched, drinking a cup of coffee, as she called from a pay phone outside. The conversation seemed to last a long time, with Ruthie waving her hand a lot.

Two hours later, we were on our way back home in Ruthie's father's Buick. Everyone was silent for most of the ride. By the time we reached the park, night had fallen. Before he let me out at the park entrance, Mr. Taggart said, "I'm glad you two are safe. But I never want Ruthie going off on one of these 'adventures' again, young man, do you understand me? She's only nineteen. We want her around for a good long while."

I wanted to let him know that I wanted her around a good long while as well. But, feeling like a whipped puppy, I could only manage a humble "Yes, sir." I glanced at Ruthie. She was sitting in the back seat with her arms crossed against her chest. She wouldn't meet my eyes. I trudged up to the Nature Center and collapsed on my bed.

"Rough day," Dwayne mumbled from the recesses of his dim corner.

I turned to the wall and, eventually, fell asleep.

Chapter 15

FEMALE PERSUASIONS

The next day, I called and arranged to have the Volkswagen towed down the mountain for repairs at a Sunoco station in town. I knew it would cost me several days of fieldwork, and probably several weeks' worth of salary—money I was supposed to be saving for graduate school expenses. Luckily, I had all the final plans for Saturday's program finished. A whittler—a friend of Ruthie's grandfather—set up a small exhibit and demonstration at the Nature Center.

I tried not to think of Ruthie and how badly I had messed up our budding friendship. I should have thought twice before traipsing off with her into the mountains in my old heap and nearly getting both of us killed. I felt as if I had violated some fieldworker code, getting involved with an informant's granddaughter. No one had brought it up in our field seminar, but I decided it really was something that we should have been warned against.

Then, to make matters worse, that same night brought a call from my dear girlfriend back in the land of graduate school. We had arranged that she would call me at the pay phone near the entrance of the park every week at a certain time. It was a bit inconvenient, but it was more private than the park office.

"Hi, Rob, how are you?" she asked, in a voice that sounded insincere. I gave her a version of the brake-failing "adventure" without mentioning a passenger. "Oh, my God," she said, "Are you all right?"

I assured her that I was. There was a brief pause. "We need to talk," she said. In my limited experience with women, this phrase always signaled trouble. I braced myself.

Fifteen minutes later, I was back in my bed again, with my face to the wall. I was beginning to memorize this particular bit of wall—the brown smudge on the badly spackled sheet rock. During the conversation with Melissa, it was revealed that Hausa was not the only thing the African engineering student was teaching her. The situation gave a whole new meaning to the phrase she had used during her visit, "feeling the language." Furthermore, he had been evicted from the apartment he shared with three other foreign students. "The landlady said they brought in roaches," she explained, "as if they aren't native here."

So, of course, he had moved into our apartment. "He didn't have any place else to go," she said, as though that were a justification.

"So, what am I supposed to do?" I asked with exasperation. "I don't think the apartment is big enough for the three of us." I was on the verge of telling her we should just call our relationship quits, but at the moment I wasn't sure if I had any better prospects.

"Well, he might get deported. His student visa is expiring this coming semester, and it might not get renewed."

So, I was supposed to wait for the whims of the State Department to decide my fate? There was another pause. Then, her voice came back with a hard edge. "You know, it's hard with you gone this summer—all summer. I've been reshifting my priorities, and just now this seems right. I guess we'll have to talk it out face to face when you get back."

I had hung up on her.

The whittling program was quite popular, much to my relief. The whittler nearly sold out of little pigs and chickens (we weren't really supposed to sell things on the park grounds, but what the administration didn't know wouldn't hurt them) and he was very happy. Several of his woodworking cronies stopped by to cheer him on, and I made arrangements to interview a couple of them. One made animal sculptures out of tree branches and other interesting pieces of wood he gathered while he was hunting. The other made wild turkey calls—small wooden boxes with lids that scraped along the sides and made a plausible gobbling sound. I wondered if these craftsmen, too, were somehow related to Ruthie.

On Sunday I decided to hoof it down the road about a mile and a half, to a church I had ridden past at least fifty times. I felt that a church service might help just now—I needed some "getting right." The preacher was a fiery hell-and-damnation type, punctuating each phrase with a labored breath until I thought he would collapse from hyperventilation. I thought of Ruthie's comment about scary preachers, and I smiled to myself.

The old-fashioned hymns had a calming effect after the wrenching sermon, and a decent choir of young people sang "Will the Circle Be Unbroken" with fervor. After the service, the ladies seated next to me invited me to coffee and cake in the basement of the church. I quizzed them about their baking skills, and they told me about the cake walks they used to hold. Numbers would be chalked on the floor, music played on a record player, and when the music stopped, the person standing on the winning number got to pick out a cake. I thought it sounded like a great activity for a program at the park. I left the church feeling much better. At least old ladies were still nice to me, the vestiges of my Boy Scouthood.

When I returned to the Nature Center, there was a note tacked to the door. It was from Ruthie: "If you still want to meet Mrs. Jenkins I can arrange it. Come down to the pool before five and we can talk." I guessed this wasn't as bad as "We have to talk." I changed to my bathing suit, put on my t-shirt, and walked to the pool. Along the way I encountered Spike, sweeping some pine needles from the pool entrance.

"Heard you had a little trouble up in the mountains," he said, arching his eyebrows. "Gotta watch those roads up there." He turned back to his sweeping. News sure travels fast around the park, I thought.

I sat down near the lifeguard chair, dangling my feet in the cool water, taking a deep whiff of chlorine. I didn't look up, but soon I heard feet climbing down the ladder and Ruthie sat down beside me.

"Sorry my daddy talked to you like that. I thought it best to give it a few days before I saw you again. Did you get your car back?"

"Are you sure it's okay to be seen with me?"

She laughed. "Actually, Granny Taggart was over when we got home. She reminded my dad about how some of the wild things he used to do when he was young gave her fits. She is your biggest defender, bud. She's really taken to you."

I wanted to ask if the granddaughter felt likewise, but she continued.

"Besides, I've had another date since." She described her date with Demond. They had gone to the one local movie theater, and afterwards to his house for coffee.

"He keeps a nice, neat house. But, he left some of his mail lying around. While he was in the kitchen making coffee, I snooped through it."

I registered mock disapproval. "Isn't that a federal offense?"

"I didn't open it or anything! Just looked at the name as printed on the envelopes. Christopher L. Demond on one." She paused for dramatic effect. "Then, bingo! Christopher Livingstone Demond on another."

Chapter 16

FAMILY TIES

On the way to Sunrise on Tuesday, Ruthie and I speculated further on the "coincidence" of Demond's middle name being the same as the FBI guy's. It hardly seemed like a middle name that someone would pick out of a baby book. It had to be a family name. But, we were both at a loss as to how to prove the connection, short of asking Demond.

Ruthie revealed that Demond had asked her lots of questions about my work, attempting to make them casual bits of conversation. Did she know whom I had interviewed? Had she been on any interviews or field trips with me? What did she know about the Boyd Jenkins story? Stuff like that.

"I told him I didn't know you, or what you've been up to, all that well. I'd only met you a couple of weeks ago, and had only seen you a couple of times, and that I really had no idea who—besides Granny Taggart—you'd been interviewing. And, that I had given you a few ideas of people to interview." I looked over at her, raising my eyebrows. "Okay, so I didn't quite tell the whole truth. But, I really don't know you that well, now, do I?"

We reached Sunrise, and Ruthie started pointing out landmarks. I had driven through the town once, out of curiosity, but without a tour guide I couldn't tell which building was the infamous store. It was boarded up, but I could still see the resemblance to the painting in Boyd's cave. Nowadays, the convenience store at the gas station on the edge of town served the purpose of the old grocery. She also pointed out the house that the girlfriend had lived in, and she assured me that she knew the way to Boyd's parents' old place out in the country, now unoccupied and run down, and would show it to me after we visited Mrs. Jenkins.

"Do you know her first name?" I asked.

"When you're in fifth grade, you never know your teacher's first name!" I remembered it, though, from the graveyard at Hangman's Chapel. Lucy, born 1920, no death date. It seemed weird to be meeting someone who already had a tombstone with her name on it.

"Ruthie? Ruthie Ann Taggart? Is that you? My, how you have grown!" I was expecting someone who looked older and more school-marmish, but Lucy Jenkins was a slim, athletic-looking woman in pressed slacks and a sleeveless blouse. I did some quick mental arithmetic—she was fifty-nine.

"Introduce me to your friend, Ruthie Ann," Mrs. Jenkins said. We shook hands and she waved us into the living room. She followed my gaze to the five paintings lined up against the sofa. "Ruthie said on the phone that you were a student interested in folk art and wanted to see Boyd's paintings, so I got them out. Would you care for a cold drink?"

While Lucy poured lemonade in the kitchen, Ruthie and I stood admiring the pictures. They were all about the same size and had the characteristic frames that I had noticed on the other two paintings I'd seen. Two of these paintings were similar in subject to the others: hunting scenes in the woods. One depicted a treed raccoon, with three hounds barking viciously, their front paws on the trunk. These hounds were more ominous than Cyrus's painting of Bob. The coon peered out from among the leaves with a defiant stare, illuminated by what I guessed in real life would have been the hunter's lantern or a powerful flashlight. Boyd had caught the gleam of the light in the coon's eyes with skill, an unearthly glow that gave me goose bumps. The other hunting scene showed a man—Boyd himself, I guessed— poised to fire a rifle at a wild turkey.

Two other paintings had different subject matter and a different style. They both portrayed wildflowers and other flora on the forest floor, and were almost impressionistic. Still, I could make out violets, daisies, ferns, and other plants I had seen in the local woods. There was nothing eerie or threatening about them. Ruthie moved quickly to them, smiling. "I like these," she said.

The fifth picture was a combination of the two styles. We recognized it as the entrance to Boyd's cave, centered among the ash trees that were just saplings then, but still made a good cover for the cave opening. You could just make out a figure in the entrance, staring out with the same defiant look as the treed raccoon. Ruthie and I looked at each other, shivering.

Mrs. Jenkins came in with the lemonade and some Lorna Doones. "What do you think of the pictures?" she asked.

"I think they are—" I searched for a word.

"Impressive," Ruthie chimed in. "They really do capture the atmosphere of that part of the forest up there—" She broke off, and I figured she was not quite sure if she should let Lucy know we'd been up to Boyd's hideout.

Lucy Jenkins raised her eyebrows, but didn't ask any questions. "I think, myself, that he was a very talented painter. For someone with no formal training, mind you, who hadn't been encouraged by anyone."

"How did you come by the paintings, Mrs. Jenkins?" I asked.

"Boyd relayed them to us—secretly of course—via a mutual friend who knew where he was. It was his way, I guess, of letting us know he was all right. Of letting us know he was safely hidden—at least for the time being—in the forest, which he always did love. We kept them hidden away until after they, uh, captured him." She reddened a little. I gathered that the bloody shoot-out was not one of her favorite subjects. She added, "Stanley, my late husband—Boyd's brother— and I would not have parted with them for anything. They are all the family has left of Boyd, after all." She paused, sipping her lemonade and looking at the paintings.

"You may wonder why I am being so sentimental about my brother-in-law—people have probably told you that he was an outlaw, a killer, and a ne'er-do-well. He was, I won't deny that. But there were circumstances that led him to all that." She looked earnestly into our faces.

I explained to Lucy that I had been collecting versions of Boyd's story from different people around the area, and asked if she would mind sharing her own version. She hesitated, asking what I was going to do with the story. I told her it would become part of the permanent record of the project, to be housed in the State Archive. She seemed pleased at the prospect, at the chance to "set the record straight" about Boyd and the Jenkins family.

"I am trusting that you are not like that other young man who came to try to persuade me to sell the paintings, and wanted 'my version' of Boyd's story to publish, so he said." She made a disgusted face. "He was quite pleasant at first, but he began to annoy me. He was quite insistent that I consider selling the paintings."

"Who was that?" I asked, as if I didn't know.

"Christopher something. I think he now sells insurance in the area. Have you met him?" She frowned a little.

"Sort of encountered him, yes," I said.

"I don't trust him, frankly. And I would appreciate it if you would not share the things I am about to tell you with him, especially those things I might tell you 'off the record' so to speak. If he wants to take the trouble of traveling to the Archive and looking up the public parts, then that's his business," she said, with a smug smile.

I asked her if she minded being recorded and she consented, with the caveat that she might ask me to turn off the recorder from time to time if she didn't see fit to make certain information public. I agreed. I had brought the cassette recorder—somehow the big reel-to-reel Nagra with mike stands hadn't seemed appropriate. I set up a directional mike on the coffee table in front of her, and said my introductions for the record, then indicated that she could start. Like most people with a complete version of the Boyd legend, she needed little prompting.

"I married Boyd's brother in 1940. We were both twenty years old. I had just finished Teacher's College, and he was a clerk at the Sunrise Savings and Loan. He had a couple of years of business college, you see. In that way, we were the oddities of the family." Ruthie and I exchanged glances. We could relate. "A very traditional family, largely unschooled, as you've probably heard. But good people, with strong moral values, especially Boyd's mother. She was as good a Christian as they come, always there to help the sick and the needy."

"There were some great musicians in the family—self-taught, mind you, it just came naturally—including Boyd himself, as I'm sure you've heard. But, of course, as with most families, there was the darker side as well. Some who maybe had drinking problems, some who were, shall we say, not the best providers for their families—I'm sure I'm not telling you anything you don't understand." She paused, and we both nodded.

"In any case, Stanley and I were quite happy. I started teaching in the Sunrise Elementary School—I switched later to the school you went to, Ruthie—and Stanley's job was good. We were not blessed with children, unfortunately, but I loved my little nieces and nephews very much and always helped out with them. I had been an only child, and so having a big family around was a new delight. There were five Jenkins children all together, Stanley was in the middle. Boyd was the youngest. There was one other boy, older than Stanley, they called him Junior. He was Melvin, Jr. He moved to the city and didn't come home much, to his mother's constant disappointment. The rest of them settled here.

"I was particularly good friends with the girls, Trudy and Emma. Trudy married a Smith, and Emma married a Hankins. Trudy was named after her grandmother on her mother's side, she was a Sharpe and she was still living at the time. She was also a dear. Anyway, Trudy and Emma had four children apiece. Some of them are still living in this area but some have also made good in the city or elsewhere. One even works in Washington, D.C.! But, I am getting off the track here, sorry.

"Anyway, as I said, it was a close-knit family, for the most part a happy family. My Stanley died young, he had a heart attack at forty-five, God rest his soul, and I do miss him every day. But, about Boyd. He was always a funny one, quiet and shy most of the time unless he was playing the fiddle. Then he was as lively as they come. He also took a hand at preaching, you might have heard that, too. He was quite a persuasive preacher, and could argue Bible quotations like a scholar. His mama was quite proud of that." Lucy sipped her lemonade.

"Boyd—although as I have said he was a quiet one—had a longing for adventure. He was like that saying, 'Still waters run deep.' Yes, every time I hear that saying I think of Boyd. They were recruiting for the Korean War then and Boyd got the bug. He saw it as a way to travel halfway across the world and see something new, I think. I guess he figured he could be a good soldier. He could handle a gun, after all, the Jenkins's were always great hunters, even Stanley. I don't think he thought much ahead of time about the killing part. Of course, everyone was so prejudiced at that time toward the Asians." She made an apologetic face.

"And so, he enlisted in the army and went off. Came back after almost two years with an honorable discharge—he had gotten a minor wound, nothing too serious. He was different when he came back. Restless, angry. Not the old, quiet, thoughtful Boyd. Even when he played the fiddle it sounded different to me—harsher, more raw. Same old tunes but with an edge of—I don't know, danger almost." She shuddered a little, then looked up and smiled. "I know that must sound strange, but I wasn't the only one who noticed. Oh, of course you could still do a square or line dance to his fiddling, and when everyone was stomping around no one took much notice of how Boyd played, I think. But, when he played for himself, out on the front porch of his parents' house where he still lived at the time, we could hear it quite clearly.

"I had a friend, she was a lovely girl. She worked as a receptionist for our doctor here in town. To tell you the truth, I felt a little sorry for her because she was from out of town and people held that against her. I knew what it felt like, because even though my family has lived in this area for three generations, we were originally from Virginia and some folks around here still don't consider me a 'native'! This girl was from Ohio, from Cincinnati, and had moved down here and got this job. Boyd met her one day when she was visiting." She looked at us, with an embarrassed expression. "Actually, I set it up, sort of fixed them up by inviting them both to dinner at the same time."

She looked away, with pain in her face. "I didn't know that she was also seeing this Tom, the grocer. Well, I knew that she had been seeing him, but I thought it was over." She looked at me and pointed to the tape recorder, making a cutting motion with her hand. I hit the pause button.

"I think I need to explain something that should remain just between us. My friend, her name was Lilly, had been having an affair with this Tom. But it was not a happy affair. He was quite good looking and had some money. But he was a cruel and hateful person. I'm sure others have told you that. I know he hit her. Maybe worse. She told me later that she desperately wanted to get out of the relationship, but was afraid of him. When she met Boyd, I think she saw a way out. He was really not much of a looker, and Lord knows it didn't look like he had much of a future. But he was gentle with her and kind. They were good for one another. They made each other laugh, and they both needed that. I guess I don't regret that I introduced them. I just wish things had turned out differently." She indicated that I could turn the recorder back on.

"Well, you have been told the rest, I suppose. Tom caught wind of Boyd's involvement with 'his' girlfriend—which was totally innocent as far as I know, she and Boyd just went out a few times for a drink—and became insanely jealous. He was that type. And the whole thing escalated until, well, the shooting. Which was, as you may also know, self-defense on Boyd's part. But Tom's father had such clout in this town that even if Boyd had stood his ground he probably would have been convicted of first degree murder. So he ran."

"It is true that a lot of people, many of them relatives, helped him stay hidden. We would get word of him from time to time through one of them. Then, one day, a man we didn't know came with a large parcel for us. It was the paintings. I had no idea that Boyd had such talent, and we were all amazed.

"We had been constantly bothered by the lawmen—local, state and particularly those FBI men. And most particularly that one, the one that stayed around the longest. Livingston, I think? He was here almost every week, interrogating us. He especially kept asking about the paintings. He had obviously come across some of the ones Boyd had traded for food and shelter up in the mountains, and I guess he figured we might have some, too. He said that any paintings we had were important evidence and we could be jailed for withholding them. He would ask different members of the family about paintings, and we all pretended not to know what he was talking about. He threatened to get a warrant to search every one of the family houses. But he wouldn't have found anything. We had them in a good hiding place."

She motioned for me to stop the recorder again. "Stanley had the key to the bank vault. We hid them there." She winked. "Of course that was totally against bank rules." She motioned again, and I turned the recorder back on.

"The rest is history, as they say. After a little over a year, this FBI man finally tracked Boyd down and that was that." She took another sip of lemonade.

"What ever happened to Lil—uh, the girlfriend?" I asked, remembering Lucy's hesitation to mention her friend's name on tape.

"Oh, she moved to the city and went to nursing school. Got married and had a couple of children. She's now a private nurse. I get letters from her, or a Christmas card, from time to time. I have even visited with her down there a few times."

"Do you think she'd be willing to talk to us?" I said "us" without thinking. I looked over at Ruthie, but she didn't seem to have registered the pronoun, or if she had, she didn't seem to be taking exception to it.

Lucy looked thoughtful, and motioned once again for me to turn off the recorder. "Maybe not on tape. I think it's still a very painful memory for her. She took the whole thing very hard, poor dear, as you can well imagine. But if I make a phone call for you, maybe she will agree to meet with you." She looked over at the paintings. "By the way, Boyd sent her a painting, too. It's the most beautiful, and it almost broke both of our hearts just to look at it. She still has it, of course, and I am sure she will be happy to show it to you."

"Do you know anyone else who has any paintings that Boyd did?" Ruthie asked. She was getting into the spirit of the search. I felt a surge of warmth toward her.

"Oh, dear. We know that Boyd painted lots and lots of pictures and traded them all over the countryside for food and other things he needed. I think that FBI man confiscated quite a number of them from people, for evidence—people who were intimidated by him.

I do know a few of our relatives up toward the Kentucky border that had some—whether they still do or not, I wouldn't know." Lucy didn't seem too willing to give us names, so we let it go.

"Here's something that might interest you, though," she said. "Remember I said that one of my nephews worked in Washington, D.C.? He's currently a member of the staff of our state senator, in fact. Well, all the nieces and nephews know about Boyd's paintings, of course. He tried to find out from the FBI what happened to the ones that were confiscated for evidence. Thinking that, maybe after all these years, they could release them back to the family. They told him that there were no records indicating anything about the paintings. Isn't that curious?"

We agreed that it was most interesting, and also puzzling. I started packing up the tape recorder. "One more question, if you don't mind," I asked. "Where is Boyd buried?"

"Well, the family plot is near the old homestead, on Hangman's Chapel Road, not far from here, next to the old church. It used to be a nice little church, but I fear it's fallen into disrepair. But we still keep up the graveyard." Her face twisted a little. "Stanley is there, and that is where I will be, too, when the time comes.

"Anyhow, Boyd is buried there, too, but we thought it best to keep his grave unmarked. The story was met with such sensation around here, we thought people might go thrill seeking, and we didn't want that. We had a time just getting them to release his remains back to the family for burial when they were done doing Lord knows what with them. We never did get back his personal effects, his gun and his fiddle. I suppose they just threw those out, like trash." She looked tired and sad.

"What about Bob?" I asked.

"Bob?" Lucy pondered the question a few seconds. "Oh, the hound dog you mean. Believe it or not, they gave us back his remains as well, and we buried them along with Boyd."

"From what I hear, he would have wanted it that way," I intoned. Ruthie gave me a perturbed look, but Lucy smiled.

"I don't know who all you have been talking to, young man, but that is very true. Boyd loved that dog, and Bob was a true friend to the end, so to speak."

We shook hands all around, and Lucy promised to get in touch with Lilly and to give Ruthie a call with her answer.

"We'll look forward to your call," I said.

"'What was that 'we,' business back there?" Ruthie said with a grin as we got in the car. "As Tonto said to the Lone Ranger, 'Whaddya mean, we, White Man?' "

I reached over and mussed her hair. "Like it or not, you're in this with me, now, kiddo." She caught my hand and held it in mid-air for a minute. If Lucy hadn't been waving us on from her front door, I would've kissed Ruthie then and there.

Chapter 17

FIREWORKS

Ruthie reminded me, as she dropped me off at the Nature Center, that the next day was the Fourth of July. Jakestown was having a chicken barbeque and fireworks after dark.

"I've been going to those fireworks since I was a little girl. They aren't the most spectacular, but they're kinda fun. Want to come?"

"You sure it's okay for you to be seen with me in public?" I said, only half joking.

"My father's temper's blown over. You can meet the rest of my family and see what you think. Granny, of course, will be thrilled to see you."

"What about Demond? He hasn't called to ask you out again?"

"I guess he got what he was after," she said, then blushed a bit when she realized how that had sounded. "Information, I mean. I don't think he's really interested in me."

I leaned into the car and put my lips close to her ear. "He's crazy, then." Her hair tickled my nose. I kissed her on the nape of the neck.

Then I heard the crunch of many little feet on the gravel of the driveway, and some muffled giggles. I jerked my head out of the window, bumping my head hard on the door frame. Ten kids clutching leaves, with Dwayne in the lead, were staring at us.

"Leaf i.d. program," he announced, deadpan, and headed them toward the Nature Center entrance.

"You get an 'A' for effort," Ruthie laughed, revving up the car engine.

The rest of the day, I kept busy making calls to the five retired loggers I had interviewed. I had cooked up the idea of having an occupational folklife program on logging, with the older loggers showing tools and skills they had used when young, and talking about rafting logs down the river and other adventures. By the end of the day, I had halfway convinced at least three of them to participate. I would have to visit each one once again and discuss the fine points, cajole them a little more, pick out the tools that they should bring. I wondered if I needed to procure a large log somewhere. Surely that wouldn't be too hard around here.

As I caught up on my field journal entries, I couldn't believe that almost half the summer had gone by. But, thinking of it another way, I couldn't believe all that I had done since arriving on that rainy day in mid-May. Dwayne came in as I was putting the final touches on the day's entry. He stood and looked at me for a few seconds.

"You and Ruthie, eh?"

"Excuse me?"

"You and Ruthie. That's cool. She's a smart lady." He passed me, went into the kitchen cubbyhole and got something out of the refrigerator, then disappeared into the recesses of our bedroom.

The Fourth was bright and not too hot. I spent part of the morning logging the Lucy Jenkins tape, but later decided to get out for a short hike before meeting Ruthie at four o'clock for the barbeque. It was a holiday, after all, and I did need the exercise. I threw a peanut butter and jelly sandwich and a bottle of orange juice into my backpack and grabbed one of the park trail maps kept in a rack near the front door of the Nature Center. I picked a trail called "Devil's Backbone" which was supposed to lead to a small waterfall. I panted up the steep hill, stopping now and then to catch my breath and look at the trees and plants around me. I wished Ruthie were along to tell me their names and their medicinal uses.

I reached the waterfall and sat down to eat my lunch. All was quiet except the rush of the falling water and the gurgle of the creek below it. A few birds twittered in the trees. The air smelled like warm pine needles. I took off my sneakers and socks and stuck my feet into the cool brook.

I started thinking about all that I had learned about Boyd so far, my mind wandering around all the facts and impressions, stories and clues. I dwelled on the mystery of the FBI man, the reason he stayed so long in the area. He clearly had some vested interest in keeping Boyd alive as long as possible. Was he doing something illegal, or merely out of the line of duty? Maybe just being out of his office and in this beautiful part of the country really did have something to do with it, I considered as I breathed in the tangy pine smell and felt the pebbles wash over my feet. Livingstone, the FBI guy's last name and Demond's middle name. Grandfather? Uncle?

I lay back on a big, smooth rock and watched a hawk make wide circles in the air. Suddenly he swooped down, returning skyward with some prey clutched in his claws. A field mouse, maybe. There was some message there, I was sure, but I was too sleepy to ponder it. I dosed in the bright sun, waking just in time to descend back to the Nature Center and take a quick shower before meeting Ruthie at the barbeque site, a baseball park just outside of town.

She touched my nose gingerly. "Got a little sun, there, bud."

"Yes, believe it or not, I went on a bit of a nature walk today. Up Devil's Backbone."

"Oh, were you trying to 'capture of essence' of the legend?"

"What legend?"

"Didn't you read the blurb in the trail map, dummy? What kind of researcher are you, anyway?"

I just happened to have brought the trail map with me, still folded to the part that showed the trails with little dotted lines. I unfolded the map and read out loud: "Capture the essence of the legend of Devil's Backbone. Local folklore says that an Indian maiden and her lover were drowned in the waterfall by her jealous ex-lover in the early years of the area's history. Legend has it that you can hear their dying moans echoing in the sound of the water if you listen hard enough." I made a disgusted face. "Who writes this crap?"

She shrugged. "I think there used to be a ranger here into heavy melodrama. He particularly had a thing for Indian maidens." She tossed her head and held it high. "I am part Indian, you know."

"Well," I said, "you'd better not let me catch you near any waterfalls with Chris Demond or anyone." She rolled her eyes.

We feasted on barbequed chicken, cole slaw, potato salad, soft white rolls and butter and very sweet iced tea, with homemade gooseberry pie for dessert. We sat and watched the children's games—sack and three-legged races, egg toss, and tug of war. We chatted with Granny Taggart about her latest quilt project. Granny gave me a number of knowing looks, and ended by saying to Ruthie, "When are you going to bring this young man around for chicken and biscuits, Ruthie Ann?"

Ruthie dragged me over to the Lion's Club baseball pitching booth. "Okay, show me your stuff." She fished a crumpled dollar out of her pocket. "Three balls, Arty," she said to the guy behind the counter.

I'd never been a great wielder of baseballs. I was a mediocre shortstop in Little League, much to my father's chagrin, and didn't even try out for the high school team. But, to please Ruthie, I gave it a try. I got the first two right on target, and was concentrating on the third when I heard a low voice near my elbow. "Don't disappoint the little lady, Anderson."

I turned to see Chris Demond with an unpleasant smile on his face. His sudden appearance unnerved me—the third ball hit just left of the target's center.

"Too bad," he said, taking out a dollar from his neat leather billfold. He executed three perfect hits, pointed to a large purple and green stuffed snake, and handed it, with a bow, to Ruthie.

"Gee, thanks," Ruthie said, making a face.

"I hear you've been consulting Ruthie on some fieldwork ideas," said Demond. "You two make quite a team. By the way, what happened to that pretty anthropologist who came to visit a few weeks ago?"

I glared at him. Ruthie looked confused.

"Well, I see you two have a few things to discuss. Enjoy." He disappeared into the crowd assembling for the fireworks.

I tried to explain to Ruthie about Melissa, how she had dumped me, how I felt nothing for her, etc., etc. What I really wanted to tell her was how much more alive, how much more real, I felt with her. How much I was growing to love this place and how much a part of the place she seemed to me, fresh and sweet and wise. But the first boom of the fireworks started as I was trying to compose the right words.

We stood a little apart. She had her arms crossed in front of her and wouldn't look at me. I watched the fireworks reflected in her dark eyes. Each crash reverberated in my head. I would gladly have wrung Demond's neck at that moment.

Ruthie went home with her family, and I went back to my lonely cell. I tried to read a few chapters of a novel I had taken out of the local library with my temporary summer card, and turned off my bedside light at midnight. The pharmacist snored softly in the other corner. The reds, whites and blues of the fireworks replayed on my closed eyelids for a long time, before I feel asleep.

Chapter 18

B E S T   L A I D   P L A N S

I finally got my VW back from the garage on Thursday and spent
the rest of the week working on the logging program, which would
be held the following week. I made the final arrangements for a
concert featuring two banjo playing brothers to be held that Saturday
evening. They were great characters who told amusing stories in
between numbers in a style reminiscent of Uncle Dave Macon. I had
to ask them to tone down the more racy stories.

I didn't see Ruthie until Friday. She sought me out at the Nature
Center after the pool closed. "I just got a message at the park office
from Mrs. Jenkins. Lilly Cummins has agreed to meet with us." She
didn't smile, but she met my eyes. "If you're still interested, that is."

I had almost forgotten who Lilly was. "Of course I am. But I can't
do it this coming week; I have a big program next weekend and I have
to go to the capital to meet with the project director and the other
folklorists on Monday and Tuesday. One of the funders of the project
is coming to town and the director wants us to describe what we've
been doing."

"Well, you've been quite busy, so that should be fascinating," she
quipped. "I have Monday after this one off, want to try for then?" She
asked. "I'll make the call if you like." I nodded. "Oh, I almost forgot,

I picked up this message for you in the office." She handed me a phone message slip.

"Some reporter from one of the papers in the city wants me to call, for a possible human interest story."

"Local celebrity in the making," she said, flatly. "Gotta go, see you next week."

I made a feeble attempt to call after her, but she slammed the door and was gone. "Next week" suddenly sounded too far away.

The banjo program went well, with only a few slipups from the brothers into forbidden subjects. Of course, the audience loved those the best, and no members of militant Christian groups came up to complain afterwards. On Sunday afternoon, I was on my way to Nashville with my latest stash of tapes and rolls of undeveloped film.

On Monday afternoon, our meeting broke up at three. I drove over to the State Archive, telling the others I would meet them for dinner later. I wasn't sure where to begin, so I consulted a reference person.

"Do you keep any files of criminal cases here?" I gave her some information, and she gave me some suggestions of where to look in the card catalogue. Since Boyd Jenkins had never come to trial, those court records didn't exist. There was nothing under Livingstone's name. There were a few entries on Boyd Jenkins, but mostly newspaper articles. And one junior high school student, whose prize-winning entry in a state-sponsored history contest, "Notorious Outlaws of Tennessee," had used Boyd as one of his examples. I was not sure what I was expecting, but this didn't help a bit.

I was crashing on Blake's floor that night, and we stayed up late talking about my latest Boyd findings. I asked him if he thought I should admit to the director that Ruthie was with me on the trip to the cave.

"Naw, that's really none of his business." He nudged me. "So, did you get any yet?"

I ignored this query, and told him the sad story of Demond's revelation of my wayward "significant other."

"That guy needs his ass kicked," Blake said in his best 'billy accent. We brainstormed some suitable revenges for Demond before nodding off. On the long drive home on Tuesday afternoon, I amused myself by refining one or two of them.

On Wednesday, I was out in the park woods with Spike, trying to find a suitable log for Saturday's program. The day was sticky and the woods were airless, but there was something even more uncomfortable about this jaunt. "What exactly you gonna do with this here log again?" Spike asked, punctuating the stillness.

"A cross-cut saw demonstration, and showing how the big calipers were used in swinging the logs around in the river, that sort of thing."

"Had an uncle was in the logging business." Spike paused to light up a cigarette and threw the still-burning match into the dry underbrush. It fortunately landed on some damp moss and flickered out. "Tree fell on him and he got squashed like a bug." He looked around. "Somewheres out here we cut down a tree this past spring. Got struck by lightning and mostly died. Left the big logs out here, burned the branches and small stuff. That work, ya think?"

We located the pile of logs, and picked out one that wasn't too marred from decay. Spike took note of the location. "I'll come back with the tractor and haul it out later." He turned to me. I could smell alcohol on his breath mingled with the tobacco, which I thought was strange for ten o'clock in the morning.

"Ya know, these woods out in these mountains are kinda dangerous. Snakes and such. Real easy to get lost. Man's been known to go out and never be found again." He looked at me, in a matter-of-fact way, flicking his cigarette butt into the bushes.

I held his gaze for several long seconds. "That's interesting, Spike. Know of any particular cases? Maybe I should interview you about them."

He shook his head, grinning. "You're a piece of work, buddy. You think everything around here is yours for the picking. I'm just warning you, there's some stuff best left alone." He turned back toward the park, muttering something under his breath that sounded like, "Damn Yankee city slickers, ain't nothing but trouble."

That afternoon, I finally found time to call the reporter from the city paper. She worked for the Style section and had been assigned by her editor to do a story on "Mountain Culture." A friend of hers—

whose mother lived in Jakestown and always sent her clippings from the local paper—had passed on the story Ed Daniels had done on the project.

"So," she gushed. "I thought you could take me on a real, well, adventure up there in the mountains to see what the culture is like, and how you collect it. As a matter of fact, someone else passed on the name of a real live ghost story teller and natural medicine expert way, way up toward Pollyville who sounds really, really interesting, and I thought you'd want to know about her. I have some information you could use, and you can help me out with this story. I'll write it from the perspective of how your work is like, well, detective work. Tracking down the best of the traditions of the area." I didn't respond, so she continued. "What do you say, is it a deal?"

I considered the positive effects of the publicity. I also considered the embarrassment if the article misrepresented the work we were doing. "If you'll let me see the article before you print it, to make sure you've gotten everything right, then I'll do it," I said. Then, as an afterthought, I added, "And we have to go in your car."

"Well, I'll have to ask my editor about seeing the article ahead of time, but of course we can use my car," she said. We picked a date the following week.

The summer was more than half over. It made me anxious to get as much as possible done. My next huge project, as if I needed any more, was putting together a small festival in mid-August. Our director had suggested, in a firm way, that we all think about such an event as a culmination of the summer's work. He showed us slides of the Labor Day festival that he had staged for several summers during his days as a seasonal naturalist in the middle part of the state. Music, cooking, storytelling, crafts, things going on in all parts of the park simultaneously. It sounded like a nightmare.

Meanwhile, even while I was putting the finishing touches on the plans for the logging program, I was busy calling people for the following weekend. I had dreamed up a "Christmas in July" program after talking with several regulars at the local Senior Citizens' Center about holidays in the "good old days." I would have to locate a cedar tree, and visitors could help make gingerbread cookies and paper and popcorn chains to decorate it. Then I would moderate a panel of seniors talking about holiday traditions. I was extremely proud of the idea.

Ruthie, on the other hand, thought it was dumb. "Here it is, over 100 degrees most of the time, and you are going to talk about Christmas?" She laughed. "What next?"

I had surprised her after she had finished work at the pool, and asked her if she wanted to get a soft ice cream at the local Tastee Freeze.

"As long as you're buying," she'd said. We were sitting on a picnic bench in the shade, licking dribbles off our fingers. The sun was still hot at almost seven o'clock.

We both avoided opening the former girlfriend topic. Instead, I asked her how well she knew Spike.

"Spike? You mean the handyman who works with George Whitelaw? Not too well. He's sort of creepy. Fond of leering at me in my bathing suit."

"Can hardly blame him for that." I lapped at a line of chocolate oozing down my forearm.

"His family, I've heard, has lived around here—mostly way up in the mountains—for a long time. Rumor has it that they used to make whiskey. In fact, rumor has it that they still do." She laughed. "Get it, they still do?" I groaned. She continued, "maybe you should interview them."

"Maybe not." I told her about Spike's warning, and about his earlier comment about the Boyd legend, and his mention of "our little trouble."

"Do you think he knows about our visit to Boyd's cave?"

"Yeah, I do. But why should he care?"

She shrugged. We finalized our plans to go to Lilly's that coming Monday and I drove her home. I asked her if she'd like to go to the movies on Sunday night, but she said that she had to babysit her young niece. I was so smitten that I almost volunteered to help, even though I didn't really care for small children. She hopped out of the car and waved goodbye.

When I arrived "back home," the sun was just beginning to set, and the Nature Center's interior was dark. I turned on all the lights, like a child afraid of spooky things lurking in the shadows.

That night, a huge thunderstorm broke the muggy weather. It came in the middle of the night, waking me from a sound sleep with its ear-splitting crashes and bright flashes of bluish light. Dwayne stirred in his bed, moaning a little. I thought of the black lightning streaks in Boyd's cave painting, and Spike's dark warning. I fell into a fitful sleep full of gloomy nightmares and woke late in the morning. The sun streamed into our room through the torn blinds like a vision of heaven.

Chapter 19

SHADOWS AT SUNRISE

A s we drove down to the city to meet Lilly on Monday afternoon, I asked Ruthie how Lilly had reacted to the idea of talking about Boyd. "What did you say to her?" I asked.

"Well, I just told her the truth. I told her that you had been talking to different people about Boyd, and you really wanted to know the whole story from as many points of view as possible. I told her that we knew that there were a lot of—well, not lies, exactly, but exaggerations told about Boyd. And we knew that she had known him from an entirely different perspective."

"And she said that was okay?"

"As long as I came along. She said that it's a story that needed to be told to another woman. But you could come, too, if you wanted."

I looked at her to see if she were kidding. She wasn't. She was looking straight ahead, with a thoughtful expression.

"I told her that you were a trained researcher, an oral historian. I didn't say 'folklorist'—that would only confuse her. And that I was a student at the university and I was from the area and always wanted to know what the truth was about the Boyd story. She laughed a little when I told her that Boyd was always held up to us as a scary figure." She chewed her lower lip. "I guess Boyd wasn't scary to her."

"Do you think she was in love with him?" I asked.

She turned to me with an exasperated look on her face. "Jeez, I only talked to her for five minutes on the phone. Give me a break!"

I raised my eyebrows at her vehemence. "Sorry!"

Ruthie had taken excellent directions and we had no trouble finding the modest white-painted bungalow in a quiet neighborhood. We parked the VW in the shade of one of the handsome old trees lining the street. I reached into the back seat for my camera case and the cassette recorder.

Ruthie looked at me. "I would leave those out here if I were you. I think she wants to talk—needs to talk—but I don't think she wants to be recorded for posterity. You can always come back out and get them if I'm wrong."

We rang the doorbell, and it was answered by a delicate-looking woman, much younger than I had expected, and still very pretty. Her blond hair was straight and chin-length. She had wide, china-blue eyes. I thought of the blue dress, the red lips of the cave painting. No wonder she had been the talk of Sunrise.

I let Ruthie do the introductions. Lilly ushered us into the living room and perched on a wingback chair. We sank into the floral couch. I glanced around the room and saw photos of her family lining the mantel, a boy and two girls advancing from childhood to high school or perhaps college graduation. The last photo was of a young baby, maybe the first grandchild. She had created a wholy different life from the one she had lived in Sunrise over a quarter of a century before. A stable, comfortable life.

"Miss Taggart—may I call you Ruthie?—tells me that you are a graduate student in history, is that correct, Mr. Anderson?"

I didn't feel like a long explanation, so I said yes. "Please call me Rob if you don't mind."

She smiled. "What do you intend to do with all these stories of Boyd Jenkins that you have been collecting?"

Since I still wasn't sure myself, I had to wing it. "I'll probably write a paper for a class. But, for now, I've been collecting the story as part of a project I'm working on, documenting the folk—uh, oral history around the state park to place in the State Archive."

She pursed her lips. She no longer wore red lipstick, but a natural shade of pink. "I'm sure that you have collected all manner of fantastic stories about Boyd. People are fond of making things up and telling them for truth."

"I have collected some of those, certainly. But also a lot of information that shows that Boyd was not just an outlaw. I'm trying to show that he was a complicated, three-dimensional human being." Ruthie looked in my direction. I amazed even myself with this revelation.

"That he was," Lilly said with a wry smile. Then her face darkened. "Much of what I am about to tell you is strictly confidential. It will certainly round out your notion of who Boyd Jenkins was, and who I was at the time—a long, long time ago. And I will not object if you use most of it in some way, as long as you don't use my name directly, and as long as you will promise to send me a copy for my approval before doing anything with it. You can take all the notes you want, but I'm glad you didn't bring a tape recorder." I wondered if she'd been interviewed before.

I agreed to all of these conditions, secretly regretting them. Her eyes widened. "Where are my manners! Before we get started with all this, would you like a cold drink? You've had a long drive."

We accepted some "Coca Cola," as she called it in an old-fashioned way, and then we all settled down.

Lilly placed her hands in her lap and looked at them. A wedding ring and diamond engagement ring sparkled on one hand. On the other was a multi-stoned "mother's" ring like the one my siblings and I had chipped in to get my own mother one year. She began, tentatively.

"I moved to the little town of Sunrise from Cincinnati, Ohio, when I was nineteen. I didn't know anyone there, really. I had an aunt who lived a few towns over and let me know that this doctor was looking for a receptionist and couldn't find anyone suitable locally. I'd learned shorthand and typing in high school, and had a pleasant speaking voice—I'd been working as a receptionist at a factory in Cincinnati for a few months before I moved down here." She sighed a little. "I had my reasons for wanting to leave. My father had died a few years before, and my mother remarried a man who—" she smiled bitterly. "Well, let's just say he was not a very nice man. Not a nice man at all."

Ruthie shifted a little in her seat. I took a sip of soda and looked at Lilly, silently encouraging her to continue.

"So, I took this job and moved down to Sunrise. It was quite a change, sort of what they call 'culture shock' nowadays, I guess. I liked it very much. It is so lovely up there in the hills. And there were some people who were very nice to me. Lucy, of course, whom you've met, and others. The doctor's wife took me under her wing. I was rather happy.

"But, of course, I wasn't native to the area and that was held against me by some. I guess they thought I had 'city airs' or something like that. But I was always pleasant and tried very hard to make friends and fit in." She fluttered her hands a little.

"I had my own little apartment at the back of the doctor's office. Did my own cooking and housekeeping, and that was quite an adventure for a young person!" She smiled at us, remembering. "Like everyone else, I did my grocery shopping in town. I didn't have a car and there was nowhere else to go." She said this almost apologetically.

"Well, I caught the eye of the son of the grocery store owners. You know that much. He was tall and handsome, and different from the other men in the town, it seemed to me. He carried himself with pride, and I know he thought himself superior. He'd been away to accounting school and thought he knew something about the 'finer things' in life. He didn't seem to mind that I was from out of town. In fact, he liked the idea. He used to tell me, 'You're not like those other girls from around here, they're so common.' That rubbed me the wrong way sometimes, because some of those people he was talking about were really my friends, but he meant it like the highest sort of compliment.

"Some tried to warn me against going out with him. 'He's no good,' they'd say. I thought maybe they were just jealous. His father was one of the most influential people in town, and his family had more money than just about anyone else.

"At first, it was fine. He took me out to the movies and to dinner in the city. We took long walks. Things like that. But little things started making me wonder what he was really like." She raised her eyes and looked out the window.

"Little things—not too unusual, but just sort of cruel. He kicked stray dogs. He spoke rudely to some of the mountain people who came into the grocery store. Then, when we'd been seeing each other for about a couple of months—" She took her eyes away from the window and fixed them on her hands again. "We'd been out for a stroll and he walked me back to my apartment. I invited him in for an iced tea. We sat down together on my sofa. Up 'till then, we'd kissed a few times, innocent stuff, but—" She broke off, biting her lower lip very hard. "I'd rather not go into details. Let me just say, I learned that day that he was not a gentleman. There was nothing gentle about him at all."

Ruthie looked angry, and I guess I looked a bit shocked. By now, I'd come to think of the guy as a jerk, but I hadn't thought of him as violent. Perhaps a rapist.

"Well, I was only nineteen. I thought maybe I had done something to make him think—" She broke off again, turning to us with tears falling down her cheeks. "My stepfather always said—"

Ruthie got up and knelt at Lilly's feet. "It's okay, it's okay," Ruthie said, gently. The older woman stroked Ruthie's dark hair. She pulled a lace-trimmed handkerchief out of a side pocket of her skirt and wiped her eyes. Ruthie rose, gave Lilly's hand a squeeze, and returned to the couch. I could see that there were tears in her eyes as well.

I felt like an intruder. I stayed quiet and let Lilly continue when she was ready.

"So, you see, that is how it was. Out of the frying pan and into the fire. I told him I did not want to see him anymore, but he wouldn't leave me alone. I was only nineteen. I didn't want to run away again. It was too hard the first time. And I couldn't talk to anyone about it. Not anyone." She wiped her nose with the handkerchief and folded it neatly, turning it over and over in her hands.

"Boyd had come home from the war in Korea, about the same time I arrived in town. I heard gossip about him, most of it not positive. They said he had been a little wild before he left, but now he was carousing, drinking too much, acting crazy. I would see him now and then in town. He always seemed to have a lost look, like he couldn't quite figure out what he was doing there. He always had his hound dog with him—that dog would wait patiently outside the barber shop, or the hardware store, until Boyd came out." She smiled a little.

"I went to a dance or two that he played for. But Tom would always show up and make my time unpleasant. He was a great fiddler, Boyd was, and I loved that old time music so." Her feet moved a little on the floor, as if to a distant dance tune.

"Lucy decided, in her own sweet way, that Boyd and I might get along. She knew I had been seeing Tom, and although I never talked to her about it, I think she suspected that he was treating me badly." She laughed a short, hard laugh. "She didn't know the half of it. So she invited me and Boyd to dinner on the same Sunday evening. It was a fine early spring day. I even remember we had fried chicken and boiled potatoes with gravy. And stewed tomatoes that Lucy's mother-in-law had canned the summer before."

"Boyd and I were shy around each other at first, but soon we began talking. In fact, we sat on the porch swing of Lucy and Stanley's house that evening after dark, talking for hours. After that, we met each other for drinks a couple of times, and we took long walks into the woods. Not just strolls like Tom and I had taken. Boyd showed me all the plants, and told me some of the things his grandmother had taught him about their healing properties. He was really very smart, and so very gentle. He treated me like a flower."

"But there's not a mountain herb on God's earth that could have healed what Boyd was going through. Nowadays I think they call it postwar syndrome or something like that. He was not much older than I was—six years, to be exact—and he had seen too much death and destruction in the war. He was there for almost two years, and it was enough to ruin him. He was a deeply spiritual person—you may have heard that he did some preaching. Well, lots of people pretend to be preachers and just like to hear themselves spout off, if you'll excuse me for saying so. Boyd was different. He truly felt the spirit, it was very real to him. I guess he just couldn't reckon it with some of the things he had to do and witness during the war. I don't think he thought about it before he went into the service. He was interested in seeing something of the world, and in doing something good for his country. The reality of it, the horror of it, was too much for him." She put her handkerchief back in her pocket and smoothed her skirt.

"This is where the story, as you have heard it, probably begins. Tom, of course, caught wind of the fact that Boyd and I were getting to be friends. We tried to be discreet since I was sure if Tom found out how much I really liked Boyd, there'd be trouble, but he found out just the same. Tom made some very unpleasant accusations and was very, very rude to Boyd's family.

"Boyd kept questioning me about my relationship with Tom, and I told him it was over as far as I was concerned. But that's not what he wanted to know. He already knew that I did not love Tom and did not want to see him anymore. What he wanted to know was if Tom had been, um, abusive in any way to me. I tried not to let him know just how far the abuse had gone, tried to act flip about it. But I'm not a good liar.

"One thing led to another. Finally, one night Tom came over, just burst into my apartment, and started screaming at me. I think he was very, very drunk. He accused me of—oh, lots of things, I don't want to go into all that. His words were abuse enough, believe me. But, then, he hit me. Hard. More than once. He had hit me before, but never like that. By the time he left, my face was terribly bruised and I cried for a long, long time.

"A knock came at the door. It was Boyd. I wouldn't let him in." She looked up, holding a hand to the side of her face, as if she were reliving that moment so long ago. "I knew if he saw me, he would know who had done that to me, and I knew—just as well as I knew my own name—that he would kill Tom for it." The tears started again, and she shook out her handkerchief to wipe them away.

"He left, but he must have asked around, whether Tom had been there or not and what people had heard. I wouldn't doubt that the next door neighbors had heard most of Tom's accusations and had heard me crying. It was summer and all the windows and screen doors were open, after all.

"Like you, I've only heard the rest of it secondhand. I stayed in my apartment and prayed that night. Prayed that nothing would happen between the two of them. But I knew my prayers had not been answered when I heard the commotion on Main Street, which was only a few blocks from my apartment. I think I had fallen asleep—to tell you the truth, I think I was suffering from a mild concussion. I didn't hear the shots. But, I heard the uproar that came afterwards.

"Soon, Lucy was at my door. 'Boyd has shot Tom,' she told me. I let her in, and she turned on the light and saw my face. She did not have to ask who did that to me. She only took me into her arms and rocked me, and we cried together for a long, long time.

"I never saw Boyd again after that. As soon as I could, I made arrangements to move here to the city and start yet another new life. It seemed that the whole town of Sunrise blamed me for something. Tom's death, Boyd's disappearance—the general disruption of the whole life of a quiet little town. People would call me on the phone and hang up. I couldn't walk down the street without someone whispering behind my back. The doctor and his wife were sympathetic, to a point, but I could tell they wanted me to leave. They even helped me out with some money to get started down here.

"I started nursing school and met a nice pharmacy student." I looked at Ruthie, thinking about our friend Dwayne, but she was absorbed in the story and didn't look back at me. "I told him the whole story, he knows everything. And, of course, there were police and even FBI men looking me up every now and again to ask me questions. That one FBI man was like a bulldog, he never let go of that case until he found out where Boyd was. He was an unpleasant sort of fellow." She shuddered a little. "Of course, I had no idea where Boyd was. He didn't try to contact me, and I had no knowledge of where he would have been hiding.

"I say he didn't try to contact me, but I suppose Lucy must have told you that he did leave me something." She brightened a little. "Boyd told me once that he wished he could paint some of the beauty he saw around him in the woods. He said the woods were like his church, that's the way he felt about being in them. As I told you, he was a very spiritual person."

She rose without speaking and went into what I guessed was a back bedroom or den, coming back with a large painting which had obviously been hanging on a wall. She brushed a light coating of dust off the top of the frame. "Lucy and Stanley made sure I got this. They said that it came to them with a note that it belonged to me."

The picture was much larger than Boyd's other paintings. Along the bottom, curving up along the sides, were lifelike representations of plants and flowers. In the center was a brilliantly illuminated portrayal of Jesus with arms outstretched, piercing eyes staring straight out at the viewer, somehow looking benevolent and ominous at the same time. At his feet on either side were forest animals, those native to the mountains: deer, raccoons, possums, skunks, even a couple of bears. Flowers ringed his head.

I remembered going to the Metropolitan Museum of Art with my high school art class, and standing in front of a huge, Renaissance painting of Christ on the cross. A feeling of awe, and sadness, and almost physical pain. And amazement at the skill of the painter who made me feel this deeply. I got the same feeling looking at Lilly's painting.

Lilly turned over the painting and let us read the inscription. "To Lilly. I had some bad inside me, and it sure came out. But you brought out the good inside me. I love you for that and wish you well always. Boyd."

"It's beautiful," said Ruthie, smiling at Lilly. "I'm sure it means a lot to you."

Lilly ran her hand lovingly along the top of the frame. "I would not part with it for anything. There was a young man, about a year ago, who came here, saying he heard I had one of Boyd's paintings. He asked to see it, said he was doing some research on folk painting in this part of the state. I don't recall his name. A tall, nice-looking young man, I think he works up your way."

Ruthie and I looked at each other. Christopher Livingstone Demond had been here, too.

Lilly continued. "I wouldn't let him in. There was something about him that made me uneasy. He reminded me, just a bit, of Tom."

Chapter 20

MAN'S BEST FRIEND

"She's quite a lady," Ruthie said, as we started back.

"That's quite a painting," I said.

"I'm glad we got to see it and Demond didn't," Ruthie said.

"That's because I'm a nice guy and he's evil," I joked.

Ruthie looked at me, her eyes narrowing. "You have your moments." We rode awhile in silence. "So, it's really over between you and the anthropologist?"

"Absolutely." I had long since decided I was moving out, African or no African.

"What about when you go back to graduate school? You may sing a different tune then." She looked out the window.

We were near a turnoff along the river. I pulled the car over, pulled her to me and kissed her. Just a little kiss, testing the waters. She didn't protest, so I took a deeper plunge. Her mouth tasted like Coca Cola and her hair smelled like fresh, crushed herbs as before. We kissed for a long time.

Finally I pulled away. "I'm here till Labor Day," I said, trying to speak normally, although I was finding it hard to catch my breath. "After that, we'll see what happens. Fair?"

Her cheeks were flushed and she looked irresistible. "Fair enough."

When we reached her parents' house, she got out and leaned back into the open window. "Your one true fan keeps bugging me. Promise you'll come to dinner Sunday evening for the legendary chicken and biscuits, or I'll never hear the end of it."

I promised, if she in turn would promise to help me with ideas for the festival program, coming up in less than a month. I went back to the Nature Center and took the proverbial cold shower.

Three days later, I was picked up at the Nature Center by the Style section reporter. She was young, maybe thirty, with reddish-brown hair cut short, and a very perky smile. Her name was Betsy Tanner. I felt less than perky myself at 7:30 a.m., which is the time she wanted to start out. I made her stop at a fast-food "drive-thru" near the Interstate so I could get some coffee and a sausage biscuit.

When I asked if she wanted a bite, she wrinkled her nose in disgust. "I'm a vegetarian."

"Sorry," I said, taking a big swig of coffee.

"And I don't drink caffeine," she said, making it sound like an illegal substance. I could tell already that this was going to be a fun day.

Betsy's directions to the home of the "real live ghost story teller" got us to the general vicinity of her home, but the final details were vague. It took us two hours to get there—the place was way to the east of the territory I had been concentrating my fieldwork on. The area was in a scenic valley dotted with small farms and orderly houses with flower gardens along picket fences. I didn't remind her that she had expressed the desire to go on a "real mountain adventure." This hardly qualified in my mind, but it was a beautiful area nonetheless.

We knew from the road sign that we were on the right road, but since we didn't have a number, and many of the houses along the road looked similar, we weren't sure which one to try. She drove up and down the road a couple of times. I finally suggested we stop and ask someone—a complete role reversal from the usual stereotype of men versus women lost on the road. She made me get out to ask.

As I approached the picket fence gate, I thought I heard a low growl but I didn't see anything. I stood still for a minute and nothing happened. With caution, I opened the gate and stepped onto the walk.

Suddenly, from under the porch, a very large dog—maybe a retriever/shepherd mix from the looks of it—leaped out. I stood very still. The dog bared its teeth and growled. I waited for it to sniff me and figure out I was not an enemy.

The dog had its own plan, and decided without the benefit of a good sniff that I was, indeed, an enemy. Without warning, it jumped on me, raking my forearm with its bared teeth, taking a nasty nip at my other arm, and nearly knocking me over. This is it, I thought. I am about to have my throat ripped out in the line of duty. What a story it would make for the perky reporter.

"Duke!" I heard a loud, authoritative male voice bellow from the front porch. The dog, who had been poised for the second attack, retreated back under the porch, snarling over its shoulder as it went. I caught my breath and looked down at my arms, both of which were bleeding. I backed out of the gate, and closed it as carefully as I had opened it, happy to exchange information from the other side.

The source of the voice, a large man in a sleeveless t-shirt and soiled jeans, approached the gate. "I'm mighty sorry, son. That dog is a menace. Can I help you?" He didn't even glance at my injuries, or offer any first aid.

"Uh—" I had temporarily forgotten my mission. I shook myself to clear my head. "We're, uh, looking for Mabel Jean Bristoe. Can you tell me which house it is?"

He pointed me in the right direction, said goodbye, and reentered the house with no further apologies. I got back into the car.

Betsy looked up from scribbling in her notebook. She took one look at my face, which must have been very pale, and then looked down at my arms, both of which were oozing. The bitten one was already turning a light purple, although the damage was actually minimal, I realized on closer inspection.

"Oh, my God!" she exclaimed. She threw down her notebook and pen and started rummaging around in her purse, coming up with a couple of Kleenexes. "What on earth happened?"

"You mean you missed it?" I said, with a note of injured pride. My latest moment of danger in the field, with a reporter along no less, and she was oblivious. I told her about the beast and my near-escape from certain serious injury, if not death. She looked back at my arms, assessing the damage.

"Doesn't look too serious to me," she commented. "But when I write it up, I can make it sound more impressive."

Cut to the quick by her indifference, I gave her the directions to Mabel Jean's house and in a few minutes we pulled into her dooryard. I made Betsy get out first.

Mabel Jean was a tall, lean and very gregarious woman with a sort of ageless look. I guessed her to be somewhere in her forties. I was expecting someone older. She installed us comfortably on a couple of well-worn wooden rockers on her front porch, and disappeared into her house to get "something" for my arms. She handed me two flowered kitchen towels with ice cubes wrapped in them. She made me rest my arms on the rocker and draped the towels on both of them. I felt like a mummy.

"Oh, that damned cur of Jackson's, he sure is a nuisance. We been telling him, all us up and down this road, to get shut of that monster for years. The rural delivery man won't get out'n his truck if he has a package for Jackson, that's the God's honest truth!" She laughed as though this were a big joke. Betsy laughed along, half-heartedly. She got her notebook poised, but didn't make the first attempt at questions.

"Mrs. Bristoe—" I began.

"It's Miss, but call me Mabel Jean, won't you?"

"Mabel Jean. We heard that you can tell some good ghost stories."

She laughed loudly—sort of a whoop, really. "Who is the confused son of a gun who told you that?" I looked at Betsy, but she didn't return my gaze. "Well, my Grandmaw was a great tale teller, she knew about all the haints up in this section, that is a fact. Now, I did inherit lots and lots of stuff from her before she died, but I surely ain't a tale teller."

Betsy twirled her pencil, making little squiggles on the notebook page, and gave me a "what now?" look.

"Well, so, what kind of information did your grandmother pass on to you, then?" I asked.

"You name it, she told me it," she offered.

The ice was getting too cold on my arms. It was also dripping on my pants. With some difficulty, I gathered one of the towels up and set it down on the porch floor. I took up the other and wrung it out, then replaced it on my raked arm, which is the one that hurt worse.

"How about herbal remedies?" I asked. Mabel Jean smiled broadly, took a deep breath, and started off.

"Now, you've heard say that you can cure warts with potatoes, I'll bet you, but you gotta know how to do it right. . . ."

Betsy started writing furiously. Half an hour later, Mabel Jean had given us at least twenty-five folk cures for everything from ringworm ("You hafta find someone who is not related to you with blue eyes and get them to wet the fingers of one hand and put them, each one, on that ringworm...") to thresh ("You know there are some that can jest blow into a child's mouth and that thresh would go away. My Grandmaw could do that and people sought her all over this section to do that.") I wasn't even sure what thresh was.

"I could go on some more, practically all day if you want," Mabel Jean said with pride. Betsy stopped writing and shook her wrist in the air. I got the message.

"Well, Mabel Jean, maybe I can come back and interview you some more about this. You certainly know a lot."

"Well, then, would you like to see my museum?" she asked, rising out of her chair. She pronounced the word carefully, "mew-zeem." It took me a couple of seconds to figure out what she meant.

Who could say no?

Chapter 21

MUSEUM STUDIES

B efore we went to see the museum, Betsy insisted upon taking a picture of me "looking like I was interviewing" Mabel Jean. Under Betsy's direction, Mabel Jean brought one of the rocking chairs close to mine, placed at an angle that would photograph well. I began to take the ice poultice off my arm, but Betsy called out from her position on the lawn, "No, leave it on!"

I could just imagine the caption: "Although in extreme pain, the intrepid folklorist continued his interview in a most professional and passionate manner."

After Betsy had snapped eight or ten photos of the pseudo-interview from different angles, the two of us followed Mabel Jean toward the back yard, shooing red and white chickens and some very bizarre-looking black and white speckled birds called guinea hens along the way. "There's such a mess of them I've plumb lost count," Mabel Jean commented. When we rounded the side of the house, we could see a small log building in a corner of the yard.

"This used to be our smokehouse. Great-grandpaw built it, and they smoked right smart of hams, bacon, sausage and the like in here in its day. But, heck, you can buy all that stuff at the Piggly Wiggly now." She whooped. "So, afore she died, me and Grandmaw came up with the idea of making the place into a museum. Kindly like a place where we could put all this old stuff that our family has kept all these years. Antique dealers and folks like that are al'ays up here, seems like, trying to get us to sell them some of this stuff, but I am not giving it up, no how."

Atta girl Mabel Jean, I thought. As we approached the building, we could see that a front porch had been added. On it, two life-sized dummies in a semblance of country dress—the male in checked flannel shirt, bib overalls and a straw hat, the woman in a calico dress, white apron and matching calico bonnet—sat in rocking chairs similar to those on Mabel Jean's real front porch. They were far more sophisticated than scarecrows, with lifelike features drawn on muslin faces, and fine, embroidery floss hair. Their hands, arranged comfortably in their laps, even had coral colored fingernails painted on.

She grinned at our surprise. "I call them Addy and Lem," she said. "That was my Great-grandpaw and Grandmaw's names." She patted Lem's shoulder affectionately. "My Aunt Sally is a real artist, I think, don't you? She makes these big dolls—small ones, too, for that matter—to sell at craft fairs and such like. Does a right smart business in them, too." A variety of farm and garden tools rested on the porch, as well as some large crockery: a churn, a ten-gallon pickle crock and some jugs. "This is jest a hint of what's inside," Mabel Jean said with a wink.

She opened the front door, which sported a hand-painted wooden sign reading, "Bristoe Family Museum, Open by Appointment" in large red letters. A smaller paper sign, curled at the edges and lettered with black magic marker, read "Inquire at front of house for appointment."

"Maybe you don't believe it, but we have had folks from all over come to see this museum," Mabel Jean said proudly, pausing at the front door. "Jest from word of mouth, y'see, no advertising involved."

We stepped inside the room, which was about twelve feet square. Mabel Jean turned on an overhead lightbulb and pulled back the calico curtains. Betsy and I looked around in amazement.

The room was filled, from floor to ceiling, with all kinds of artifacts of country living. They were arranged in no particular order, it seemed. There were several large pieces of furniture, in very good condition: a pie safe with punched-tin floral designs, two simple but elegant cherry bureaus, a Hoosier kitchen with built-in flour sifter, a corner cupboard probably of poplar. Covering the tops of each of these pieces—and crowded in all corners, piled on shelves, and stacked one on top of each other on the floor—were slaw cutters, butter molds, wool carders, baskets, and an assortment of other items. On three quilt racks in one corner hung quilts, coverlets, lace doilies, and rag rugs. Other small items hung from pegs on the wall. There were also more farm implements: scythes, wooden hay rakes, grain cradles, froes, even a flail. A large deer head with cobwebs on its antlers hung high on one wall. The rafters were strung with dried herbs and more baskets.

"My mother would go nuts here," I mused out loud. I turned to Mabel Jean. "You don't sell any of this, ever?"

She frowned at me, as if I had just asked her if I could buy something, which was not my intention.

"I mean, it's a wonderful thing that you have saved all of this. This is a wonderful, wonderful collection." Betsy was scribbling in her notebook. I hoped she had gotten down all those "wonderfuls."

I continued looking around, marveling at the good condition of all of the pieces. I avoided tripping over a small spinning wheel on my way to the far wall. Something hanging there in the half gloom above my head caught my eye.

It was a Boyd painting. By now I knew the characteristic style, the rough frame. But this one depicted chickens and guinea hens not unlike those we had shooed on our way through the back yard. There were five of them, three with heads down, scratching at some grain on the ground, and two looking directly at the viewer.

Mabel stepped carefully over to me. "Jest looks like they could step right out o' the picture, don't it?" She studied the painting. "You heard of him, I guess, if you been collecting stories down there toward the park. I knowed he was from Sunrise, that ain't too far from where you're staying."

I nodded. "Boyd Jenkins," I told Betsy, who had come over to see what we were discussing. She looked at me blankly.

Mabel Jean explained, "He kill't a man down in Sunrise. And he was on the lam, hiding out here and there all in this section. Mostly, I guess, in some cave or other way west of here. But, he was here, too—that he was." She paused dramatically and added in a half-whisper. "Fact of matter is, he stayed right here in this smokehouse for nearly a month."

Despite myself, I imagined a sign Mabel Jean could have hung on the front door. "Boyd Jenkins Slept Here." I didn't suggest it, however. Instead, I said, "Tell us about it, Mabel Jean."

Betsy made a face and glanced down at her watch. I ignored her signals, pulling up three chairs with woven corn husk seats.

Mabel Jean smiled at me. "Here's what it was. I was jest a kid, but I remember him. I was visiting Grandmaw—this was her place, did I tell you? I stayed with her mostly, my maw had sort of a nervous condition when I was young. One night, it was late fall, we got a knock at the door 'round about midnight. I was already in bed, but I sneaked down the stairs to see who was callin' so late. I thought maybe it was somebody whose wife was having a baby—did I tell you my grandmaw was a midwife?

"Anyways, it warn't somebody having a baby. It was a strange man. He was sort of rough-looking and looked run down. Had long scraggy hair and his clothes were dirty. I was scairt. My grandpaw asked the man what he wanted.

"'I'm Boyd Jenkins,' the man said. 'Cain't blame you if you turn me away, but I need a place to sleep and maybe a bite to eat if you can spare it.' He had a satchel with him—I later found out that was what he kept his painting stuff in.

"Grandmaw took one look at him and turned to Grandpaw. 'Lucas,' she said, 'This man is ill. We cain't turn him out.' That was my grandmaw all over. She could tell what was ailin' you jest by looking into your eyes. And, she was a nat'ral born healer, she had that in her. No matter if this man was a criminal or a saint, she was bound to minister to him.

"So, to make a long story short, Grandmaw made Grandpaw fix ole Boyd up a pallet in the smokehouse, and put in a kerosene heater 'cause the nights was getting cold. Grandmaw nursed him, washed his clothes, and give him a barbering. When he got better, he said he would like to make us some pictures and what did we fancy?

"I asked for the chickens and hens." She wagged her head up toward the painting. "But Grandmaw had something else in mind.

She showed Boyd something she had been workin' on for many a year. It was a book with all these ole remedies in it. What this plant and that was used for and all. 'Course she had told lots of that to me, jest telling me and showing me, like I told you. But she wanted to get it down on paper, too. I guess she wasn't too sure about me carrying it all on when she passed." She smiled with the memory.

"So, Grandmaw shows this book to Boyd, and he takes a good look at it. Turns to one of the pages, like he's reading Grandmaw's mind, reads the writing, takes out his paints and brush and does a fine picture of tansy. That's what the writing on that page told about, and Grandmaw had left a space on the page jest big enough for the picture. It was almost as if she knew he would come and he'p her out with that book." Mabel Jean smiled.

"Do you still have the book?" I asked, fascinated.

She looked at me with a "What do you think?" scowl. "I'll show it to you directly. But I ain't done with my story yet.

"Like I said, Boyd stayed here nearly one month. For two solid weeks he painted in Grandmaw's book until he had painted all the plants she had written up. Then, he commenced to painting other pictures. He could crank out five or six a day, painting way into the night by kerosene lantern. He let me watch him sometimes.

"'Mabel Jean,' he would say to me, 'Hold on to these pictures. Maybe they will be worth something someday.' Then, one morning we woke up and he was gone. He had taken a few of the pictures with him, but left us about fifteen of them.

"Couple days after, a man with a fancy black suit came to call. Said he was from the FBI, searching out the 'fugitive' Boyd Jenkins. Had we seen him? Grandpaw and Grandmaw said no, they had not set eyes on the likes of him. He looked them straight in the eye, but they never backed off that lie. Then he looked at me." Mabel Jean bit her lip. "He must've seen something in my face.

"'I must warn you,' he told us all—I can still remember his highfalutin' words—'This man is a killer and is dangerous. If you are harboring him, you are committing a crime and I can and will arrest you.' Grandpaw kinda snorted at that. The man looked sharply at him. He said he was 'obligated to search our premises.' He took Grandpaw for a country fool, you see, but my Grandpaw weren't one.

'You need a warrant for that,' Grandpaw answered, 'And I don't see no warrant.'

"The feller felt in his pocket and brought up some piece of paper. He was trying to bluff Grandpaw, counting on him maybe not knowing how to read. But Grandpaw called his bluff. 'This ain't no warrant, sir,' he said, handing the piece of paper back to this FBI feller.

"Gosh darned if that feller didn't camp jest outside our fence for almost three days. Of course, Boyd was long gone by then anyways. So, the FBI feller left, but in two more days he was back with a proper warrant. Grandmaw and Grandpaw had hid the paintings in places we figured he'd never find them, jest in case. But darned if he didn't find five or six of them anyway. He was turning the house and outbuildings upside down looking for more, but we had the others hid good. He finally gave up trying to find any more and gave us a 'severe warning' not to give shelter to Boyd Jenkins again or he would find out about it and stick us all in jail. I had nightmares for weeks after, about being hauled off to a cell by this feller.

"So, we still had about ten or so of those paintings of Boyd's."

"Do you still have them?" I asked.

Mabel Jean looked sad and suddenly older. "I sold them off, here, last year, all except this one."

"Why? To who?" I stammered, surprised that Mabel Jean would ever sell anything from her collection.

"Grandmaw was real sick, and I didn't have enough money to keep her in the hospital," Mabel Jean explained. "I was about to start selling off all this stuff." She waved her hand around the room. "But, this was Grandmaw's and Grandpaw's, and Great-grandmaw and Grandpaw's stuff." She wiped a tear from the corner of her eye and sniffed.

"Then, like a miracle from Heaven, this guy come along. Said he heard I had some paintings that ole Boyd did. Don't know how he knew that, but then so many's been through the museum, I guess maybe that was the way. Said he was working for somebody that would pay me big money for any that I would sell. 'How big?' I asked him. Said up to two hundred and fifty dollars for one of them, depending on what shape they were in. I remembered what Boyd had said, 'Hold on to them, someday they may be worth something.' I jest figured that day had come.

"Still, he was kind of a rough-looking feller and I didn't trust him. 'I might have some that I could sell you, buddy,' I told him. 'But I ain't showing them to you unless you can pay me right up straight, in cash.' He took a big bankroll of twenty dollar bills out of his back pocket. You coulda blowed me over with a feather.

"So, I kept the chickens and hens. That one was mine and no amount of money could make me part with it. Sold all nine of the others and made enough money to keep Grandmaw comfortable till the end." She sniffed again.

"Certainly no one can blame you for that," the reporter said, giving me a stern look.

"What did this guy look like?"

"Like I said, sort of rough-looking. Medium tall, looked like he worked out of doors. Blondish-red hair, long and not very neatly kept. Looked like he hadn't shaved in a few days. Smelled like tobacco—and whiskey. That's why I didn't trust him at first, but when he showed me the color of his money. . . ." She trailed off, embarrassed.

Despite the heat of the day and the stuffiness of the small building, I got a sudden chill. She had just described Spike to a T.

Chapter 22

SETTING THE STORY STRAIGHT

Both women looked at me with concern. "Are you all right, hon?" Mabel Jean asked, taking my arm.

I did feel a bit queasy. "I think I just need some fresh air." I stumbled out onto the porch, joining Lem and Addy.

"It's them dog bites, prob'ly," Mabel Jean said, bustling out behind me. "You didn't get you any of that dog's hair, did you?"

I looked at her as if she were speaking another language.

She laughed. "Don't tell me you ain't never heard about the 'hair of the dog that bit you!'"

"I thought that was a hangover cure," I said.

"Well, some use it in that sense now, but they used to say that if a dog bit you, put a mess of its hair on the bite and it will cure it. But I have something else that will help, just a minute." She went in through the back door of her house and came out with an old baby food jar with something whitish and gooey-looking in it. "Jimson weed salve'll fix you right up." Before I could protest, she spread the goo on both my arms. It smelled like lard, which was probably its base.

"If I could find my grandmaw's ole mad stone, I would rub it on you as well. No telling what that ole dog has been into."

I got the gist of this, without knowing exactly what a mad stone was. What if the attack dog were carrying rabies? I'd have to have all those shots in my stomach? I grew even paler at the thought.

"No matter. We haven't had a mad dog in these parts for twenty years or more." She looked at Betsy and me in turn. "You two must be hungrier than a boxed coon. I'll rustle up some dinner here directly." She turned and went back into the house, not hearing—or pretending not to hear—Betsy's protests.

"So, what was that all about?" Betsy asked.

"What?"

"All that Boyd Jenkins stuff. And the paintings being sold. You know more about all that than you're letting on."

I feigned a "Who, me?" gesture. I didn't want to get into the whole Boyd story with this prissy reporter. On the other hand, I couldn't wait to mull it over with Ruthie.

Betsy took out her camera and snapped some photos of me looking at the logs of the museum building, which were quite remarkable in their width. She screwed on a flash and took some pictures of the interior of the museum, then me posing with Lem and Addy. She even took some of the chickens and guinea hens, still wandering around the back yard, pecking at the bare earth.

Mabel Jean came out and showed us the herb garden near the house, the fruit trees and the vegetable garden. Betsy took a few more pictures. Our hostess picked several big, red tomatoes and a cucumber, and signaled us to follow her into the house. She served up ham, green beans and cold corn bread, with the sliced tomatoes and cukes, and—of course—sweet tea with plenty of ice and a few sprigs of fresh mint in each glass.

"Jest some stuff left from last night's supper, sorry it isn't much," she apologized.

Betsy pushed the ham aside and fished all the salt pork out of her beans. I ate all that was on my plate and didn't turn down seconds when they were offered. Dessert was big slices of lemon pie, satisfyingly tart.

I could have stayed the rest of the day, asking Mabel Jean all sorts of questions, but Betsy said we had to be getting back. "Wait!" I protested. "I'd like to see the book that Boyd illustrated."

Mabel Jean brought it out to the front porch. Betsy stood, tapping her foot, as Mabel Jean placed the book carefully in my hands. It was amazing. There were about seventy-five pages, with Mabel's grandmother's fine handwriting describing each medicinal plant, and a lifelike illustration of each by Boyd. Somewhere he had gotten some watercolors, and the pictures were delicate and detailed. I leafed through some of the pages. Sassafras to thin the blood; yellowroot for sore mouths; catnip for colds; mullein for sprains. "This is a treasure, Mabel Jean."

"I know, hon. I know." I handed her back the book, and she hugged it to her breast. Betsy fairly pulled me down the stairs to the car, after we politely thanked Mabel Jean for the tour and her hospitality. She stood waving, the book still in her arms.

I called Ruthie's house that evening, but her mother told me that she was out shopping with a friend. I was dying to tell someone. I went back to the Nature Center and gathered up all my change. I dialed Blake's number, no reply. I went back "home" and took up my field journal. Getting a beer out of the fridge, I sat down to write about the adventures of the day. Two hours later, my still-throbbing arms slathered with jimson weed goop that Mabel Jean had insisted I take, I fell asleep reading the novel from the library.

I woke the next morning in a minor panic, thinking about all the work I had to do if I was going to pull this festival off in a few weeks. I put the Boyd mystery further out of my head and went to the park office to start making phone calls. I had just set up an appointment to see a guy with an old-fashioned bee gum which, I had been told by other beekeepers, was a hollowed out log used for a beehive before the more modern type caught on, when the receptionist motioned to the phone on her desk.

"Call for you on the 6883 line," she said. I punched the button. It was Betsy.

"Listen, Rob, I have a draft of the story done. My editor said it would be okay if I let you fact-check it, and I need to get it to you a.s.a.p."

"That was quick," I marveled.

"I'm working on a deadline," she said, with a hint of annoyance in her voice. "They want to run the story this Sunday if possible, on the front page of Sunday Style. That is sort of a coup. I'd appreciate it if you could help me out with this. I think I can wire it to your local newspaper office if you can go pick it up there."

We agreed on that, and after a few more phone calls, I drove into town to pick up the story. "Hitting the big time, huh?" Ed Daniels joked as he handed it over. I took it back to the park office to make a Xerox I could mark up. In the middle of copying, the receptionist called to me.

"The sheriff's on the phone saying you called him about borrowing a still?" she said, with a look of disbelief on her face. I smiled and picked up the phone. While I was on the phone trying hard to convince the sheriff that, no, we weren't going to make whiskey on the park premises but, yes, we would like to borrow a confiscated still for a display at the festival, etc., etc., Spike walked in. He sauntered back toward the room with the Xerox machine, which also had a rest room.

It took me ten minutes to get the sheriff to agree to at least consider the idea—if the park superintendent would call him personally, and if we would sign an affidavit stating that we were absolutely not going to use the still, which had been confiscated on the Kentucky line, for any illegal purposes. Before I was off the phone, Spike left, giving me a dark look on his way out.

When I retrieved my copies, I noticed the smudge of an oily black thumbprint on one of the pages.

I took the story back to the Nature Center and ate my lunch while reading it over. As I could have predicted, it was gushy, making my work and life sound a great deal more exciting than they actually were. The dog episode set me up as heroic, carrying on in the face of danger and pain. My friends would love it. My mother would, no doubt, inquire whether I didn't want to find a new line of work.

In the last paragraph, Betsy had attempted to interpret the Boyd story and described the book with the illustrations, the one remaining painting, and the pictures Mabel Jean had sold for her grandmother's medical expenses. I put big "delete" marks over this paragraph, suggesting instead that she write more about Mabel's gardens, or a further description of the museum. When I called her an hour later to go over the changes with her, using the pay phone to ensure some semblance of privacy, she protested. "You're supposed to be fact-checking, not rewriting. That's a great story, Rob. What's the matter with printing it?"

"It's just possible—well, I'm not sure of course—but, um, the guy that bought the paintings—uh, I think there might be something not quite on the up and up about it." I realized that I sounded pretty incoherent.

"Do you have any proof of that?" she asked, with a reporter's curiosity.

"Well, no. But, I still don't think printing anything about that whole transaction would be a good idea."

"I'm not sure I'm following you."

I thought of another angle. "Well, for one thing, we don't want to encourage other people to sell off their Boyd Jenkins paintings, if they have any."

"Why not? If they need the money like Mabel Jean did, and can get a fair price for them, who are we to stop them?"

I sighed. "Look, just trust me. Get rid of that paragraph, please." I read her my suggestions for an alternative paragraph. She grudgingly agreed to my request.

The story came out in Sunday Style, under the title, "Folklorist Lets Nothing Stand in His Way While on the Job" with a big photo of me talking to Mabel Jean, holding the ice to my wounds, and a smaller picture of me "measuring" the logs of the museum quite unprofessionally with my outstretched hand. A third picture showed the interior of the museum, with the Boyd painting clearly visible. To my chagrin, the caption read, "Collections of the museum include a painting by notable local outlaw, Boyd Jenkins."

Chapter 23

SUNDAY BEST

I got to Granny Taggart's house exactly at two, wanting to keep in Granny's good graces by being punctual. I was dressed in the one nice pair of pants and shirt that I had brought with me for church functions. I even had black, dress-up shoes. Ruthie answered the door in a pair of cut-off jeans and a college logo t-shirt, barefoot. "My, my! The celebrity arrives!" She waved a copy of the Style section, which she had been reading.

"Sounds like you and this female reporter hit it off," she said, with an emphasis on the gender designation.

I raised my eyebrows, then laughed. "She was a royal pain," I assured Ruthie. "I'll tell you all about it sometime—" I lowered my voice with a nod toward the kitchen "—when I can add the proper expletives." She smiled.

"What about that Boyd Jenkins painting?" she said, matching my whisper and pointing to the picture of the museum interior.

"You don't know the half of it," I told her, still whispering. "But it can wait."

Mrs. Taggart came in, wiping her hands on her flowered apron. "Welcome, welcome! I am so glad that you could take a couple of hours off to come have dinner with me and Ruthie. Ruthie helped me make the chicken and biscuits I told you about. She showed me the piece in the paper, sounds like you had quite a time up there!"

Soon we were seated at the table, chatting away like old buddies. I told Ruthie and Granny (she insisted I call her this instead of "Mrs. Taggart") about the herbal medicine book that Mabel Jean's mother had put together. I didn't tell them about Boyd's illustrations—I would share that later with Ruthie.

"Why, my own mother used to know a lot of those, but she never got it down in a book. But it sounds like this woman's grandmother was what they used to call a healing woman. Did she tell you—could her grandmother stop blood and blow out fire? I mean, if someone got cut or burnt, she could cure them?"

"Yes, she told us about that. And she was a midwife, too."

Granny nodded her head. "Old Mother Elizabeth Riggins, we used to call her, did all that type of stuff around here years ago. People would pay her in whatever they had, sometimes a bushel of Irish potatoes, sometimes a dozen of eggs, sometimes a peck of meal. Do you remember her, Ruthie Ann?"

Ruthie shook her head.

"She delivered your daddy, in fact," Granny said.

"What did you pay her?" Ruthie asked.

"I don't recall, but your grandaddy was making cash money back then working for the CCC outfit that built the park, in fact, so we probably paid that way." She laughed. "She did accept cash, too, if anyone had some!"

I had no idea that Ruthie's grandfather had worked for the Civilian Conservation Corps crew that had dammed up the small creek to make the park's lake, built the stone picnic shelters and some of the cabins, and forged roads through what was then farmland and forest. I asked Granny about it, and we had a lively discussion. She told me that she had some photos he took while on the crew, and she could show them to me after dinner. He was one of the few locals on the crew, and he often invited some of the men who were far away from home to dinner at their house.

She winked. I was getting used to her winks by now. "Kind of like you, huh? And guess what? My youngest sister up and married one of those CCC boys that worked with him, too!"

Ruthie looked at me and rolled her eyes. She got up and started clearing the dishes. I rose to help.

"Granny and I have a surprise for you, for dessert. We are going to teach you how to make fried pies." We assembled in the big, bright kitchen. "You told me to think about stuff you could do at your festival, and I thought maybe this would work out. But we thought we'd try it on you to see what you think."

The ingredients were lined up on the kitchen counter. There was a deep cast-iron skillet on the stove, with grease melting in it. Ruthie showed me how to roll out the biscuit dough into a circle about the size of a medium-sized dinner plate.

"That's good, but you've got it too thick on this side." She reached over me and rolled the dough out smooth and even. Granny stood watching and smiling, turning down the heat under the skillet when the grease started smoking.

"Now, take this filling—it's made from dried apples that Granny put up herself last fall—and put it on this side. Fold it over, that's good. Take the fork and seal it. There, you've got the idea."

Granny was in charge of the frying. "We used to use lard, of course, but hardly anybody does that any more. It's bad for the arteries, you know. I use Crisco, myself. Take it and brown it nice on one side, then turn it. It's best to turn it just once." She put the finished product on a paper towel to drain. I was so anxious to taste one that I burned my mouth. Even so, the tangy apple filling and flaky crust were delicious.

We made a dozen of them—Ruthie had promised to bring some home with her—and settled back in the dining room to eat the fruits of our labor. Ruthie had managed to get flour on her nose and was flushed from the heat of the skillet. I thought she looked good enough to eat, herself.

"We always made these when I was a kid," said Granny. "And stack cakes. Now, there's a good thing to have, too, Ruthie."

"Stack cakes, of course," said Ruthie. "How could I forget? They're the best!" She described the cake to me. Four or five layers of a cookie-like dough, baked until golden brown in round cake pans. Layer it with the same cinnamon- and nutmeg-laced dried apple filling that we had used for the fried pies, and let it set for a day or so to "mellow."

"Okay, so you two are in charge of the stack cake and fried pie demonstration. I think we could do it in the Nature Center, don't you?" The three of us worked out the details, and then discussed other ideas. Granny suggested a jam, jelly and pickle contest, "like they have at fairs." She said that the county home demonstration agent, an old friend of hers, would probably be happy to act as judge.

I suggested a cake walk and pie auction. They thought those were great ideas. "The Volunteer Fire Department is always trying to raise money, maybe they would take the pie auction on as a project. My Uncle Arliss is in charge of that sort of thing. There's this guy who's a really good auctioneer in town, maybe you've heard of him. He'd be the one to get. The firemen's wives could bake the pies," Ruthie offered.

I told them about the comparative beekeeping display I was planning, using the bee gum and a modern wooden beehive borrowed from the folks I had interviewed my first day on the job. "A fellow that teaches agriculture at the Voc-Tech school has one of them things that shows the bees behind glass," Granny suggested.

I asked what I would need if I wanted to have a hominy-making demonstration. "Oh, one of those big old washtubs, if you want to do it like we used to. And some dried white corn, and some lye and lots and lots of water," Granny answered, describing the process. "You have to wash it and wash it or it's no good. Then put some salt and whatever else you want to flavor it with. You can show how to can it, too, if you want."

We exhausted all of our ideas, and Granny offered to bring coffee out on the front porch. Ruthie and I moved out there, sitting together on the white porch swing suspended from the ceiling. "I like all this folklore stuff," she admitted. I brushed the flour off her nose. I wanted to tell her more about Mabel Jean, but I was afraid Granny would come out with the coffee at any moment. But Granny seemed to be dragging her feet with the brewing, and I thought I knew why.

"She really does like you," Ruthie said. "I think it's because you're interested in all this old stuff. She loves to talk about it."

Finally, Granny came out with a tray. We jumped up to help her. "Hey, Granny, tell Rob about the time the rooster clawed up your red dress."

"Lord, that old story," she blushed a little. "It's a fact that roosters get angry when they see red, just like they say bulls do. I had me a brand new Sunday dress, and it was redder than red. My mother got me dressed up for church and then told me, she said, 'Now Ruth, stay inside and don't get your dress mussed.' New dresses didn't just grow on trees back then, you know. I think it was Homecoming Sunday, that's why I got a new dress to begin with.

"Well, I was only a little kid and I wanted to go out so bad. It was a lovely late summer day and I wanted to go across the yard and pick myself an apple off the tree. When my mother wasn't looking, that's just what I did. Out of nowheres, our big old rooster came charging out and just started jumping on me, tearing the skirt of my beautiful new dress to shreds with those sharp claws. The dress had a puffy crinoline slip under it. That's the only thing that saved me from getting scratched bad. My mother heard my screams and came running, chasing that old rooster away with a dish towel. Oh, if I didn't get a dressing down for that! And I was scared to cross the yard for weeks after." She laughed.

"Tell us another, Granny." Ruthie and I were swinging in a pleasant rhythm. For a second, I wished I had my tape recorder. Then I realized that this experience would be totally different if I were recording it as a professional folklorist. I eased back and enjoyed the moment for what it was. I felt a warm feeling of belonging.

"Here's one I'm not sure you ever heard, Ruthie Ann. It happened to your great-great-grandmother. One afternoon she wanted to bake a cake, so she went out to gather some eggs. She only had one hen that was laying just then, so she looked into the nest. What do you think she saw?" Granny asked us, as if we were schoolchildren. We both shrugged.

"She saw a huge black snake laying in the nest. He had swallowed all the eggs, and you could see them as four or five knots in his belly."

"Yuck," commented Ruthie.

"I guess that was the end of that cake," I said.

"No, sirree," countered Granny. "She was determined that no dog-gone snake was going to get the best of her. She got the garden hoe and killed that snake dead. Chopped its head clear off, in fact. Then what do you think she did?"

Again we shrugged in unison. But then Ruthie widened her eyes. "Oh, Granny, don't tell me!"

"Yes, Ruthie Ann. She squeezed on that snake body until she got all those eggs out. And only broke one. And her family had cake that night for supper, none the wiser about where the eggs come from to bake it!"

Ruthie and I both made disgusted noises, and Granny laughed loud and hard.

"You young'uns today, you don't have any idea what life was like, even when I was a child. We had to make do. You couldn't be always running to the store for this and that."

We watched the sunset from the porch swing, while Granny did the dishes, refusing our help. I reached for Ruthie's hand. "This is nice," I said.

Ruthie wanted to know about my trip to Mabel Jean's, but I said it would have to wait. I needed to get back to the Nature Center and work on festival plans. I went in and thanked Granny for the dinner, the ideas and the stories. She made me take some cold biscuits with me in a plastic bag, for my breakfast, along with a jar of homemade blackberry preserves. Ruthie walked me to my car.

"So now that you've sampled the chicken and biscuits, what do you think?" she asked with that twinkle in her eyes.

"I think I'd like to sample some of your other wares," I said with a wink.

Chapter 24

DRAWING IT OUT

I now had less than three full weeks to get this festival thing off the ground, plus I had to carry out two small weekend programs. My last two programs, the logging one and Christmas in July, had been quite successful. But, judging from all the work even those single programs had been, I could hardly imagine pulling off this three-ring circus I was planning. I was bound and determined to impress the pants off our project director, however, so I pressed on.

On Monday morning, I got a call from him while I was in the park office looking up some phone numbers. "Rob, how goes it?" he asked jovially.

"Coming along," I answered.

"Heard you got some fine local publicity this weekend," he said with genuine appreciation. "Sorry to hear about your war wounds."

I laughed. "Well, they're almost healed."

"That is so fine. It made a great story. Listen, I wanted to let you know that I'm sending Blake out to help you with your festival in a few weeks."

Thank you, God, I thought.

"He'll come in on the Thursday before if that works for you."

"That works," I said, trying not to sound too relieved.

I stopped by the newspaper office for a few minutes, to ask Ed Daniels if we could get some advance publicity this week on the upcoming festival. He took down some information. "Nice piece in the Sunday paper," he commented. I thought he sounded a little miffed.

"I guess," I said. Before I left, I asked him if he knew anyone who kept mules and a wagon. He brightened.

"Not many people left who do. But Harlen Sears, who lives out near Downings, has a bunch of them and a wagon, too. He has taken that rig to the county fair in the past, I know. You probably could convince him to come down to the park, if that's what you have in mind. Want me to call him for you?"

I agreed, although I preferred to do my own calling. Ed talked to Harlen like an old buddy for a few minutes, then put me on. We made a date for that afternoon.

I was almost out the door when I got a sudden inspiration. I turned back to Ed. "Did you cover the Boyd Jenkins story for the paper back when it happened?"

Jenkins looked perturbed. "Don't tell me you're still on that kick. I wrote some of the stories that were in the paper then, yes. Why?"

"Didn't it ever seem strange that this one FBI agent stuck around for so long?"

"He got his man, finally, didn't he? I always figured that Boyd was a wily one and gave the guy a good run for the money. He knew every survival skill in the book—learned at his daddy's knee and honed in the army, after all. Why?"

"Just curious. You don't know if there's any connection between Chris Demond and this FBI agent, do you?"

He looked at me then as if I had lost my mind. "Seems like you'd have better things to do than hunting this Boyd nonsense to death. I think Demond, like you, was just interested in the story. It's a good one. But one that needs to be put to rest." He turned back to his work, and I left.

In the next few days, I lined up the County Home Extension Agent for food judging, cajoled the bee gum guy into lending it to us for the demonstration, convinced Harlen Sears to bring a mule team and wagon to give rides around the park, and made appointments to see Ruthie's Uncle Arliss, his fund-raising committee, and a woman whom the Home Extension Agent suggested for the hominy demonstration. I had to start thinking crafts and music.

A square dance on the Saturday night of the festival would be good, and we could use the same group that came when Blake was here. They seemed to be very popular, and hopefully they were available. A gospel sing on Sunday afternoon would be a nice touch— since my first program, I had met a number of other family groups who seemed interested in participating. I was thinking about all this, sitting at my desk at the Nature Center when Dwayne came in. He reached in his pocket and handed me a slip of paper, offering no comment.

It was a note that Blake had called and to call him back. The office was closed for the night, so I gathered up my change once again and headed for the pay phone.

"Rob, my man!" Blake's hearty voice was a welcome sound. "I have three words for you. Country and western."

"Country and western what?" I asked, as if this were some sort of riddle.

He snorted. "Music, of course. We need some at your festival. I can arrange it, too. I could have bands there all day and night if you like."

"Hmmm . . . have you run this idea past our esteemed project director?"

There was a moment of silence. "Not exactly."

I hated to discourage his enthusiasm, and the offer to take over some of the planning was tempting. I knew all of Blake's arguments for including c&w in the program and agreed with them in theory. My change was running out.

"Tell you what. If you can get that one group we heard—the ones that played some old-time stuff along with the newer stuff—to come for the Saturday night dance, you're on."

I could almost hear his grin. "Deal made, my man. I will have it all arranged by the time I get there, week from next Thursday. Keep a candle burning."

Something about all this made me nervous.

Things were going almost too smoothly. Everyone was agreeing to do the things I asked them to do—even the sheriff had agreed to lend us the still, and, as it turned out, the bee gum owner knew a thing or two about stills and could double as an interpreter of "old-timey" whiskey-making traditions. I had simple programs lined up for the intervening two weekends—the tatter I had interviewed a while back for one, and a father and son fiddle and guitar duo for the other. The way was clear to finalize the festival plans.

I got a dozen sheets of white poster board at the local "five and dime" and tried my hand at designing a poster for the festival. I kept it pretty generic since I wasn't sure that some of the planned events were going to actually happen. I would put the finished products up in strategic locations around the park and in town. I was beginning to obsess that no one would come to this extravaganza after all my hard work.

The result of my attempted artwork was pretty horrid. Ruthie came in, finished with her lifeguarding shift, while I was trying to make the fiddle I had drawn look less like a Coke bottle with strings. "Pretty sad," she said, surveying the damage. "What about something like this?" She took a new piece of poster board and make some quick sketches. She copied my written information in steady, almost calligraphic, script and filled in the sketches with the different colored magic markers I had bought. The result was impressive. I marveled at this woman of many talents.

"Can you do ten more just like it?" I asked.

"Only if you take me out for a milkshake."

"You work cheap," I commented.

"You've also been promising me information for over a week now. I must have it!" She promised to take the posters home and finish them that night. We drove to the Tastee Freeze and sat on a picnic table.

I gave her the full report on the trip to Mabel Jean's, telling her everything I could remember. When I told her about the illustrations in the book, she almost choked on her milkshake. "That would be perfect—absolutely perfect—for my senior honor's thesis. Do you think she'd let me use it?"

"How could she resist a nice girl like you?" I said. I felt a rush of relief. Ever since I had seen Mabel Jean's book, I knew that someone had to do something with it. And I didn't want that someone to be Demond.

I saved the sale-of-the-paintings story for last. Ruthie looked thoughtful. "There's something really, really sad in that," she mused. "Here's this woman who all her life helped heal others, and in her last illness, her granddaughter has to sell off something so precious in return for her health care."

"Yeah," I said. "But I've been thinking that there's something strangely appropriate in it, too. A sort of a barter. Almost like she traded the paintings for the healing. Like your granny was saying people used to pay the healing woman in potatoes or whatever they had. Or, like Boyd himself did for food and shelter."

She scowled. "Maybe, sort of. But it's still a shame she had to sell them. Who bought them, anyway?"

"That's the damndest thing." I gave Ruthie the description that Mabel Jean gave me. "Does that sound like anyone we know?"

"Well, that could describe half the guys in three counties around here, bud!" she laughed. Then she got serious. "But, if it was anybody we know, it sounds like Spike."

"Yes!" I exclaimed. A heavy-set woman at the next table with an incredible beehive hairdo looked at me with a frown, and I lowered my voice. "But why? And who was he working for?"

Ruthie shrugged and drained her milkshake cup, making loud slurping noises with her straw. "Well, Sherlock Holmes, we don't even know for sure that it is Spike."

"But it makes sense. He tried to warn me off the Boyd legend. And he knew about our visit to the cave, we think." I suddenly remembered the cigarette butts at the base of the stump. Maybe it wasn't a logger's lunch, after all.

"What? You look like you're on to something." My mind was racing ahead. I told Ruthie about the smudges on the draft of the newspaper article. We agreed that we'd both been stupid, and that— if our suspicions were correct—Spike was way ahead of us.

"Demond is part of this. Has to be," Ruthie said.

"I've been thinking and thinking about it," I said. "The only thing Peter Livingstone could have been after—the only thing that might have some value—was Boyd's paintings."

We looked at each other, clouds of doubt passing over our faces. "Value to whom?" Ruthie asked.

"Even back then, there must have been collectors who were interested in that sort of thing. I mean, look at Grandma Moses's pictures, they've been worth a bundle for a long time."

"Hate to tell you this, buddy, but Boyd wasn't exactly Grandma Moses."

"Yes, but his pictures have a certain—I don't know. But I know you feel it too."

She looked at me and smiled, and was about to say something. Just then, one of her friends spotted her and came over to get introduced. The friend was in a chatty mood. I said I had to get back to work, and the friend said she would give Ruthie a ride home. "I'll come by and get that poster stuff later," Ruthie promised, giving me a wink.

I had almost forgotten that I was due to meet with the volunteer firemen that evening to discuss the cake walk and pie auction. I left a note for Ruthie at the Nature Center and dashed back out. By the time I returned, she had been there and gathered up the poster-making supplies. The Nature Center was dark and ominous. Dwayne was out somewhere. I settled down to do more festival planning, burning only the single desk lamp. I jumped when a large moth dived into the light and fluttered angrily. I found myself wishing that the Nature Center door had a lock.

Chapter 25

FESTIVAL FANDANGO

The next couple of weeks were consumed with plans for the festival—no time to speculate about Spike, Demond, their connection to each other and to Boyd. Once all of the program elements were in place, there was more publicity to do, supplies to be purchased, things to be picked up and stored, sound systems to check and a million other little details to go over and over.

Blake showed up after dark on the Thursday before the big weekend. I was so glad to see him that I gave him a big hug. "Hey, you really must be lonely up here," he joked. "What's the latest with your woman?"

I had been so busy, that I had barely seen Ruthie since she had dropped off the finished posters the week before. She was helping me behind the scenes, calling pie and cake bakers and buying the supplies needed for the cooking demonstrations. We had communicated by phone and by notes left at the office. Once or twice I had breezed by the swimming pool to get some information from her. One day, she told me that Dwayne was going to let her head an owl-calling program the weekend after the festival. I had nodded, with no idea of what she was talking about, but in too much of a hurry to get an explanation.

"Hello, you still there?" Blake roused me from my daze. "She has your head that messed up, huh?"

"No, not at all. It's this festival thing, it's driving me nuts. So tell me that you have the band all lined up for Saturday night, and that everything else will go smoothly."

"Well, I've been meaning to call you about that."

"No, no, I don't want to hear it." I knew something was going to go wrong with this plan.

"The proverbial good news and bad, my friend, no need to panic. The good news is I have a band for Saturday night. The bad news, it was not your first choice."

I hadn't remembered having a second choice. Blake had booked one of the more contemporary c&w bands when he found that the one I had suggested couldn't make it. I remembered them, a bunch of young guys in leather vests and tattoos and not one but two electric guitars.

"Well, at least the project director won't be here to see this," I said with relief.

"Oh, that's the other thing I was going to call you about. He's due in Saturday, late morning."

The day of the festival arrived, all too soon. Every inch of the park, it seemed, was covered with some kind of traditional activity. At least that's the way it looked on the crude map that I had drawn to pass out along with the program. Blake was at the office Xeroxing mass quantities of these while I cleaned the Nature Center stove. The dirt of the ages seemed to cling to every inch of it. Public Sector Folklore, the Glamour Profession, I thought, almost passing out from the ammonia fumes.

After the stove was as clean as I felt it could ever get, I went back to my check list. Blake had made the final calls to the three gospel groups scheduled for Sunday afternoon. I hoped he hadn't secretly replaced any of them with the Country and Western Gospelaires, a real group that I had seen written up in the local newspaper several weeks before.

Everything seemed in order. I couldn't do anything about the Saturday night group at this point, but I didn't think the project director would object much to the rest of the line-up. I walked down to the office to see if any last-minute phone calls had come in for me. Along the way I saw George Whitelaw. "Told Spike to find you some good firewood for that hominy demonstration," he said. "We got the pot hung up on the stand just now."

"Thanks, I'll go take a look at it," I said. Most of the park personnel had rallied for this massive event, for which they would have my eternal gratitude. The receptionist had been a sport about taking the endless messages. The two rangers had volunteered to help with parking and crowd control. Even Dwayne had agreed to oversee the beekeeping and still demonstrations. I hadn't seen much of Spike. I preferred to go to George with my buildings and grounds requests.

I got hardly any sleep the night before the event, thinking of every detail I might have forgotten. Did I have an extension cord for the sound system at the picnic shelter? Had I told the firemen where to sign in when they came? Should I have arranged to send someone to pick up the bee gum guy, who was ancient and had a car to match? I tossed and turned and was up at dawn, going over my list one more time and worrying. I made some instant coffee, boiling the water in my one all-purpose sauce pan, and sat in the half-darkness. Soon the sun rose, a comforting sight. At least the weather was cooperating.

About an hour later, Blake stumbled in, rubbing his eyes. I offered him some coffee and made myself another cup. "Today's the day," he said, slapping me on the back. "Don't worry, it's going to be fine."

"Easy for you to say," I said.

All morning I ran from site to site making sure the final preparations were in place. Participants started arriving at nine, and the general public at eleven. The mule team got there at the very last moment, resplendent in their polished harnesses. The wagon looked newly painted, bright red and yellow. "Jock was a little reluctant this morning," Mr. Sears said around his wad of chewing tobacco. He gave the mule on the left a pat. I could sympathize.

The chair-seat weaver needed a bucket of water. The hominy maker needed running water. I took the bucket of water from the hominy-making site and gave it to the chair-seat weaver. As I was passing the Nature Center, looking for George to see if we could get a hose at the hominy site, Blake sauntered over. "The thing you wanted the bee guy to put the display on is too high. Can we find anything lower?"

It was like that all morning and into the early afternoon. Finally, just as everything started settling down and a huge crowd of people were milling around, I felt a drop. I looked up, and another plopped into my eye. The forecast, which I had been studying for the past week, said there would be a twenty percent chance of afternoon showers. This couldn't be happening.

But it was. The drops started coming faster and faster, until a total downpour let loose. Everyone was running for cover. I started dashing from site to site, making sure that anything perishable was covered with one or more of the big garbage bags I had placed at each area "just in case."

In the midst of this chaos, I saw the project director marching toward me in a bright yellow rain poncho. I was glad to see he had come prepared. "Sorry I'm late, got stuck in some construction on the Interstate. Can I help somehow?"

I sent him to check on the beekeeping/still site. As I rushed around trying to make sure everything and everyone was as safe as possible, I thought of one good thing that could come of the rain— maybe it would cancel the evening concert. Just then, the rain started letting up and the sun broke through. When I looked up, I saw a perfect double rainbow painting its way across the sky. I recalled some weatherlore one of my informants had related the week before: "Rainbow in the afternoon, no more rain that day."

I went from area to area once more, assessing the damage. The fire under the hominy pot was smoldering, sending curls of pungent smoke into the air. The demonstrator was cheerful about it, though, already trying to revive the fire with someone's newspaper.

In fact, everyone had taken the rainstorm in stride. We had lost a significant part of the audience, but more were coming. The ranger on parking duty estimated that five hundred people had been at the peak. Attendance figures could reach a thousand by the end of the day, he said. He was smiling. "We should do this every year."

As long as I didn't have to organize it ever again, that would be fine with me.

I stopped by the Nature Center and had to wade through a crowd. Ruthie and Granny were furiously frying pies and cutting them into small pieces for people to taste. No one had told me we couldn't give people samples, so I had assumed it was okay. Hopefully, no one would get ptomaine poisoning and sue the Department of Conservation. Ruthie brushed the hair out of her face with the back of her hand. "God, it's hot in here. Everyone jammed in during the rain, and they all wanted a taste. When there's free food around, you always have a crowd." She looked at me, with a good-natured grin. "Whose idea was this, anyway?"

She put a finger on my t-shirt. "Bud, you are soaked through. You look like one of those contestants in a wet t-shirt contest," she winked at me. "Better go change into some dry stuff before you drive all the ladies wild."

I winked back and flexed a bicep for her amusement. I hadn't even thought about how wet I was. I ducked back into the bedroom and changed everything, down to the soggy underwear. I sat on my bed for a minute, wishing I could crawl into it and go back to sleep. Instead, I put my dry-socked feet into my spongy sneakers and hurried back into the fray.

Chapter 26

AFTERWORDS

The rest of the afternoon happened quickly. Before I knew it, it was time to set up for the evening dance. "So who are these guys, anyhow?" the project director inquired as he helped me set up mikes. I looked at Blake who stood nearby hooking up an extension cord to an amplifier, but he ducked his head and looked away. I was not going to take all the heat for this, I thought.

"Well, it's a group that Blake discovered when he was here. It wasn't my first choice," I said, aiming the words in Blake's direction, "but I think they'll be a real crowd pleaser."

When the group arrived, I could see the displeasure in the project director's face. They were too young, too scruffy-looking and they had amplified instruments. I braced myself for the worst, but he didn't say a word.

As I had predicted, the crowd was huge. And rowdy. From the first twangy chords, the audience was on its feet, whooping and dancing the two-step, calling out requests. They were young to middle-aged, with a few older couples. "This is the folklore of now, my friend," Blake commented to me, moving his feet to the music. He nudged me, "I gotta surprise for you later. You're gonna love it."

He picked out a lone woman in the crowd and asked her to dance, disappearing before I could reply.

Ruthie materialized through the crowd and beckoned to me. "What do you need?" I called to her over the din.

"I need you to come dance with me!" she laughed, moving her hips. "This is a great group!" Ignoring my protests that I couldn't dance worth beans, she pulled me into the swaying bodies. She attempted to show me how to two-step, but it was a lost cause. The next dance was a slow waltz. We stood looking at one another for a moment, then I pulled her to me and we slow-danced awkwardly. I tried not to step on her feet. Before the song ended, we were doing better, and I had my face buried in her curls. I caught a whiff of fried pies.

At the end of the song, I broke away. I wasn't happy with the sound level. Blake came up to us and asked Ruthie for the next dance. He winked at me as I headed for the stage. I was truly getting sick of all these winks.

I stood backstage a while looking into the crowd. The project director came up to me. "Well, it's not exactly the group I would have liked to have seen here tonight," he said. "But the rest of the day was terrific, and I'm sure tomorrow's gospel sing will be great, too. Congratulations." He shook my hand.

I surveyed the audience and saw two familiar figures over to one side. Demond was standing, hands on hips, watching the dancers. Spike was lighting a cigarette, walking toward Demond. He sidled next to him, and they started a conversation, not looking at one another. Demond waved Spike's smoke out of his face. He looked angry. Spike ground his cigarette butt savagely under his heel, and walked away.

As I watched, Demond walked into the crowd and I lost sight of him for a few seconds. Then, he emerged dancing with someone. Ruthie. I shuddered as they twirled around and around. Just then, Blake tapped me on the shoulder. "Listen up," he said, grinning.

The group stopped playing and the leader took the mike. "This program, folks, is part of a project done this summer by the Department of Conservation, as you may know. There is a folklorist here at the park collecting information, and if you have some good ole stories for him, you'd better get in touch with him while he's here. Rob

Anderson, if you are out there, come on up here and let them see your face!"

The project director waved me on. Embarrassed, I stepped into the stage lights we had set up and gave a little wave. People clapped. The leader continued, "I'd also like to introduce Blake Taswell, the coordinator of the project, who got us to come out tonight to entertain you all." Blake bounded up on stage, and another flurry of clapping started.

"We would like to dedicate this next tune to Rob and Blake, who collected it from a gentleman named Cyrus Daniels. It tells the story of Boyd Jenkins, who lived around here, and many of you have probably heard your parents or grandparents speak of him. I know I have."

I looked at Blake with amazement, and he grinned back. We retreated backstage as the band started a souped-up version of Cyrus's song about Boyd. They made the first stanza into a chorus, and added a couple of instrumental breaks to fill it out, but the song's words came out clearly and the tune was close to the original. "I got them a copy of the tape," Blake whispered in my ear.

The project director came up to us as the song was finishing and the crowd exploded with applause. I couldn't read his face. Then he burst into a smile and shook both our hands. "Nice work," he said.

I looked out into the crowd, but couldn't see Demond or Ruthie. I felt a little panicky, but then caught sight of Ruthie standing near her grandmother, giving me a thumb's-up sign.

The Sunday gospel sing was an anticlimax after the intense activity of the day before. I had thrown in a few craft demonstrations to round out the day—a family of basket makers, a braided-rug maker, and one of the whittlers who had showed up at my earlier whittling program. When the afternoon was over and all of the equipment was packed away, Blake and the project director helped me clean things up. "We call this 'redding up' where I come from," Blake joked. I growled at him a little, jealous of his energy level. We hadn't gotten much sleep the night before—too busy analyzing the good and bad points of the festival over a six-pack.

Blake and the project director both left early that evening, after we ate dinner at the park restaurant. At my request, Ruthie came along.

She matched us all joke for joke, and regaled us with stories from the fried pie front.

"This little boy came in and he and his grandma stood in line for about ten minutes waiting for a taste. Then, when he finally got one, he said, real loud, 'Grandma, this ain't nothing but an old fried pie. You made me wait all this time for a fried pie?' We all laughed. Blake threw me a look.

"You got it bad," he whispered later as he got into his car. "Good luck with that one." I felt like belting him.

Ruthie and I were finally alone. "Great program," she said, looping her thumbs in her jeans. "You look beat. Go get some sleep."

"I will," I said, "but not until I hear about you and Demond."

She looked puzzled. "Oh, the dance. He just grabbed me and we danced. He's a pretty good dancer."

"That's all?" I asked, suddenly exhausted.

"No more, wish it was more exciting than that. We danced once, and then I didn't see him again. End of story."

Still, I felt uneasy as I climbed into bed. Even though it was only seven o'clock, I fell right asleep and didn't wake up until eight the next morning.

I was sluggish from too much sleep. I faced the task of writing about the festival experience in my field notebook. I dug my copy of the program out of the pants I'd been wearing the day before, and looked at my scribbled notes. Some of them were obscured where the rain had soaked through. At least a dozen people had come up to tell me that they would like to be interviewed for the project, or they knew someone that I should not miss interviewing. I copied down the names, addresses and phone numbers in my log book, knowing that in the three weeks I had left on this job, I wouldn't get to interview half of them. I already had a list of more than twenty other likely prospects I hadn't been able to contact yet.

I felt depressed. I had a bunch of ideas for programs, and only three more weekends to carry them out. I took myself out to breakfast, delaying any decisions of what to do first.

As I was driving back to the Nature Center, I remembered the project director telling me that he wanted all of the folklorists to write an article about some aspect of their fieldwork for the Department of

Conservation's monthly magazine. I had asked him if I could write about the Boyd Jenkins legend and Boyd's paintings. He had agreed.

Starting this article seemed like more fun than thinking about all the other work left to do. There was something subversive about it, knowing that my old friend Demond had indicated he might still want to "do something" with the legend. I hoped he would be pissed as hell when I sent him a copy of the published article. By then I would be long gone, back in the sanctuary of graduate school. And Ruthie would be back in college.

I tried not to think about that as I got out some notebook paper and attempted an outline. I tried out several lead paragraphs and ended up throwing them all into the trash. I got out a clean piece of paper, and finally wrote something I thought would do for a start. "Boyd Jenkins was a notorious outlaw. At least that is the way most people in Eastern Tennessee think of him. But to a small number of people who actually knew him, Jenkins was much more. Brother, friend, hunting buddy, preacher, and talented folk painter. It is his paintings, more than anything else, that Jenkins leaves behind as a tangible evidence of his complex life. Stirring and realistic, these paintings are a precious legacy of a man that many felt acted in self defense—and defending the honor of a loved one—when he shot Tom Atkinson dead on that fateful night in the little town of Sunrise."

It already felt like a sweet revenge.

Chapter 27

THE BIG SPLASH

I decided on my last three programs, and concentrated most of my fieldwork on gathering the information needed for them. The first would be a program on tobacco: growing it as a crop, harvesting it, preparing it for market or home use, and its many traditional uses. Not too many people grew it in the area anymore, but I had met a few. As a bonus, at the festival a man named Leonard Fentriss had introduced himself, saying he still could "rive out" tobacco sticks like the ones they used for hanging up the crop in barns to dry. "Use 'em for tomater stakes nowadays," he explained.

I interviewed two farmers who had small patches. They walked me through the growing and harvesting process. Then their wives gave me lists of ailments you could cure with tobacco: put the leaves in linens to keep insects out; put chewed tobacco on snake bites or sores (also useful for swellings, boils, bites, stings, or toothache); use the juice for warts or to get rid of head lice on children. "Not that my children ever had head lice," one wife told me, reddening.

Ruthie agreed to help me plan another program. I was intrigued by the idea of children's folklore—the things that country children in the area knew how to do that city kids didn't. She came over after her pool shift and dictated a list that included crawdad catching, June bug baiting, mumblety-peg, and "rolly hole" marbles. She told me about play-party games, which weren't common in the area anymore. "But the ring games that we played when we were kids still use a lot of the same old songs," she said. She promised to introduce me to her nieces, nephew and younger cousins to get more ideas. Meeting more of her family would be fun.

Then I discussed my ideas for a Labor Day weekend program. I didn't want to do anything elaborate—I didn't have the energy left after the festival.

"I think you know the program we have to do," she said.

"What program?"

"Remember you said that one of the other folklorists on your project suggested you should have an exhibition of Boyd's paintings?"

I grimaced. "They're spread all over. It would take me a week just to gather them all up and then another week to get them back."

She hit me on the head with her wet bathing suit. "Well, lazy-bones, I have an idea. We could invite Mrs. Jenkins to bring her five; I think she would do it if I asked her. That in itself would be a good little exhibit. But we could also put something in the paper inviting other people who own them to bring them in."

"You keep saying 'we.' " I smiled.

"Well, I'm in this thing up to my eyeballs, too. Summer's almost over and we still haven't quite figured out what Demond and Spike are up to. We're pretty sure it involves the paintings, and money, and there's something wrong about it, and this little scheme might just smoke them out."

"How?" I asked.

"Well, maybe if some people come in with paintings, we could ask them whether anybody has tried to buy them. Get a description and see if it matches Mabel Jean's, or Lilly's for that matter."

"We could also urge them to keep the painting in their families," I added.

She thought a while. "I guess I really don't feel that's our job, after all. If they want to sell them, that's up to them. But I still would like to know who's buying them and why. And, if all this leads us back to the FBI guy."

I agreed to think about it. Then I remembered what she had told me about leading a nature program that weekend. "What's this about calling owls? How do you do that, with a telephone?"

"If you must know, you have a recording of different owl calls, and you go to the edge of the woods and play it. If you're lucky, some owls call back."

"Sounds exciting," I joked. She looked hurt.

"Well, it's my first public program. Look, here's my name on the announcement." She took a crumpled piece of Xerox paper out of her pocket. "So, it's not exactly fame and fortune, or even a big festival," she poked me in the ribs. "But it's a start."

I tried to get back into her graces. "Ah, this is great. I really always wanted to hear an owl up close. What owls do you usually hear?"

"Barn owls and screech owls, mostly." She folded the paper and put it back in her pocket. "I have to go now and read up on my owls." She still looked a little mad.

The tobacco program which I had scheduled for Saturday afternoon went well, with about thirty-five people attending. Many had never seen anyone splitting wood with a froe and mallet before. "I saw some of those in a museum once, and I always wondered what they were used for," commented one young woman toting two small children behind her. Much to my delight, the kids watched with fascination.

I had been feeling slightly "peaked," as Granny would have said, all week. I attributed it to festival aftermath. By the end of the program, I felt truly awful. My head ached and my throat felt raw. Just what I needed, I thought. By the evening, it was clear that I had come down with some sort of bug. Ruthie stopped by to see if I still planned to come to her "debut" as an owl summoner. "You belong in bed," she said, leading me in that direction.

I knew I had a fever because I was feeling very lightheaded and hot. "Too bad you can't join me," I said.

"Be quiet and take this." She handed me two aspirin that she had found in the medicine cabinet and a glass of water. She slipped my shoes off and pulled the covers up to my chin.

"I'll come check on you after the program," she said. "And tomorrow, I'll bring you some chicken soup."

After Ruthie left, I stripped down to my t-shirt and jockey shorts. I drifted off to sleep, waking up now and then in a feverish stupor. I thought I was dreaming when I felt a hand lifting me into a sitting position. "Ruthie?"

No response. I opened my eyes, but that didn't help much. The room was very dark, since Ruthie had pulled down all the shades and night had fallen. Something was placed between my lips. A bottle.

"Drink this." A male voice said in a flat tone.

"What is it? Who are you?" He was very close and even though my nose was stuffed up, I could smell tobacco and alcohol.

I felt something cold and sharp at my neck. "Drink it, I said." There was menace in the voice now. He poked the sharp thing into my flesh just enough to make me obey the command.

I took a swallow from the bottle. I had never tasted any liquor that strong. It burned all the way down, making me gag. "More," he said, impatiently. I forced down some more of the nasty stuff. "Made it myself," he said, with an evil little chuckle. Before he was done, he had forced me to drink the whole contents of the bottle, which I judged to be a pint. My head was swimming. I thought I would vomit, but I tried not to, thinking of the pointy thing. The last thing I wanted to do was make him mad.

He put something over my head which made the room even darker. The world was already revolving in slow, sickening circles when he picked me up and threw me over his shoulder like a sack. His back smelled sweaty. I tried not to pass out, but I was losing the fight.

The outdoor air was chilly on my bare legs. My back brushed some tree branches. We were walking along the road, I thought, try-ing hard to orient myself. I tried once or twice to struggle out of his grasp but I could barely move. Gravel crunched under his feet. We were crossing the road. Bump, bump, bump. Down some stairs. He opened a chain-link gate and I smelled chlorine. He set me down on some cold concrete and tore off the thing on my head and my t-shirt.

"Nice night for a skinny dip," he said. "Have fun." He raised my head and brought it down hard on the concrete.

Chapter 28

QUESTIONS AND ANSWERS

An angel was bending over me. Her head was framed by a bright halo of light, but otherwise she looked like Ruthie. I thought I could hear her calling but her voice seemed far, far away. "Rob, Rob—can you hear me?" I was very cold and my head was filled with pounding waves. Then, darkness again.

I woke up next in a room full of white. It didn't take me long to realize that it wasn't heaven. It may have been the bright green plastic chair next to the bed that tipped me off. Or the smell of antiseptic. A nurse came in. "Awake, are we?" she said, fussing with my pillow. "There's someone out here who wants to see you. Should I let her in?"

I tried to nod yes, but my head hurt so badly I just managed to smile a little. She took that for a yes.

Ruthie came in with a big bouquet of white, pink and red gladiolus. "Late ones, from Granny's garden," she said softly, as though the sound of her voice at its normal volume might bother me. "You were almost a goner there, bud. Do you remember anything?"

It took me a moment to find my voice, which came out in a croak. "Whiskey. He poured it down my throat. And carried me someplace."

"Was it Spike? Because from what I hear, he's disappeared. Didn't report for work yesterday and his truck is gone from his house. None of his family has seen him or heard from him." She gave a little ironic smile. "Or so they say."

"I can't be sure. It was dark." My head was throbbing, and when I swallowed, my throat felt as if it had been scraped from the inside with broken glass.

"Well, whoever it was made it look like you'd gone for a midnight dip in your jockeys," she smiled. "But I convinced them that you'd been sick in bed and weren't too likely to be interested in a skinny dip. I think he wanted to make it look like you'd gotten plastered and banged your head on the edge of the pool. He even left the bottle by the side of the pool for effect. Pretty clever if you ask me. I didn't think Spike was that resourceful. Then again, maybe he had help."

"You saved me?"

"Well, me and Dwayne. Good thing we are both trained in life-saving and first aid. We were coming back from the owl program—the owls weren't cooperating, and we just gave up after awhile—"

"Thank God for uncooperative owls," I rasped.

"So, anyway, we were coming close to the pool and we heard a loud splash. Then, some footsteps. It was a really still night, you could hear everything. 'That's funny,' I said to Dwayne. 'Sounds like some-one jumping into the pool.' We ran down there in case some kids had gotten in, you know, fooling around where they weren't supposed to be. Instead, there was you, floating face down." She made a face.

"Mouth-to-mouth resuscitation?" I asked, sounding hopeful.

"Yes, as a matter of fact. But I hate to burst your bubble. Dwayne did the honors. I did jump in and pull you out, though, if that's any consolation." She smiled, and that naughty twinkle danced in her eyes.

I tried to sit up in bed, but my head hurt too much.

"Just take it easy. There's a policeman here who wants to ask you some questions, but you should get some more sleep after that. They think you can probably come home day after tomorrow."

Home. I wondered where that was. The Nature Center?

"Granny says you can stay at her house for the rest of the time you're here, if you like," she said with that uncanny way she had of reading my mind. "Oh, and I took the liberty of calling your parents, got the number off your job application. Mr. Bird had a copy.

I thought they should know what sort of trouble you were getting yourself in and out of down here. I told them you were going to be okay and not to worry. Hope you don't mind."

I smiled, showing her I didn't mind. "We need some answers," I said, fighting to stay awake.

"Plenty of time for that when you feel better." She planted a tender kiss on my forehead and left the room.

Several days later, propped up on some pillows in Granny's guest room, I was taking a stab at writing in my log book. Ruthie came in with a glass of water.

"So, you think tomorrow we could go?"

"I think I'll be up to it. Did you check to see if he's still around?"

"He is. Maybe we were wrong about him being involved."

"I don't think so. Should we call ahead, or just pop in?"

"I say the element of surprise is in order here." We discussed a few more plans, and I showed her the draft of the Boyd article that I had roughed out.

"You've been busy. Must be Granny's good cooking that has revived you this fast."

The next day, after Ruthie had scoped out the situation, we drove the short distance to the little blue house outside the park grounds. The Honda was parked in front, so we walked through the gate and knocked on the door. Demond answered after a minute or so. "Come in," he said, as if we had just popped in for tea.

"I was expecting you. I guess you'd like to ask me some questions. You're so good at interviewing people together, after all."

"Cut the crap," Ruthie said in a tight voice. I raised my eyebrows, forgetting how much it still hurt to do that.

Demond sighed. "Well, what I am about to tell you will clear up any mystery you think you might have stumbled upon. I think you'll find it interesting, but probably not as satisfying as you'd like."

"Try us," said Ruthie.

"Number one," Demond started, "I have not done, nor have I ever done, anything illegal." It sounded as if he were practicing to testify in front of a grand jury. He paused, seeming to ponder exactly where to start.

"I am, as I told you, Anderson, really a trained folklorist. I began my studies in 1974, and I truly enjoy the field. But, as you yourself know, it is not likely to make you rich." He smiled, twisting his face. "I was pretty much resigned to that fact. I really wanted to teach on the university level. I like the intellectual atmosphere.

"When I passed all my comps and reached the dissertation stage, I went home to Bethesda, Maryland—that's where my family lives—for a visit. I was going to do some research at the Archive of Folk Song at the Library of Congress, narrowing down my topic. My mother recruited me to help her clean out her brother's, my uncle's, house. He had died and left his row house in Georgetown to her. She was his only sibling and only living relative."

Ruthie shifted in her seat. I leaned back against the cushions. My head was throbbing a bit, but I wanted to hear this.

"He had been an FBI agent. That much I knew. But he didn't—really, couldn't—discuss his work. I just knew him as Uncle Peter. A jolly fellow. Giver of expensive Christmas presents." Demond laughed mirthlessly. "Peter Livingstone. But you already know his name, I'm sure. And the fact that I might be related to him. You've been spending way too much time trying to figure all this out. By the way, Miss Taggart, when you leaf through someone's mail, try to remember to put it back in order. You both could have saved yourselves a lot of trouble if you'd have just taken my advice. And Spike's." He smiled that annoying smile again. "But, I digress."

"Uncle Peter was on the Jenkins case, as you know. He stuck around this part of the country for quite awhile, as you also know."

"That was before you came down here. How did you find out?" I asked.

"Excellent question, Mr. Anderson. You two have been at a handicap in this little mystery. I was more fortunate. I had the job of going through Uncle Peter's personal papers. Among them, I found a most interesting notebook filled with names, addresses and dollar figures. I also found canceled checks from someone in New York City, someone I'd never heard of. Lots of checks, and lots of money for the time period, the mid-1950s.

"The addresses in my uncle's book were all in northeastern Tennessee and southeastern Kentucky. Some of the places were so small, they weren't even on a regular road map. There were some notations next to the names as well, like 'five from these, may have more,' or 'know they have some but weren't budging.' "

"People with paintings," Ruthie commented.

"Very good, Miss Taggart. But you're getting ahead of me." He continued.

"I tried to find out from the Bureau what case my uncle was working on around those years, but they wouldn't divulge the information. A bit of sleuthing in the library's newspaper files helped me figure out that it was probably the Boyd Jenkins case he was working on. My mother confirmed that he had gone to someplace in Tennessee for almost two years around that time."

"The whole thing was intriguing me. Of course, I recognized—like you did, Anderson—that the Jenkins story was sure to be ripe with folklore possibilities. But the checks still had me stumped. I wrote to the address on the checks, explaining my curiosity and assuring this mystery person that any information he could give me would be kept strictly confidential.

"I got a phone call almost immediately, and I went to New York for a meeting—all expenses paid. This guy, as you have probably guessed, is a collector of folk art. He divulged his arrangement with my uncle. It seems that my uncle had sent some Jenkins paintings, which he came across as pieces of evidence on the case, to a friend who owned an art gallery in Georgetown. He wanted to know if his friend could tell him anything about the paintings that might help with the case. I see you sneering, Miss Taggart. Obviously, you have been thinking the worst of my uncle, but I assure you he was innocent up to this point.

"In any case, his friend gave him some general information, such as what type of paint Jenkins must have been using and other useful clues. But she also let slip that she knew a collector in New York who was paying well for the type of folk art that Jenkins was producing. Quite well. She convinced my uncle to let her show the paintings to the colllector, who was coming into Washington for a visit. 'Just to help authenticate them,' you know.

"Well, you can guess what happened next, I suppose. When my uncle found out how interested the folk art collector was in the paintings, and just how much he was willing to pay for them, he was seduced. The FBI didn't pay that well, after all, and he was a man with expensive tastes.

"So, as far as I have been able to reconstruct, he kept enough paintings coming to the FBI lab to satisfy them, and sold the rest to the buyer, through his gallery owner friend. Jenkins, you've probably found out, was prolific. And most of the locals were easily convinced to give up their paintings as 'evidence.' "

Demond continued. "He was afraid, though, I think, that if he kept it up too long, someone would find out what he was doing. So, when he had made a tidy sum, he blew the whistle on Jenkins, and—well, you know the rest."

He said it so matter-of-factly that I wanted to punch him. In fact, if I had felt up to it, I would have. But the story wasn't over.

"Enter me. I thought the Jenkins story was fascinating and would make a great dissertation topic. Really. And, in anticipation of funding my research, I made a deal with the collector—who still prized his Jenkins paintings and welcomed more of them—that if I found anyone willing to sell any remaining paintings, I would let him know. And, of course, he is even richer now than he was back when Uncle Peter was dealing with him, and was willing to make it worth my while.

"It's a whole generation later, after all. If Jenkins's paintings meant something to the people that he gave them to twenty-five years ago, they mean little to most of the people who now find them while cleaning out Aunt Hattie's attic. Most were more than willing to make a tidy little sum selling them to me."

I saw Ruthie's fists balled in her lap. She seemed ready to punch him herself. I put a hand on her elbow. There was more.

"Oh, don't look so 'holier than thou.' You know that I was doing some of those folks a big favor by buying the paintings. Like dear Mabel Jean Bristoe, whose granny would have been evicted from the hospital if it hadn't been for the sale of the paintings.

"Business was so good, in fact, that I needed to hire some help. I had Uncle Peter's book, after all, so I knew the names and addresses of all of the people who he suspected still had Boyd paintings. And I couldn't be everywhere myself. I decided to take it slow, and stay in the area awhile to prove my sincerity. I knew it would take some time to find all the paintings I could, and the collector was patient.

"I got this insurance gig, not a bad job for my purposes. Local gossip is rampant, as you've discovered, so it wasn't hard to find a willing helper. My local man, Fred, a.k.a. Spike, Dooling had some heavy gambling debts to pay off and was quite happy to get this job 'moonlighting,' as it were. He had an aptitude, too, as it turned out. Not too intimidating, just a bit menacing. Flashing cash was his idea. He's not as dumb as he looks.

"So, things were going along pretty smoothly until you showed up, Mr. Anderson. And, you managed to involve Miss Taggart, here." He made a tsk-tsk sound. "You really should be more careful—you could have gotten her injured. Spike and I, in our own ways, tried to warn you to leave the Jenkins story alone. But you had to pursue it. When verbal warnings didn't work, Spike hatched the plan to stage your mishap coming down the mountain from Jenkins's cave."

"And here everyone was blaming your poor old Volkswagen." He laughed curtly. "I assure you, I had nothing whatsoever to do with that, or the nasty business at the swimming pool. I am still deeply sorry for both incidents. But Spike felt you were getting too close. And he has such a flare for dramatic violence. I think he watches too much television." He smiled to himself.

Demond leaned over and lowered his voice. "Some advice, in case you two plan to go into the detective business, you have to be more careful in the future. You leave a trail behind you that is ever so easy to follow. Notes at the park office. Articles at the Xerox machine."

Ruthie let out what sounded like a growl. I looked at Demond with disbelief. All the time we thought we were being so clever, discovering things about him, he and Spike were always one step ahead of us.

"Spike thought that you were writing a story for a newspaper, or magazine, or both—urging that people with paintings by Boyd Jenkins should hold on to them for historical purposes. He could see his cash cow drying up, and he was more desperate than ever for money. I tried to tell him that very few people around here would actually read such stories, even if they did get published, but he wasn't convinced." He couldn't resist a smirk.

"So, I guess that brings us up to date. You've cost me a tidy sum, I suppose, but I've been at this for a year and a half. I won't tell you how much I've managed to squirrel away, it's really none of your business. The Contemporary Folk Art Gallery in New York has been wanting to convince the collector to organize a major exhibition of Jenkins's work ever since they caught wind that some new pieces had been 'uncovered.' This guy is one of their biggest benefactors. So, the time seems right for me to move on and curate it. They intend to pay me well for doing so. The catalogue will form a good basis for my dissertation, which I fully intend to finish. Having a Ph.D. never hurt anyone."

We were both dumbfounded for a full minute, while Demond sat calmly, enjoying his moment of triumph. I felt pretty woosie and wanted to get out of there as soon as possible.

"By the way," Demond said. "The collector knows all about my uncle's less than legal obtaining of the paintings. But he has some very good friends at the FBI. If you know what I mean."

Ruthie was the first to get up. She walked over to Demond, and slapped him full and hard on the right cheek. If I had felt better, I would have followed it with a punch to the left one.

Chapter 29

EXHIBITION SPACE

Ruthie and I decided to carry out our plans for a modest exhibition of Boyd's paintings as a final program on Saturday. It was Labor Day weekend, and both Ruthie and I had to get back to school the following week. There were so many loose ends, with only a few days to tie them up, I hardly knew where to start. But we both needed this program for our own sense of closure.

I would go ahead with the article, too, without mentioning anything about the FBI man, or Demond's upcoming "major exhibition." Ruthie and I agreed that only a select few should be told the whole story. Someday, maybe, we would find a way to get back at Demond. Not just for our own sake, but for the sake of Boyd and all of the people who had known and loved him.

Ruthie had to finish her stint at the swimming pool, but in the evenings she accompanied me on visits to Lucy Jenkins and Cyrus Daniels. Both received the news of the FBI man's "doings" with a minimum of surprise. We convinced Lucy to bring the paintings to the park that Saturday, and Ed Daniels graciously gave us front-page coverage on short notice, running a photo of one of Lucy's paintings. The article invited anyone with a Boyd Jenkins painting to bring it for others to view. Ruthie got someone else to cover the pool for the day.

On the morning of the exhibition, Lucy, Ruthie, Granny and I sat admiring the paintings, which George Whitelaw had directed his new assistant to hang on the Nature Center wall, when the first visitor came in. He had something under his arm.

"My name is Grant Wilkins," he said, unwrapping the bundle. "My mama told me to hold on to this painting. She told me the whole story of Boyd Jenkins and the way he had been wronged. I treasure this piece, I sure do, and the story that goes with it." In less than an hour, four more people brought paintings. About an hour and a half into the program, there were twenty-five people, all comparing each other's paintings and swapping versions of the legend. Ruthie and I went from one person to the next, gathering the stories the best we could.

"He taught me how to shoot," said one man, who was twelve when Boyd came into their coal camp for shelter.

"I petted Bob," said a woman, pointing to a picture that showed the bobtailed hound.

"My uncle, who used to raft logs, said he once gave Boyd a ride in his john boat," said another man.

"My granny said he once preached in their church—way up in the mountains, it was when the regular preacher was called away," a younger woman told us.

In the midst of all this hubbub, a slight woman walked in with a big bundle under her arm. Ruthie and I ran to greet her. When Lilly undid the sheet she had wrapped up her painting in, all eyes in the room turned to see it. The whole room seemed to be holding its breath. Seeing the painting again, I couldn't help wondering what Demond would have made of this one. I was sure that it was Boyd's "magnum opus" and it would have made a stunning centerpiece for his New York exhibition. I laughed to myself. Ruthie looked over and gave me a knowing look. I had no doubt she was thinking the same thing.

I photographed all of the paintings, and gave a little speech about how wonderful I thought it was that everyone in the room had seen fit to keep the art work in their families. One by one, the painting owners left, until only Ruthie, Lilly and Lucy remained. Even Granny, who was tired from all the excitement, had gone home.

We helped Lucy and Lilly wrap up their paintings. "Thank you for calling me, Lucy. I wouldn't have wanted to miss this."

Lucy nodded, her eyes shiny. She turned to Ruthie and me. "Are you young folks free? Lilly and I would like to take you for a little ride."

We nodded, not quite sure where they were going to take us. We piled into Lucy's Oldsmobile and drove until we came to the road I had stumbled upon early that summer, which now seemed like an age ago. Hangman's Chapel.

We got out of the car and Lucy took some flowers arranged in a large cut-glass vase out of the trunk. We followed her to a corner of the graveyard where a small patch of what looked like weeds were growing. Ruthie knelt down and fingered some of them. "Pennyroyal," she told me. "Mullein, tansy, yellow root, goldenrod." I recognized the names from leafing through Mabel Jean's book.

"Our family all helped dig them out, up in the mountains, and plant them here. They're all healing herbs, you know," Lucy said. She placed the vase of flowers at the center of the plants. She put her arm around Lilly, who was crying silently.

I looked over at Ruthie and saw she was crying, too. I took her hand. We all stood there for a long time, gazing at the unmarked grave, thinking our own thoughts.

Lilly wiped her tears away with her handkerchief, and blew her nose. "He was no saint," she said, "but he was a good man, nonetheless."

There could never have been a more fitting epitaph for Boyd Jenkins.

Chapter 30

LAST THINGS

I spent the next couple of days putting finishing touches on tape logs, getting my final field log notes in order, and packing. Tuesday, my last day, was cloudy, with a hint of impending fall in the air. I walked down to the office to type up my article draft and say goodbye to the staff.

While I was there, I got a telephone call from Ed Daniels. I had noticed him at the Boyd exhibit, but I had only caught his eye for a moment among the crowd and commotion.

"Son, I want to thank you," he said.

"You're welcome," I said, pausing, with no idea what I was being thanked for.

"I know I discouraged you from pursuing the story of Boyd Jenkins. I thought you were just after the sensational side of it. But that painting exhibit you organized put a whole new light on Boyd Jenkins for me, and I think it did that for many others, too." He paused a moment. "I took down a bunch of the names of folks who brought their paintings, and we're going to run a human interest feature each week for the next two months on their stories."

I would have liked to have told him the whole story, but it would have taken longer than I had. Maybe some day. For now, the promise of a local follow-up on my summer work would suffice. A legacy of my labors. "You'll send me copies?" I said, hoping the little catch in my voice wasn't too evident.

"Of course. Good luck, son. Will we see you next summer?" He was about the twentieth person to ask me that in the past couple of weeks.

"Well, the project was only funded at the park for this summer, and will move to another park next year, but I really would like to come back, at least to visit." The words had a ring of insincerity. I wanted more than anything to come back, but I had no idea if I ever would. Next summer, I'd probably be in a completely different part of the region, if not the country, working on a new project.

I dragged my feet back to the Nature Center, sighing. I stood outside the low, ugly structure, trying to fix it in my mind forever. The front porch where Ruthie and I had sat, being eaten by mosquitoes. The large front room, home to weekend programs and Ruthie's visits. The little cubbyhole which was my "office" where I had copied tapes for Ruthie. The cramped kitchen, where I had fixed Ruthie iced tea, and where she and Granny had fried pies. And, the sleeping quarters, with the two regulation metal camp beds and scratchy grey wool blankets, where I would have gladly entertained Ruthie given the chance.

Dwayne, who had taken and passed his pharmacy license test, had already vacated. He had been offered a job at the new branch of a chain drugstore in a town just south of the city, not far from his parents' home. Ruthie and I had taken him out for dinner at the park restaurant to celebrate. His final words before he roared off in his old powder-blue Chevy Impala were a deadpan, "Did I say decadence? Maybe the folklore of the eighties will be self-absorption." He pumped my hand, and broke into a sly grin for one fleeting moment. It was the only time I'd seen him smile all summer.

Ruthie and I had planned a farewell picnic. Granny had invited us to dinner, but instead Ruthie had talked her into providing us with the picnic food: fried chicken, deviled eggs, potato salad, homemade rolls and home canned dill pickles. Our fat, salt and starch quota for the month, Ruthie had joked as she placed everything in the otherwise naked Nature Center fridge that morning. During my last visit to town, I had purchased the best bottle of champagne available at the local liquor store. Not exactly Tattinger's, but it would have the same effect, I hoped.

With nothing left to do, I sat rocking on the Nature Center front porch, awaiting Ruthie. She had volunteered to help close down the swimming pool for the season. George Whitelaw pulled up in his pickup, got out and came over. "Just dropped by to say so long," he said. I gestured to the empty chair beside me.

"Been a pretty good summer, I'd say," he commented, lighting up a Camel. "I am sorry about that trouble with Spike. Guess he hasn't turned up yet, or at least he's laying low. It'd be hard to nail him on anything, I 'spect, though."

George was right. The bottle of moonshine, I had learned, bore no fingerprints besides my own. He had been smart enough to wear gloves, and to make me hold the bottle. Since I didn't actually ever see my assailant to make a positive i.d., and no one else saw him leaving the scene, it would be hard to prove that it had, indeed, been Spike. Smell, apparently, was not admissible evidence.

The local police promised to bring him in for questioning if he turned up, but I doubted they would put much effort into finding him. Half the countryside was related to him, and they would hide him if needs be just like Boyd's family had hidden him.

"Well," I laughed a little, "unless they can trace that whiskey."

George laughed. "Lord, Lord, likely every moonshiner in these hills has that recipe."

We sat in amiable silence for a few moments. Flies buzzed and the sun broke out of the clouds. "What will come of all this old stuff?" he asked.

"All the documentation goes into the State Archive," I began my usual spiel, thinking he meant the "old stuff" I had been collecting that summer.

He flicked away his Camel with an impatient gesture. "No, no, I know all that. So, there's a mess of papers and photos and tape recordings at the State Capitol. I mean, what becomes of it here? Young folk don't seem interested. All newfangled ways and McDonald chains and farms going belly-up and stuff bought at department stores instead of made by hand. People watch television, they don't tell stories anymore. Old folks dying off and their stories and know-how with them." He stared across the small parking lot.

I didn't have an answer for that. I don't think he expected one. The only thing I could think of to say was, well, a few young people are interested and do listen. But would listening to the old stories and learning about old skills change our lives? Would we ever turn to the old wisdom, to the old ways, in preference to our modern conveniences? Was it enough to appreciate them, to try to glean messages from them? To encourage others to appreciate them and try to spur a desire to pass on as much as possible? I was still pondering this when George stood up and called, "Hey, gal!"

Ruthie stepped up and shook his hand. "Sorry to hear about your Uncle Earl." He bowed his head.

"Yeah, well. I'd better be getting going, leave you two young'uns to yourselves." I shook his hand, and he climbed into the truck and waved.

"Earl?" I asked.

Ruthie frowned. "Died last night. Peacefully in his sleep from what I hear. You interviewed him, didn't you?"

I swallowed, a thick feeling in my throat. "Yeah. He was a great storyteller."

"Also, in his day, he was one of the finest jaw harp players in the county. And grew the finest gourds for dippers and martin houses this side of the mountains." She sighed. "Granny got some seeds from him one year to try to grow her own, but they never did as well as Earl's. She said she should have spit some tobacco juice on them."

"He never mentioned playing the jaw harp or growing gourds," I said.

Ruthie looked at me, with a little smile. "You just have to learn to ask the right questions."

"I hope I don't have to smell chlorine for the next year! Let's grab that picnic and get out of here."

Ruthie had promised to take me to a "mystery spot" which would fit the occasion. She tugged me in the direction I had taken that midsummer afternoon—up Devil's Backbone. We took it slow—I was still sore from my recent "accident." Finally, we reached the spot near a small waterfall. There was a clearing there, surrounded by fragrant cedars. Ruthie set out a tablecloth and all the goodies. I managed to open the champagne without putting out an eye. I had rummaged around at a secondhand shop in town and found a couple of mismatched wine glasses.

"Truly elegant!" She grinned, piling food on paper plates.

I poured the champagne and cleared my throat. "A toast. To us, Ruthie and Rob, partners."

She clinked my glass, and downed her champagne in a gulp, gesturing for me to do the same. Then she carefully placed the glasses down, and moved closer. I met her kiss halfway.

We shoved food, picnic basket and all aside and came together in each other's arms, laughing and kissing. We lay side by side, looking into each other's faces, and the kissing became more intense, more urgent. I reached under her sleeveless t-shirt and slipped it over her head. She raised herself a little and started taking off her bra.

"Whoever invented these things ought to have been shot," she joked, fumbling with the hooks. We took off the rest of our clothes, and lay looking at each other for a few moments. I traced the line of her tan across her shoulders and chest, and she shivered. Then, we were all arms and legs, kissing and laughing and licking. I groaned a little when her elbow hit my sore head, and we slowed down. We made love looking into each other's eyes, and I felt a tenderness and purpose I had never felt with my friend the anthropologist. Or with anyone else before. It felt right, so very right, and I wanted that feeling to last forever.

Afterwards, we lay munching on the picnic foods the ants hadn't found, and sipping more champagne, our t-shirts thrown carelessly over our naked bodies.

"Umm, it doesn't get better than this," I said, drowsy in the afternoon sun, which had emerged from the clouds again.

"You mean Granny's cooking, or what?"

"Granny's cooking. You. This place. All of it," I said, kissing her nose. She rolled onto her back and looked up at the sky.

"Do you believe in a higher power?" she asked.

"God, you mean?" For a moment I thought she was going to reveal a conservative religious side of her personality, harkening back to the beekeepers I had interviewed on my first day on the job.

"Yeah, but more than that. I mean, a power that makes things happen."

"Uh-huh. I think it made the earth move a few minutes ago."

She continued, ignoring my bad joke. "I think something brought us together. A force to do something good. Maybe not to save the world, but to save a little part of the world for a few people. To right a memory. That was important. I couldn't have done it alone. You couldn't have done it alone. We did it together, and it was good."

I smiled. "It was good. The whole summer was good." I kissed her again. "I do feel it," I said with fervor, imitating one of the local preachers. Ruthie swatted me on the shoulder.

We were silent for a few moments, both looking up at the sky, listening to the rushing sound of the waterfall. Then I said, "Seriously, we did the right thing. It won't show up in my field notes, or the documentation that goes into the State Archives. It's ours. And Lucy's and Lilly's and Mabel Jean's and Cyrus's and all the others who knew Boyd. Really knew him. And Boyd's, too."

The sun burst full force from behind the clouds, now, directly on us. Ruthie got up, flung off her t-shirt blanket, and dragged me, laughing and protesting at the same time, into the pool. The water was ice-cold and felt wonderful. We giggled and splashed like little children.

When we couldn't stand the icy water any more, we lay back down, making love again. Ruthie gave a little moan just as the sun passed behind a cloud. The hair on the back of my neck stood on end, and I realized that I was thinking about the fate of the mythical Indian maiden and her lover. Also about Boyd and Lilly. I buried my face in Ruthie's dark curls and tried to forget about both the fabricated and the real legends, and everything else. But, lovely as the moment was, ghosts lurked just below the surface. They would always be there.

Chapter 31

LEAVING

Wednesday morning, I was on my way back to the capital to turn in my tapes, field note book, undeveloped rolls of film, and equipment. The VW's radio had mysteriously begun working again, and I tuned into Country Station WHIL and turned up the volume, singing along with the choruses. The songs were all about lost loves, unfaithful wives, and abusive husbands, which didn't help my mood much. I felt as though I were forgetting something, although I knew I had checked and double-checked all the Nature Center nooks and crannies at least three times. I sensed, however, that it wasn't something tangible.

Granny had packed me some biscuits with butter and honey, a Coca-Cola and some early apples, despite my protests. "I know that you'll stop at some fast food joint and eat something greasy and bad for you otherwise," she clucked.

"He will anyway, no matter what you pack for him," Ruthie had joked. She handed me a wrapped package about the size of a shoebox. "Open this when you're far away—out of Tennessee and all the way back to school if you can stand the suspense," she whispered.

I handed her my own present. "Open this up anytime after I'm gone, and promise to start using it as soon as possible," I countered. It wasn't a very original gift—a large box of stationery with my school address printed on the inside lid, and one hundred stamps. But, in my desperate attempt to stay attached to her, to this place, to the summer, it was all I could think of to give her.

Granny had given me a long, crushing hug, and kissed me on the cheek. "You'll be back here before long, I 'spect," she said. "In fact, I know it. This place is in your blood now." She smiled. "You'll always be welcome, I hope you know." She turned and went into house, leaving Ruthie and me alone.

"Safe trip," said Ruthie. She sniffed a little. "Get going now, I hate long, drawn-out good-byes." We kissed, hard and long, and I left.

WHIL went out of range and I couldn't find another country station. In fact, the only station that came in clearly was an all-news one and, having been out of touch with current events for most of the summer, I found I didn't want to re-enter the world quite yet. I let my mind wander, and it turned to school thoughts. I wasn't sure where I was going to spend the night when I got there, and how I was going to juggle finding a new place to live with starting classes a couple of days late. I started thinking about the classes I was going to take, and how I should be narrowing down a dissertation topic in the next year. I tried to muster some enthusiasm for getting back to school, but I was having a hard time. Thirty miles out of Nashville, I found another country station and started singing again.

When I got to the Department of Conservation, I found that I had missed saying good-bye to my fellow folklorists. Ann had to go back to school early, and Jack was staying an extra week at his park to finish off some fieldwork. The project director had our fieldwork photos, black and white contact sheets and color slides, laid out on one of the tables in his overcrowded office. I had only seen the first month's worth of mine, which I had picked up at our second meeting in Nashville.

As I went over the photos, squinting at each through the eye loupe, the whole summer seemed to unfurl. It took me almost four hours to fill in the blank spaces on my photo logs, even though I had tried to keep up with the forms as I took the pictures. There were some very bad photos, too dark, blurry, or showing nothing but the back of someone's head. But there were also some decent ones, and some I considered very good. I was especially adept at inanimate objects. Mrs. Billings's baby doll heads and the figures crafted by Cyrus stared back at me as hauntingly as they had in real life. I wondered what the archivist processing this collection would think of them.

I got to the slides of the trip Ruthie and I had taken to Boyd's cave. I spent so long looking at the picture of Ruthie sitting on the log, eating her apple, that my eye started burning. I wished I could just take it with me, slip it into my pocket without anyone noticing. How long would it take for the archivist to figure out there was a picture missing? Who would care?

Blake came in while I was staring at the photo and nudged the eye loupe from me, taking a look for himself. He chuckled. "I should've known." He looked up, grinning. "You can request a copy, you know. It'll just take about ten days. Think you can wait that long?" I wanted to punch him.

By the time I finished logging the photos and completing my other business at the Department of Conservation, it was time for a late dinner. Blake and I drove in his clunky Matador to a barbeque joint, and afterwards hit one of his favorite c&w bars. We listened to the house band in silence, Blake occasionally picking a young lady out of the crowd to dance with.

"You look glum, my friend," he observed, downing a draft in three gulps. "Cheer up."

"Easy for you to say," I mumbled, trying to match his beer-drinking prowess. I nearly choked.

"Ho, ho. You think I've never missed a women before?"

I looked at him. He had a big silly grin on his face, and he refilled our glasses from the pitcher on the table, draining it. "Here's to the end of it."

"The end of what?"

"Whatever you need an end to." He clinked his glass against mine and drank the last of his beer. "Let's get out of here," he said.

We wandered around the quiet city a while, surprising drunks on doorsteps and getting propositioned by a few middle-aged prostitutes. We walked all the way to his apartment stopping a couple of times to pee on some trees. Even though it was a distance of nearly three miles, I was so anesthetized from the beer that I didn't feel sore any more. "I'll get the car tomorrow," Blake said, as if he did this sort of thing often.

Back at Chez Blake, we sat on the couch. My head was buzzing. Blake put on a tape, and it took me a few minutes to realize that it was the recording of our evening festival program. He grinned. "I made it for you, to remember me by."

"How could I forget you, you Bozo?" We both laughed.

The Boyd song came on. It was the last straw. Before I knew it, I was crying. Not just a single, silent tear, but bawling like a baby. I looked at Blake, embarrassed beyond words.

"Hey, guy," he said. "Go ahead. You deserve it." He fished out his handkerchief, shook it out and handed it to me. "Only slightly used," he said.

I started laughing and crying at the same time. It had been that kind of summer.

I called a graduate school friend on Thursday morning and made arrangements to crash on his couch until I found a new place to live. I arrived in the university town just before sunset. It looked like an alien world, bathed in a surreal golden light.

In a few days, I would be back in the graduate school routine: going to class, reading a ton of books, writing papers, proofreading scholarly articles submitted to the journal for which I was the graduate assistant. Summer would dry up and blow away like the oak leaves on the wide lawns of the university's Student Union. I could write a paper for my Folk Art in Modern Life class on Boyd's art. But maybe not. I might lack scholarly objectivity about the subject at this point. I felt tired and depressed.

I arrived at my friend's apartment, and had to socialize for awhile, really wanting to be alone. He had spent the summer working at the library and taking seminars with visiting professors. The seminars, he said, were "extremely stimulating," but they sounded pretty boring to me. I tried to explain my own summer, but somehow my description of the mountains and the folklore I had collected, and people I had met, fell flat. I could see him glazing over. He suggested we go to have some coffee at our favorite haunt. I told him to go ahead, and maybe I'd catch up with him a little later.

With remarkable restraint, I had saved Ruthie's present until I got here. Being around Blake, and working with my field materials, had maintained enough of the connection back to East Tennessee to keep it real. Now, here, it was already beginning to fade. I hoped whatever was in the box would bring it back, bring Ruthie back.

I unwrapped the box and looked in. I lifted out a small photo album. In it were photos that Ruthie had taken at the Boyd exhibit, with a little note that said, "My brother had to go to into the city, so I made him take my film to one of those one-hour photo places. It cost a fortune, so you'd better appreciate this." In each picture, a painting owner posed with his or her Boyd piece. On the opposite page was a neatly written synopsis of the story the person told us. She was much better at photographing people than I was. Her photos not only documented the exhibition, but caught a little bit of each painting owner's personality. The next to the last page was a picture of me interviewing one of the painting owners, looking earnest and absorbed. The last page was a picture of Ruthie herself, which she had taken by aiming the camera lens into a mirror. I traced the blurry outline of her face with my finger and smiled.

The second item in the box was a bottle of some liquid with sprigs of herbs floating in it, with a note attached. "Granny says this liniment is a cure-all. Rub it on any part of your body that you dare, and you'll surely feel better. But, whatever you do, don't drink it." I unscrewed the top—it smelled horrendous, like licorice and kerosene. I replaced the lid and screwed it on very tightly. I could just imagine Ruthie laughing at me.

The third item was a sealed envelope. I opened it carefully. It contained a thick, three-inch lock of dark, curly hair, tied with a blue ribbon. I sniffed it and the fresh, herby smell brought back a wave of memories. The note with it read, "I know you have this thing about my hair. Clairol Herbal Essence is the secret. Sorry if you imagined some old mountain herb concoction." It went on. "There's an old belief Granny once told me, that possessing a lock of someone's hair binds you to them. What do you believe?"

It was an intriguing question. What did I believe? At that moment, I believed that I had lived through the most important summer of my life. And no matter what happened in the months and years to come, it would always be with me.